PRAISE FOR THE NOVELS OF NINA BRUHNS

Winner of the National Readers Choice Award and three-time overall winner of the Daphne du Maurier Award for Excellence in Mystery/Suspense

RE

"Bruhns starts off her new . . . Her characters are sexy and . . . they continue to grow on many levels . . . you through page-turning action and suspense. The sexual tension is palpable and when Bruhns's latest couple gets together, sparks fly." —*RT Book Reviews* (4 stars)

"A taut thriller . . . The freshness in this exhilarating tale is the location and the heroic Russian who is a wonderful, unique protagonist . . . Readers will relish this tense story as love puts an exclamation-point end to the remnants of the Cold War." —*Genre Go Round Reviews*

"A great cast of characters and the heated sexual tension between the hero and heroine keeps this romantic suspense story moving . . . A perfect blend of romance and suspense." —*Fresh Fiction*

"Nina Bruhns excels at writing romantic suspense with plenty of action and incendiary passion between her main characters." —*Romance Novel News*

A KISS TO KILL

"Greg and Gina are one of the hottest couples I've read lately . . . There's not one thing I didn't like about this book. It's fast paced. It's got an intriguing and complex story and mystery. It's got fascinating characters on every page. It's sexy and sensual and then some."

—*Wickedly Romantic and The Unread*

HILLSBORO PUBLIC LIBRARIES
Hillsboro, OR
Member of Washington County
COOPERATIVE LIBRARY SERVICES

continued . . .

"A thrill ride of fast action and hot sex in the steamy Louisiana bayous, Nina Bruhns's latest delivers it all!"

—CJ Lyons, bestselling author

IF LOOKS COULD CHILL

"Nonstop, edge-of-your-seat action that never lets you down . . . The relationship between Marc and Yankee Tara was H-O-T . . . There was never a moment that I wanted to put it down."

—*Joyfully Reviewed*

"If you like a thrill a minute, you will enjoy *If Looks Could Chill*. The gripping tale is well written and filled with intrigue and passion."

—*Romance Reviews Today*

SHOOT TO THRILL

"Suspense just got a whole lot hotter with Nina Bruhns's dynamite romantic thriller. A hero to die for and a heroine to cheer for . . . An awesome, sexy story."

—Allison Brennan, *New York Times* bestselling author

"[A] fast-paced thriller . . . Powerful chemistry."

—*Publishers Weekly*

"Sexy, suspenseful, and so gritty you'll taste the desert sand. A thrill ride from start to finish!"

—Rebecca York, *New York Times* bestselling author

"A provocative, sexy thriller that will get your adrenaline pumping on all levels."

—Tamar Myers, award-winning author

MORE PRAISE FOR THE NOVELS OF NINA BRUHNS

"Shocking discoveries, revenge, humor, and passion fill the pages . . . An interesting and exciting story with twists and turns." —*Joyfully Reviewed*

"[A] delightfully whimsical tale that enchants the reader from beginning to end. Yo ho ho and a bottle of fun!"
—Deborah MacGillivray, award-winning author

"This is one you will definitely not want to miss!"
—*In the Library Reviews*

"Nina Bruhns . . . imbues complex characters with a great sense of setting in a fast-paced suspense story overladen with steamy sex." —*The Romance Reader*

"Gifted new author Nina Bruhns makes quite a splash in her debut . . . Ms. Bruhns's keen eye for vivid, unforgettable scenes and wonderful romantic sensibility bode well for a long and successful career." —*RT Book Reviews* (4 stars)

"The kind of story that really gets your adrenaline flowing. It's action-packed and sizzling hot, with some intensely emotional moments." —*Romance Junkies*

"Nina Bruhns writes beautifully and poetically and made me a complete believer." —*Once Upon A Romance*

Berkley Sensation Titles by Nina Bruhns

SHOOT TO THRILL
IF LOOKS COULD CHILL
A KISS TO KILL
RED HEAT
WHITE HOT

WHITE HOT

NINA BRUHNS

BERKLEY SENSATION, NEW YORK

HILLSBORO PUBLIC LIBRARIES
Hillsboro, OR
Member of Washington County
COOPERATIVE LIBRARY SERVICES

THE BERKLEY PUBLISHING GROUP
Published by the Penguin Group
Penguin Group (USA) Inc.
375 Hudson Street, New York, New York 10014, USA
Penguin Group (Canada), 90 Eglinton Avenue East, Suite 700, Toronto, Ontario M4P 2Y3, Canada
(a division of Pearson Penguin Canada Inc.) • Penguin Books Ltd., 80 Strand, London WC2R 0RL,
England • Penguin Group Ireland, 25 St. Stephen's Green, Dublin 2, Ireland (a division of Penguin
Books Ltd.) • Penguin Group (Australia), 250 Camberwell Road, Camberwell, Victoria 3124, Australia
(a division of Pearson Australia Group Pty. Ltd.) • Penguin Books India Pvt. Ltd., 11 Community
Centre, Panchsheel Park, New Delhi—110 017, India • Penguin Group (NZ), 67 Apollo Drive,
Rosedale, Auckland 0632, New Zealand (a division of Pearson New Zealand Ltd.) • Penguin Books
(South Africa) (Pty.) Ltd., 24 Sturdee Avenue, Rosebank, Johannesburg 2196, South Africa

Penguin Books Ltd., Registered Offices: 80 Strand, London WC2R 0RL, England

This is a work of fiction. Names, characters, places, and incidents either are the product of the author's
imagination or are used fictitiously, and any resemblance to actual persons, living or dead, business
establishments, events, or locales is entirely coincidental. The publisher does not have any control over
and does not assume any responsibility for author or third-party websites or their content.

WHITE HOT

A Berkley Sensation Book / published by arrangement with the author

PUBLISHING HISTORY
Berkley Sensation mass-market edition / August 2012

Copyright © 2012 by Nina Bruhns.
Excerpt from *Blue Forever* by Nina Bruhns copyright © 2013 by Nina Bruhns.
Cover art by Kris Keller.
Cover design by Annette Fiore DeFex.
Interior text design by Laura K. Corless.

All rights reserved.
No part of this book may be reproduced, scanned, or distributed in any printed or
electronic form without permission. Please do not participate in or encourage piracy of
copyrighted materials in violation of the author's rights. Purchase only authorized editions.
For information, address: The Berkley Publishing Group,
a division of Penguin Group (USA) Inc.,
375 Hudson Street, New York, New York 10014.

ISBN: 978-0-425-24398-5 4968 2908 09/12

BERKLEY SENSATION®
Berkley Sensation Books are published by The Berkley Publishing Group,
a division of Penguin Group (USA) Inc.,
375 Hudson Street, New York, New York 10014.
BERKLEY SENSATION® is a registered trademark of Penguin Group (USA) Inc.
The "B" design is a trademark of Penguin Group (USA) Inc.

PRINTED IN THE UNITED STATES OF AMERICA

10 9 8 7 6 5 4 3 2 1

If you purchased this book without a cover, you should be aware that this book is
stolen property. It was reported as "unsold and destroyed" to the publisher, and neither the
author nor the publisher has received any payment for this "stripped book."

ALWAYS LEARNING   **PEARSON**

This one goes out to all the Hermits,
who are always unfailingly supportive and the
best buds imaginable.
Thanks for all you do,
and for your invaluable friendship, Hermits!

1

////////////

For a man on the run, the fog was both a blessing and a curse. It hid you from your enemies . . . but it could also turn against you.

For the past week, U.S. Navy Lieutenant Commander Clint Walker had been grateful for the recurring blanket of mist as he'd scrambled to stay two steps ahead of his pursuers, island-hopping his way along the Aleutians toward mainland Alaska. So far he'd managed to evade the tangos hot on his trail—a Chinese black-ops team determined to retrieve the stolen military plans in Clint's possession . . . and no doubt kill him for their trouble.

But that would only be the beginning of the trouble for the U.S. Navy—and for the country—should the Chinese succeed in stopping him from delivering those plans.

A severe storm had left Dutch Harbor under a dense shroud of gray that blotted out the pale rays of the midnight sun and cast the surrounding landscape in an eerie, impenetrable glow. It seemed like he'd been jogging through the thick soup for miles, getting nowhere.

As he ran, the hairs on the back of his neck prickled. His grandfather would say it was the breath of the bear. But this was more like the breath of the dragon. Drawing on the lessons Grandfather had taught him during those long-ago summers they'd lived on the land using only the gifts nature had given them, he focused every sense on the danger lurking out there in the mist. Clint even knew the dragon's name: Xing Guan, commander of the Chinese black-ops team of trained assassins that had been sent to bring back, at any cost, the small data storage card that had been stolen from their navy.

Clint had yet to see Xing Guan's face. But he knew his ruthless reputation from the scatter of reports that had come across his desk at Naval Intelligence regarding the notorious commander. The man was brutal, relentless, and smart as a fox. And he was out there right now. Close by. *Stalking him.* Clint could feel his pursuer's menacing presence down to his very marrow.

It wouldn't take a rocket scientist to guess where he was heading. The biggest airport in the Aleutians was here in Dutch Harbor. The Chinese operators tracking him might already be hiding there, lying in wait for him to show up. But he'd have to risk it. He needed to get the micro SD data card containing the stolen plans back to Washington, D.C., ASAP.

If he could find the damned airport.

After four days of stinking hell working his passage on a fishing trawler, Clint was dead on his feet. All he wanted was to find a way back to Washington and his apartment, grab a steaming hot shower, and sleep for twenty-four hours straight.

He stopped jogging long enough to catch his breath. And listen. He could hear the shallow waves of Iliuliuk Bay sucking at the nearby shore, so he knew he was still on the right road. In the distance, a foghorn's low, mournful moan did a duet with the distinctive metallic clank of anchor chains from the dozen or more ships that were moored along the piers lining both sides of the harbor. The sharp smell of raw fish filled the air but gave no clue as to whether he was closer to the airport or to cannery row. Of course, with just one change of clothes, it might be himself he was smelling.

Hell. He couldn't see a goddamn thing in this fucking pea soup. He must have missed the turnoff for the airport. Maybe. He was on his last legs, and both his SEAL training and the hunting instincts learned at the knee of his grandfather were rapidly failing him tonight. He needed to focus.

He glanced around. Because it was the middle of the night, the airport runway lights had been turned off, and there were no other visual or auditory clues to indicate direction. The entire island seemed to be closed up tight as a clam and wrapped in cotton wool. Thankfully, it was the height of tourist season; by dawn the airport would be humming with activity. He had to be close.

Rather than risk running into the enemy black-ops team, he'd hunker down for the night. First thing in the morning he'd scout out a plane to hitch a ride on to Anchorage or Seattle.

Unless they found him first . . .

He froze. *Footsteps?*

No. Just the rustle of leaves.

He'd spotted his pursuers back on Adak Island. There'd been three of them, moving in concert through the harbor to hunt him down, a stealthy, efficient killing unit. The Chinese *really* wanted those plans back. That was when Clint had decided he'd rather face the wrath of a fishing trawler captain as a stowaway and work off his unplanned passage than risk being taken by Xing Guan. He could not lose that data card.

On it were top secret Chinese plans for a revolutionary new long-range guidance system for their ever-growing fleet of unmanned underwater vehicles, or UUVs. Information crucial that the United States acquire, for the protection of our North American coastlines. We were already vulnerable. Without countermeasures to the silent, deadly, nearly undetectable UUVs, it would be open season on our coastal cities.

Pulling down a deep breath, Clint started to jog again.

Sonofabitch. He was getting too old for this shit. If he managed to make it back to D.C. in one piece, maybe he'd actually accept that Pentagon job the commander had been dangling in front of his nose for a few years now.

Or not.

Even in his midthirties, as a former Navy SEAL Clint was not exactly enthralled by the idea of sitting behind a desk from nine to five. Although right about now, a warm, clean office sounded damn good, even if it did come with a ball and chain. Maybe he could even start thinking about a family. Grandfather was long gone, and there was no one else. No wife, no clan, not even a rez any more—not since the casino mafia had driven the honest folk off the reservation.

Suddenly the faint whisper of hushed human voices floated out from the fog. *Not* leaves. And not his imagination.

Again Clint halted in his tracks and listened. *One, two, three speakers.* Male. He couldn't hear the language they were speaking, but it didn't sound English. *It sounded Chinese.* And the men didn't sound happy.

He swore silently and veered off the road. Folding himself into a patch of low juniper, he waited. Moments later, three mute black silhouettes glided stealthily past.

He swore again. *So much for the airport.*

He assessed his options. There was only one road off Amaknak Island into Dutch Harbor proper. The sea lapped at one side of it, and when the fog lifted, the stunted tundra shrubs on the other side wouldn't hide a large cat. Going forward, an ambush awaited; to the sides, total exposure.

Nowhere to run. Nowhere to hide.

Fucking hell.

There was only one thing left to do.

He turned and started to sprint, heading back the way he'd come.

Time for plan B.

Captain Samantha Richardson heaved the last insanely heavy box into place on top of a seemingly endless row of crates and cartons. She and most of her ship's crew had spent the past three hours restacking them. Who knew biscuits weighed so damn much?

A freak summer storm had swept across the Bering Sea yesterday, pounding *Île de Cœur* with fifteen-foot waves and wreaking havoc in three of the seven cargo holds in the bowels of the old tramp freighter. They were only three-quarters full, and anything not nailed down had been tossed about like confetti.

Samantha had already fired and booted off the chief mate, the merchant marine officer responsible for overseeing the loading and securing of the cargo in Japan. Or rather, *not* securing it. She didn't want to think his neglect had been deliberate, but she wouldn't be surprised. There were those in the company who were diehard old school—men like her father and her ex-husband—and believed a woman's place was raising children, changing sheets, and meeting a man at the door with a martini and a smile when he came home from three months at sea. Anything but being the captain of her own ship, spending three months at sea herself.

Her chest tightened briefly. *What. Ever.*

Île de Cœur was now a man down, but Sam would manage. If this was a sample of the chief mate's handiwork, good riddance to him. In reality, she'd been glad for the excuse to fire him. The guy'd had a real attitude problem, and she desperately needed this transit to go smoothly. She'd put all her eggs in this single basket. Or rather, her father had. This transit would make or break her career.

Samantha surveyed the evenly distributed and well-secured stacks of crates that she and the crew were now standing on top of. "Finally," she muttered. She tipped back the old-fashioned yachting cap she always wore and wiped the sweat from her brow with a sleeve. "I thought we'd *never* finish."

Luckily, she'd spent three years as a chief mate herself

en route to her captain's license, and *Île de Cœur*'s second mate, Lars Bolun, was taking the captain's exam this fall, so together they knew how to expertly redistribute the load so it wouldn't shift again.

At her sigh of profound relief, a weary chorus of "Amen!" came back at her from the five men and one woman heading for the ladder up to the orlop—the lowest regular deck—Second Mate Lars Bolun, Carin Tornarsuk the oiler, and four able seamen, Johnny Dorn, Frank Tennyson, Jeeter Pond, and the old salt Spiros Tsanaka.

It was well past midnight, and if they all managed to climb out of the cargo hold, grab a bite to eat, and fall into their bunks without losing consciousness from exhaustion first, it would be a pure damn miracle. Before this, they'd cleaned up hold five, where three pallets of Sapporo Reserve had slipped their ropes and crashed into each other like cymbals, leaving glass bottles shattered and beer sprayed over everything. And before *that* they'd had to completely unload and reorganize hold two, which was filled with vehicle tires, spare machinery parts, and lethally sharp logging equipment, all of which were supposed to be neatly arranged according to purchaser, and had been, when they'd left Sapporo. After the storm, hold two had looked like a cyclone had gone through it. It had been a nightmare to match up the shipping labels—printed in Japanese, naturally—with the lading bills so the orders could be unloaded and picked up quickly when they reached Nome, Alaska, which was their last port of call before heading home to Seattle.

All this lifting had been done by hand without the aid of their deck crane, the top of which had been nearly ripped off during the storm by a killer wave. The crane was useless until the chief engineer, Shandy, could repair it. Hopefully he'd get it working by morning.

Either way, they had to shove off by oh-six-hundred. Sam absolutely, unequivocally, without fail, must get this cargo to Nome before noon on the Fourth of July. In hold three they were carrying the precious order of special fireworks she'd managed by hook, crook, and more than a few shady side deals to scrounge together last week for the new mayor of Nome and his self-aggrandizing election celebration.

The new mayor was the founder and owner of Bravo Logging Corp, Richardson Shipping's biggest client, with eyes on the Alaska governor's mansion. Sam's father, Jason Richardson, had promised the mayor his fireworks—even though at this late date every firework in Japan and China had long since been spoken for and shipped out. Then dear old Dad had deliberately given Sam the assignment of fulfilling the order. Knowing she'd fail. *Or so he thought.*

But dear old Dad didn't know her well enough. One thing father and daughter shared—"failure" was not a word in either of their vocabularies.

Well, other than in marriage. Neither of them had done so well in that department.

She swallowed down the spurt of unwilling hurt that shot through her. After a lifetime of hurts, you'd think she'd be used to it by now. But this last one, Jim's betrayal, had really knocked the wind from her sails. But such was life.

She straightened determinedly and headed for the ladder.

Bringing in this cargo, intact and on time, would ensure at least one part of her life stayed on track—her career. Her father and his fossilized cronies would be forced to end her infuriating "trial contract" and hire her on permanently at Richardson Shipping. Those who wanted her gone from the family business would be effectively robbed of the ammunition they needed to convince her father to fire her—despite her being his only child. Even if he'd never formally acknowledged she was his, other than allowing her his name at birth.

He didn't give a damn about blood ties. She knew better than to think he wouldn't show her the door, with half a reason. She intended to see he didn't have a reason. Not even a fraction of one.

Seaman Johnny Dorn's expressive moan brought her out

of her frustrating thoughts. "I am never, ever, *ever* going to eat another White Lover as long as I live," Johnny Dorn declared, collapsing back against the steel bulkhead as the crew waited for her to catch up to them at the ladder. "Even after drinking a *hundred* gallons of beer."

Everyone was too wiped out to laugh at the raunchy play on words. The inevitable ribald jokes about the unfortunately named Japanese biscuits, combined with the spilled beer, had kept them amused for the first fifteen minutes of lifting and heaving cartons. After that, the humor had fizzled under the weight of the task.

"Hell, Dorn, maybe you ought to hang on to at least one White Lovers box," seaman Frank Tennyson taunted with a grin as they climbed the ladder and he hoisted himself up through the man-sized hatch onto the deck above. "Might be the only chance you get to—"

"Okay," Sam interrupted with a chuckle, *really* not wanting to hear where *that* conversation was headed. Frank was Brad Pitt to Johnny's Bernie Mac, and their verbal exchanges were often hilarious, but always off-color. "Mixed company here," she said dryly as she hung up the clipboard with the cargo manifest on a wall hook beside the metal bulkhead ladder.

She grabbed the ladder and followed them up. The cargo holds were down in the very lowest depths of the ship, below the orlop—or the engineering deck—which was in turn below the huge garage-like ro-ro deck where the roll-on roll-off cargo was parked and tied down. Above the ro-ro deck was the main outside deck, or weather deck, where five railroad containers were secured along with an old Malaysian trolley car headed for San Francisco. That was also where the currently disabled deck crane was positioned. Rising up amidships from the weather deck was the ship's midstructure, which housed the crew deck, then above that the quarterdeck that housed the mess, galley, and lounges. Above that, perched atop the midstructure like a penthouse, was the bridge. Thank God the big stuff on the weather deck had all been tied down correctly. Talk about a potential disaster. She reminded herself to quadruple-check the railroad containers in the morning.

She reached the hatch and stretched up to grab the rim. "Hey, how 'bout someone up there giving me a hand?" she called up. Normally she'd rather chew off her own arm than ask for help, but her muscles felt like limp spaghetti. She was actually afraid she might slip and fall.

Lars Bolun knelt and reached down, trying to slip his arm around her torso as she climbed up another rung and popped her head through the hatch.

"Just relax, Cap'n," the second mate said with a lopsided smile. "I can pull you the rest of the way up."

She snorted and batted him away. "In your dreams, mate." She did, however, grab his hand to steady herself as she hauled herself up onto the orlop deck. She wobbled a bit, and he put a hand to her waist to keep her from toppling.

She straightened away from him, forcing her rubbery legs to carry her weight whether they wanted to or not. She adjusted her cap. "Thanks, Mr. Bolun. I'm good."

He gave her an amused look. "One of these days, Captain, you'll fall willingly into my arms."

At that, everyone *else* snorted.

She rolled her eyes. "Wouldn't hold my breath, mister." They all knew he didn't stand a chance.

Not that he wasn't a good-looking guy. Tall and muscular, with a shock of long, blond hair, and smart to boot. But she was his boss. It just wasn't going to happen.

Besides, he was steady, earnest, and resolute. In other words, the kind of man who'd be looking for clean, folded clothes, a martini at the door, and a lifelong commitment from a woman.

Sam didn't trust commitment. Not anymore. Men threw away commitment like it was yesterday's newspaper. They were far better at betrayal, and her heart couldn't take another one of those.

Suddenly, there was a shout from the top of the narrow stairway leading topside to the main deck. "Capdhain Richardson! You need dho come up here!"

The distinctive East Indian accent belonged to Matty, the wiper—the young greenhorn seaman who got all the dirty maintenance and gopher jobs on board. But Matty had turned out to be a natural mechanic, so Sam had unofficially elevated him to assistant engineer, which was why he was on deck helping Shandy with the crane instead of reloading the cargo with the rest of them.

"What's going on, Mr. Shijagurumayum?" she called back. His full name was Mahatma Shijagurumayum. The others called him Matty for obvious reasons. She'd had to practice in her cabin for half an hour before she'd gotten her tongue wrapped around his ridiculously long and unpronounceable last name.

"Ginger just saw a guy climbing up dhe aft mooring line!" Matty singsonged excitedly. Matty's accent always deepened when he was excited. Ginger was the cook, and a good one, too. "Some idiot must be trying to stow away."

"What?" She stared at Matty for a second in surprise, wading through his accent. Then she made a beeline for the companionway—the main staircase running the whole way up the center of the ship. A *stowaway*? *Hell*, no. That was not going to happen, either. "You didn't let him get on board, did you?"

"No, ma'am. Mr. Shandy's waiting at dhe dhop of the line to grab him."

"Good." She bounded up the metal stairs two at a time. The sound of her footfalls echoed like a popgun. She hadn't thought to post a guard on the dock—she hadn't thought she needed one. With the threat of terrorism and piracy worldwide, security at all their ports of call was normally tight as a barnacle on a hull. No unauthorized persons should be able to get to the cargo docks.

How had this stowaway made it past the gate?

She burst up onto the weather deck, followed closely by the others. They all ran aft across the mist-shrouded deck where Shandy stood at the port rail peering down at the ghostly dock twenty feet below. His gaze swept from side to side, searching the thick black void between the ship and the cement dock. The mooring line cut like spider silk through the dark gap up to the hull. But no one was clinging to it like an insect. Or rather, a rat.

"Where is he? Did you get him?" Sam asked Shandy breathlessly, scanning the dockside. The dock lights were just glowing spheres of yellow in a shroud of shimmering gray. In the swirling fog, even with the feeble help of the midnight sun, it was impossible to see anything but the dim silhouettes of buildings and equipment.

Shandy looked up disgustedly. "Gone. He must have heard Ginger shout to me and taken off."

Sam's anxiety, along with her shoulders, notched down a fraction. "You're sure?"

"Trust me, Cap'n, nobody got past me." Shandy lifted a hand, which was clutching a big, oily wrench.

Sam winced a little but was grateful for his vigilance. "Okay. Good. But let's set up a watch tonight, yeah? I'll call the harbor cops and report an intruder."

"I'll take the watch tonight," Lars Bolun volunteered. "I can sleep tomorrow."

"Thanks, Mr. Bolun," she said, grateful. She could always count on the second mate to step up when needed. "I'll send Ginger out with a plate of food and some coffee." She turned to the others. "Hit the hay everyone. We sail at high tide. That means six a.m., not six fifteen."

They all groaned as she started back inside to the companionway that went up past the crew deck, all the way to the bridge.

"Maybe we should just let the fucker come on board and work him like a dog," Frank grumbled. "We *are* a man short. . . ."

She threw him a withering smile and kept walking. "Right. Because we really want a desperate criminal or a terrorist working side by side with us."

She made her way up the two flights to the bridge, where the ship-to-shore radio was located, and placed the call to the harbor police. Then she retired to her stateroom for a quick shower.

At last she sank onto her bunk and closed her eyes with a tired sigh. She was so exhausted her head was spinning.

Despite that, sleep refused to come. She just couldn't put the intruder out of her mind. Who was he? An escaped prisoner? A terrorist? Or just some poor, homesick fishing bum or park rat who didn't have money for passage to Nome or Seattle? Was he still out there somewhere, waiting to try again?

She shivered and pulled her blanket tight up under her chin. Of all the ships in Dutch Harbor, why had he chosen *Île de Cœur* to stow away on?

She thought about her sidearm, a shiny new Glock 23. It was stored in the bulkhead safe, and so far—thank goodness—had only come out for cleanings and her weekly sessions at the gun range. It was Richardson Shipping policy that all company ships keep a supply of firearms on board, so in addition to hers, there was also a gun safe with a half dozen pistols and three rifles in the officers' lounge. Pirates were an ever-present concern. Okay, maybe not so much in the north Pacific. This was definitely not the South Seas—but better safe than sorry.

Finally she gave up, slid out of bed, and fetched the Glock from the safe. She even loaded the clip. But she drew the line at racking it. Setting the gun in a cubby next to her bunk, she got back into bed and firmly closed her eyes. She was going to get some sleep if it killed her.

She'd just sunk into that floaty twilight zone between waking and sleeping, her body relaxed and her lids heavy as lead, when there was a soft knock at her stateroom door.

She dragged up her eyelids and frowned. "Who is it?"

No one answered.

"Who *is* it?" she repeated, alarm creeping through her muzzy mind. She struggled up and groped for the Glock.

"It—It's me," a deep voice said softly.

She blinked, her hand hovering above the weapon. Who the hell would—"Bolun, is that you?" she snapped. *Really?*

"Open the door," he said, his voice muffled, but more cajoling than demanding. "I, um, need to . . ."

Oh, for godsake. She rose from the bunk and grabbed her robe, wrapping it tightly around herself. At the last second, annoyance made her pick up the Glock. Padding to the door, she cracked it open and peeked out.

"What is it?" she asked. "I thought you were on watch."

He was standing a few feet back. In the near darkness of the passageway, she couldn't see more than the outline of his large body.

Except there was something wrong. His hair . . . it should be blond and pale, even in the dark. Instead it was black as the midnight sky.

Oh, crap. *Not Bolun.*

She gasped and slammed the door.

Too late.

The man moved like lightning. He slapped his palm against the door, preventing it from closing, then pushed his massive frame into it so it flung open and she flew backward onto the bunk.

Suddenly she remembered the Glock in her hand. She whipped it up.

"*Don't,*" he warned.

Her heart slammed to her throat.

A large, black pistol was pointing right back at her.

2

There was a woman in the captain's quarters.

A woman with a gun in her hand.

What the hell?

The woman froze, her sleepy face showing a mix of terror and panic, but her gun was aimed squarely at Clint's chest. Even in the dimly lit corridor, he was a sitting duck.

Shit.

Why was this always happening to him? He was the fucking *good* guy.

"Put down the gun, ma'am. I'm not here to hurt you," he said calmly.

He slowly reached for the credentials in his back pocket. He should have thought to get them out earlier, but after he knocked on the door he'd been so surprised to hear a woman's voice coming from the stateroom that his tired mind had been temporarily wiped blank.

That, he had not expected. *A female captain.* He could have sworn the nameplate on the door had said Captain Sam Richardson. Then it dawned on him. *For Samantha.*

The irony of his stereotyping didn't escape him. He, of all people, should be free of preconceived notions.

"Hey!" she protested as his fingers dipped into his back pocket. "Hands where I can see them!"

He halted, and asked, "What could I possibly be reaching for that's worse than this SIG I already have aimed at your heart?"

She blinked. Looking . . . *Damn*. He hadn't expected *that*, either. She looked, well, adorable.

Gradually, he lowered his weapon. "Relax. I'm just getting my identification." He dug, and flipped open the thin wallet. "I'm Lieutenant Commander Clint Walker, and I work for U.S. Naval Intelligence. Mind if I come in?"

Her jaw dropped incredulously.

Not wanting to be seen by anyone else, he didn't wait for her to regain speech. He stepped all the way into the stateroom and closed the door behind him, plunging the space into total darkness.

"Hey!" she squeaked again. "What are you—"

He didn't relish being shot by accident, so he sidestepped and silently approached her. In a swift movement he relieved her of the pistol. He heard her panicked intake of breath and realized she was about to—*Hell*.

Even faster, he holstered his SIG and slapped his hand over her mouth to stifle her scream. She started to struggle. He ended up sitting in a tangle next to her on the bunk, the back of her head pressed hard into his shoulder. In the dark, her warm staccato breaths were amplified, and the slight tremors in her limbs seemed like earthquakes. He tried not to notice, but . . . damn, she smelled really nice, too. All warm and flowery and feminine. And her body . . . God, was she *naked* under that robe?

With difficulty, he wrangled his highly inappropriate thoughts back on task.

"Please don't scream, ma'am. Honest to God, I'm not here to hurt you. I just need your help."

She wriggled against him. Her soft hair tickled his chin and cheek. The silk of her robe glided across his skin.

God*damn*.

Light. He needed light.

He set her weapon down on the bunk and groped the bulkhead for the inevitable dome light switch. He flicked it on, and the stateroom filled with a dim glow. He looked down. The first thing he noticed was the pretty color of the hair under his chin. Flaxen blond, like liquid gold. Then he peered farther down. And saw her breasts. Naked, pale, and creamy white, tipped by rosy points. Her robe had gaped open, exposing them along with the satiny expanse of her concave belly.

Sweet Mother of God.

He slammed his eyes shut, fighting the instant urge to touch.

Damn, he'd been in the field *way* too long.

He fumbled for her weapon, retrieved it, and pressed it back into her hand. "Here," he said, and let her go as though burned by the feel of her skin instead of being so turned on by it. "Please. Just shoot me now." He ground his palms into his eyes.

She leapt off the bunk, and he half expected to feel the bite of a bullet in his flesh. Which he fully deserved for bungling this so damn badly. But none came.

After a moment he dropped his hands and looked up at her. She'd fixed her robe—*thank you, Jesus*—and was holding the gun firmly in one hand. But it was pointed at the floor, not at him. In the other hand, she held his creds. Her gaze flicked between them and his face.

"You're really Naval Intelligence?" she asked, her voice still hoarse from fear, or possibly from being awakened in the middle of the night. By a maniac.

"I really am," he confirmed with a shade of embarrassment.

She scowled. "So this is how Naval Intelligence officers usually conduct themselves? Bursting into the captain's cabin, taking her hostage, and scaring the crap out of her?"

He flashed her an apologetic smile. "Uh, not usually, no. Only when they're being complete morons. Sorry."

Her scowl didn't even crack. "How the hell did you get onto my ship, anyway?" She tossed back his creds, and he caught them. "I have a guard posted."

He gave her a wry look. "I wouldn't be very good at my job if I couldn't get past one guy pacing the deck drinking coffee and looking bored."

Her lips thinned briefly. He did his best to ignore how plump and lush they were when they relaxed again. Jesus, what was *wrong* with him?

She stooped to pick up an old, once-white cap he must have knocked to the floor, and hung it back on a peg next to the door. "You said you need my help. All right, talk."

Sitting on her bunk was a bad idea. Her scent clung to the bedclothes, making it impossible not to think about that glimpse of her gorgeous breasts. He dragged his gaze up to her eyes and for an instant struggled to remember why he was there. Because it *wasn't* for what he was thinking.

"Are you the intruder who tried to climb up our mooring line earlier?" she prompted when he didn't speak right away.

Right. He focused. "Yeah. That was me." He raked a hand through his short-cropped hair and stood. Immediately she backed up against the door and gripped the gun harder. He stayed where he was. "The thing is, I need to bum a ride to the mainland."

Her gaze turned incredulous. "That's it? You need a ride? *That's* why you broke into my cabin at gunpoint?"

"I did knock first," he pointed out. Lamely.

She rolled her eyes. "Wow."

At least she wasn't scowling any more.

"I thought I heard someone coming. I don't want to be seen," he said.

"Why not?" she demanded, her suspicion back in full force.

He debated how much to tell her. Too little and she wouldn't understand the urgency. Too much and he'd be putting her in danger. Even more danger than his mere presence on board her ship engendered.

"There are some men chasing me," he finally settled on. "They want to kill me."

Her brows flared. "Why does that not surprise me? What did you do to them?"

"Nothing." He shifted on his feet. That much was true.

"Then why do they want to kill you?"

Damn, the woman was persistent. "Sorry. I can't get into that. Classified."

She regarded him evenly. "In that case, sorry, I can't give you a ride."

He pursed his lips. How to handle this? "What if I said it's a matter of national security?"

She hesitated. "Is it?"

Thank God, a patriot. He nodded. "Yes, ma'am, it is."

Apparently the look on his face was serious enough that she didn't dismiss his claim out of hand. "Would your superior officer confirm that story if I called and asked about you, Lieutenant Commander Walker?"

So she'd been paying attention to his introduction. He was mildly impressed. Under the circumstances most people wouldn't remember his name, let alone his rank. "No doubt he'd deny any knowledge of my existence," he said. "It's a sensitive mission."

She blew out a breath. "Naturally. So I'm just supposed to trust you about all this."

He gave her a faint smile. "I'd be grateful if you did, ma'am."

Though still annoyed, she seemed to come to a decision, and relaxed a fraction. "Captain Richardson."

"Ma'am?"

She glanced down at the gun in her hand. "Not ma'am. I'm Captain Samantha Richardson. I know it's protocol, but I hate it when people call me ma'am. I keep looking over my shoulder for my mother."

He regarded her. "Trust me, you're the only one thinking of anyone's mother," he murmured.

Hell. Had he said that aloud?

"I also dislike guns," she said, ignoring his sideways

compliment. She crossed the short distance to the bunk, and unracked and placed the Glock in a shoebox-sized night cubby built into the bulkhead.

That she trusted him this far was definitely progress. Especially since his own weapon was still tucked in its holster under his arm. "So. Will you help me, Captain Richardson?"

For the first time she looked straight at him, and her eyes met his. They were green, like celery. He loved celery. "God knows why I believe you," she said with a tight sigh. "But I do. So, yeah. I'll help you, Lieut—"

He held up a hand. "Since we're doing names, when I'm undercover I prefer Clint. And thanks for trusting me."

She ignored that, too. "I think the word I used was 'believe,' not 'trust,' Lieutenant Commander."

He took a step toward her, holding her gaze. "I'm serious. Call me Clint. No rank. Only you can know I work for the navy. I wasn't kidding about the national security thing."

She regarded him for a long moment. Finally she said, "Tell you what, Mr. Walker. Since you're a navy man, I assume you've served as a ship's officer."

He nodded, giving up for now on the name. And, unconsciously, on anything else. Obviously she had no interest in being friends. Or anything else. Not that this was the time or place to indulge in such things.

"I just fired my first mate, so I'm a man short," she went on. "You can take over his place on the crew until we get to Seattle."

"First mate?" Another surprise. Although he was an officer, he'd been a SEAL and knew more about explosives and oxygen mixes than ordering around sailors. Or whatever a first mate did on a civilian vessel. "Not sure I'm up to that task on a merchant ship," he admitted. "I have no idea what the position entails."

She waved a hand. "I've already put Second Mate Bolun in charge of the cargo, so basically you'd be responsible for the safety and security of the ship and crew. Right up your alley, I'd think."

"Security I can handle," he affirmed with a small curve of his lips. At least it wasn't dragging in putrid-smelling fishing nets.

"You'll need a uniform," she said, frowning at his ragged, grubby attire. "Jesus, what'd you do before this, stow away on a garbage scow?"

He winced. "Not far off. Fishing trawler. They had me chumming and hauling nets. Sorry about that. I could definitely use a shower or three, and a change of clothes. Not to mention a bed."

His gaze caught hers, and yet again he was reminded of her naked body under that flimsy robe. Apparently she remembered, too. He saw a light flush sweep her cheeks. But this time she didn't look away.

They stared at each other for a taut moment, but before he could decide if and what he should do about it, she turned abruptly. "You can take the chief mate's stateroom. It has a shower," she said pointedly. "I'll show you."

He eased out a breath of disappointment, all the while berating himself. Well, what had he expected? That she'd invite him to share hers? The way he looked—and smelled? Get real.

"Thanks," he said. "It's been a rough week. I could probably sleep all the way to Seattle."

She shook her head as she padded barefoot to the cabin door. "Not on my ship, you won't." She glanced at the glowing dial of the wall clock. "Since it's nearly two a.m., I'll give you a break and let you slide on your first watch." He knew that traditionally the first mate stood the oh-four to oh-eight hundred shift, at least on navy ships. "But we depart at six a.m. sharp. I'll expect you on deck."

"Yes, ma'am," he said agreeably, and just smiled at her annoyed glance. Two could play the name game.

Reaching for a long, gray coat that hung by the door, she muttered, "I'll dig up a spare uniform so you can burn those clothes. God forbid we have to smell them all the way to Nome."

Hello.

"What?" In two strides he'd reached her. He put a hand on her arm. *"Nome?"*

She jerked away from him, startled. "Yeah. Nome. We've got a ton of cargo to offload there, and we're on a strict schedule. Is that a problem?"

Yeah. It was.

"It's imperative I get to Seattle ASAP," he said. That was the closest naval base, where he could finally catch a ride on a military transport plane to D.C. without risk of running into Xing Guan and his team of assassins. His commander had told him to take the time to get home alive, but the navy really needed the data card he was carrying. Like, yesterday.

"Well, it's imperative *I* get to Nome ASAP," she countered. "You're welcome to find another ship to stow away on, if you don't like our schedule."

He let out a groan. "Fuck."

She hiked an eyebrow.

"Sorry."

The intel on the micro storage card in his pocket really *was* a matter of national security. A growing number of the compact, torpedo-sized Chinese UUVs were already being detected running sorties along the North American coast. Used for both intelligence and military purposes, UUVs were rapidly replacing their much larger, more visible, and massively more expensive submarines. The sooner Clint got the plans for the new Chinese guidance system to D.C. and the navy's experts, the sooner they could start designing countermeasures against the all too real threat of coastal incursion, industrial and military espionage, and even sabotage.

He couldn't tell her that, though.

He also couldn't phone in the plans, or e-mail them, or use any other unsecure, unencrypted method of communication to transmit the top secret intel to the navy. He was under strict orders from the brass. He had to *personally* get the storage card to D.C., or at the very least Seattle. Which was not proving easy. After jumping off a Russian submarine ten days ago, he'd been forced to traverse the most remote, sea-swept ends of the earth, with no money, no map, and nothing but a wetsuit, a small dry-bag, and sweat equity to trade for transpo across the two thousand miles of frigid, largely unpopulated Aleutian Islands just to get this far. It had been an adventure—right up until that damn fishing trawler. That he could have done without.

"If this mission is so damn important," Samantha observed, "why don't you just call the navy and have them send a helicopter or something to pick you up?"

Like he hadn't already tried that. Twice. But a combination of the navy's newly mandated budget cuts and always fanatical bean counters, the great distance to the nearest military base, and the usual bullshit of bureaucratic and jurisdictional red tape, had made his commander throw up his hands and decide, fuck it, it would be faster and safer for an ex-SEAL to make his way back home on his own. Even with nothing but lint in his bartered pockets.

Clint agreed. With Xing Guan and his henchmen hot on his heels, he'd take his chances on his grandfather's lessons, his SEAL training, and his own ingenuity on the run, rather than cool his heels, exposed and vulnerable, waiting for transport to be procured and sent the two thousand miles from Seattle.

"Yeah, the helo didn't work out," he merely said, frustration starting to whir in his gut once again.

This entire week had been one long series of frustrations. Which in itself was aggravating as hell. Not so long ago, none of this would have bothered him in the least.

Jesus, he really was getting old and crotchety.

Or horny.

Maybe that was why he felt so damn frustrated.

He looked pointedly at Captain Richardson. *Samantha.* "So. About that bed . . ."

She astutely avoided his gaze. "Yeah." She turned, grabbed her long coat, and slipped it on as she slid into a pair of battered deck shoes. "Come on."

He was both disappointed and glad that she'd covered

herself up completely before taking him to his stateroom. If she hadn't, he'd be sorely tempted to—

Never mind. He had to stop this. He wasn't *that* horny.

Except he was, which was totally unlike him. What the hell was it about this particular woman that got his juices flowing and his thoughts veering into places they seldom inhabited? Normally it would never occur to him to slam the door and rip that ugly coat off her, and then open that flimsy robe, and—

Fucking hell.

She gave him an odd look as she led him along the passageway to another stateroom two doors down. Way too close to hers.

She opened the door and flipped on the light. "Head's over there." She pointed. "The shower's the size of a breadbox, but the water's hot."

"Don't suppose you'd like to join me?" he asked, unable to stop himself.

She blinked. Then gave him a long, assessing look. Her focus started at his hair, dropped to his shoulders, then his waist, and then his— He cleared his throat as her gaze continued down his thighs, then slowly traveled back up to his face.

To his shock, she said, "Tell you what, Mr. Walker. Ask me again when you don't smell like a bilge rat."

With that, she turned and went out, closing the door behind her.

3

The next morning as she got ready for the day, Sam was still wondering what on earth had possessed her to make such a blatantly suggestive comment to Lieutenant Commander Walker.

Sam had a firm rule against fraternizing with her crew, on or off the ship. No matter how incredibly sexy the man in question happened to be.

And no matter how depressingly lonely she'd been feeling since her ex-husband, Jim, had left her.

But a ship's captain was supposed to be a leader. Set an example. Be beyond any whisper of scandal. It was why she called everyone "mister" or "miz," to keep a correct personal distance firmly in place. Some skippers went out of their way to be buddies with their crew members, but Sam couldn't do that. Because of her very precarious position in her father's company, she must scrupulously avoid even the perception of weakness or undisciplined behavior. She knew only too well that even if he didn't fire her, the old man would use any excuse to bust her ass down to an office job—the proper place for a woman in the company, according to him. Even his daughter. Hell, *especially* his daughter. The only reason he'd given her this chance at her own ship was because he knew damn well if he didn't, she'd walk out of his life for good. He was still trying to convince himself that he was making up for three decades of being anything but a father.

Good luck with *that* delusion.

But she had to admit, the sight of Clint Walker's enticing bedroom eyes and his hard, muscular body was making her ask herself what harm would come if she indulged in a small indiscretion. Just this once. It *had* been nearly three years since her bastard ex-husband had departed for greener—make that *younger*—pastures, leaving her essentially alone in the world. Wasn't she entitled to a little human comfort? Even a little pleasure? She'd been so hurt, so utterly blindsided and betrayed by Jim's leaving, there'd been no other man since. The thought of starting another relationship made her break out in a cold sweat. It was that trust thing. But she just didn't have the stomach for one-night stands, or vacation flings, or indiscriminate bar pick-ups. She didn't have anything against such things—for other people—they just weren't for her.

Normally.

Until Clint Walker had come barging into her stateroom waving a gun and looking so gorgeous her mouth actually watered thinking about him. *Lord* have *mercy*. The lieutenant commander was walking, talking sex on a stick.

As long as you plugged your nose.

He'd made it pretty darn clear he was interested in her, too.

And, after all, she reasoned, who would know? If they were careful and kept their short, no-strings affair under wraps, no one would be the wiser. And as soon as *Île de Cœur* hit the dock in Seattle, Clint Walker would be gone like a shot, out of her life for good.

The ideal man.

Hot and temporary.

She'd have to give his proposition—or had it been hers?—some serious thought. . . .

When she finished dressing and made her way to the mess hall for breakfast, Walker was already there, wearing dark blue pants and a white uniform shirt complete with the gold stripes appropriate to his newly assumed rank. An old navy peacoat was draped over the back of his chair. As promised, last night she'd scrounged a spare set of clothes from the storage room, and quietly sneaked into his stateroom to leave it on his bunk—*after* putting her ear to his door and hearing the shower running.

Chicken.

Warmth flooded her cheeks like a schoolgirl's as Walker caught her gaze from across the mess hall and smiled. He stood, for no other apparent reason than that she'd entered the room. Wow. Was that good navy training? Or a good mother . . . ? She gave him a quick smile back and kept walking.

She wasn't the only one who noticed his gentlemanly behavior. Lars Bolun frowned, pausing with a forkful of eggs halfway to his mouth. Ginger came around with a pot of coffee and Sam's favorite ceramic mug, filled it, and set it in her usual spot at the head of the long Formica table. But Ginger's eyes never strayed from the newcomer.

"Can I top yours up, too, Clint?" she asked him with a subtle flutter of her eyelashes.

A sudden, intense, and completely irrational spurt of jealousy stabbed through Sam. Mortified, she tamped it down, even as she noted with satisfaction that Walker's eyes were still glued to *her* rather than Ginger as he took his seat again.

Lars Bolun noticed that, too, and his frown deepened. He really needed to get over it. She glanced down the table at Carin, who was watching *him* . . . unnoticed as usual.

"Thanks, Ginger," she said, striving for normalcy in her tone and actions. She stuffed her cap into her coat pocket and strode to the buffet that had been laid out on a table along one wall. "I see you've all met Mr. Walker. He'll be joining us as first mate until Seattle. Mr. Bolun, I'd appreciate if you show him the ropes this morning before you go off shift."

The rest of the crew had straggled into the mess after her; now eight curious pairs of eyes cut from her to Walker and back again.

"Where the hell *he'd* come from?" asked Frank, ever to the point.

"Fuckin' A!" Johnny exclaimed. "He's not the fuckin' *stowaway*, is he?"

"I believe I made my opinion of stowaways known to everyone last night," she evaded, keeping her back to them as she filled her plate. "The company feels we should have a full contingent on board. Mr. Walker showed up early this morning." It was a fine line, but neither statement was a lie.

Walker followed her lead, shrugging at their skeptical looks. "The fishing trawler I was working had to put in for extensive repairs here in Dutch. What can I say. I got bored waiting."

"Funny, I didn't see you come aboard this morning," Lars Bolun said with dangerously narrowed eyes.

Again Walker shrugged. "I didn't see you, either. Were you supposed to be keeping watch?"

Bolun's mouth parted in affront, but Spiros Tsanaka preempted him. "Which trawler?" he demanded suspiciously.

To her relief, Walker answered promptly with the name of a small vessel owned by a local family, one familiar to all of them. "Captain Ryan's a good guy," he said, paused, then added, "but their cook stinks. This," he said, lifting a forkful of Denver omelet, Ginger's specialty, "is the best meal I've had in weeks."

The tension broke a little, and there were even a few chuckles. Most of them had met and liked Captain Ryan, and everyone in Dutch knew that Ginger was the best cook on the line. His compliments were a point in his favor.

"So," Bolun began.

Glancing at the clock, Sam cut him off before he could

get started with an inquisition. "Mr. Bolun, what else needs to be done before we're secure for departure?"

Sam didn't exactly blame them for questioning the whole stranger-showing-up-in-the-middle-of-the-night-right-after-an-intruder-scare thing. She'd been terrified herself last night, she reminded herself. But she also didn't want the crew interrogating Walker. The last thing she needed was word of her somewhat iffy decision to let him stay on board getting back to her detractors at Richardson Shipping, or to her father. Not before she could explain her reasons, anyway.

Aside from which, it was getting close to their six a.m. departure time. The clock was ticking.

Bolun looked briefly put out by her interruption. But he got over it and, with a note of pride, recited a very short list of things left to do before the tide peaked.

"Seems like Mr. Walker wasn't the only one bored last night," she said approvingly. Lars had taken care of much of the prep work on deck during his stint on watch. "Thanks for that."

"Just doing my part," he returned somberly. "I know how much is riding on this transit." He didn't add, "for you," but the implication was clear from the way the statement hung meaningfully in the air.

Sam didn't dare look at Walker. Or at Bolun. She didn't feel like making explanations. And she sure as hell didn't want either one of them getting the wrong idea about the other. Which was when she decided that escape was sometimes the better part of valor. She gulped down her coffee, grabbed a buttered roll to go, and stood. "Think I'll go down and check on Chief Shandon's progress with the deck crane," she said. Tugging on her cap, she beelined it for the exit.

"Don't you people have work to do?" she called over her shoulder. "Because if you don't, I can find you something."

Their grumbles echoed after her.

She emerged on the narrow poop deck behind the mess and got her first glimpse of the day outside. The weather had been crazy for the whole month of June. Hopefully July would be better. But it was impossible to tell from where she stood.

One of the things she'd loved best about growing up in Alaska was the sparkling yellow sun. It lit up the grand panorama of the state's natural wonders in an endless rainbow of brilliant colors. The wide, limitless sky was often so blue it hurt to look at it, the forests a green so deep and varied that it defied description. The crystalline lakes, the pristine white snow, even the wild animals were painted in a vivid palette of colors not found anywhere else in the world. That she had been forced to abandon her beloved Alaska for gray, colorless Seattle was just one of the myriad reasons she hated her ex-husband. Unfortunately, even the whole state of Alaska wasn't big enough for her and Jim to inhabit at the same time.

Not in her opinion, at any rate.

As she clattered down the ladder to the weather deck to check on Chief Shandon, she grimaced. Despite the ubiquitous summer sun that wouldn't set at all for another week or two, this particular day promised to be another of those awful, foggy, foggy, island days she'd grown so weary of enduring. They seemed to suck the life right out of her, and the crew, as well. With any luck, once they'd cruised out from the shallow waters of the Aleutians and entered the cold, crisp depths of the Bering Sea, they'd leave the fog behind.

"Hey, Chief," she greeted Shandy. "How's it going with the crane work?"

He glanced up wearily. He looked like absolute shit warmed over. His eyes were bloodshot and sunken, his tan skin lusterless, and his mouth etched in a downward curve. He couldn't have gotten any sleep at all last night.

"Not great, Skip," he muttered. Shandy was the only one she allowed to call her "skipper," out of respect for his age and his vast experience and knowledge of everything having remotely to do with the workings of a ship. "I've managed to replace most of the worst-bent parts, but there's still a ways to go to put them back together and get the thing in a useable state again. Plus we seem to be out of a critical size of bolt I need to secure that last section."

They both looked up at the very tip of the crane arm, which was listing at a precarious angle from the rest of the rig. From it hung a steel cable, attached to a giant metal claw-hook that secured the large steel mesh net that was used to load cargo onto the ship. It was swinging back and forth over the deck like a pendulum. If the arm broke off and the hook and net fell, someone could be seriously injured, or even killed.

"You're a wonder, Chief. I'm sorry I have to put you through this. I wish we'd had the time to do these repairs in Dutch." She felt guilty as hell about that. But if they'd stopped, they'd never make it to Nome in time.

He shook his head. "Heck, it's my job, Skipper, and I don't mind doin' it. I'm just worried about the weather's all."

She sighed and looked around for Matty. "Where's Mr. Shijagurumayum? Isn't he helping you?" They really had to get this thing fixed. Or at least immobilized so it wasn't a danger to the crew.

"Poor kid was falling over. I sent him up to his bunk for a few hours' kip."

She took in his rough condition. "What about you? I'm betting you've been up all night," she said. It was obvious he was on the verge of falling over himself. "You should get some sleep too, Chief."

He shook his head. "Can't. With no bolts, I gotta get that top section welded, while the weather's still good. Don't want to take a chance of it turning nasty again. Been too unpredictable."

It was a legitimate concern. Regardless of the forecast, you never knew what the Arctic would throw at you. Especially lately, what with the ravages of global warming.

"Can't someone else do it?" she asked, nonetheless concerned for his safety. The man was dead on his feet. Her hair rose at the thought of him climbing that broken crane arm with a welding torch.

Shandy sighed tiredly. "Ain't no one else."

"I can do it," said a voice from behind her.

She turned. Lieutenant Commander Walker was standing with his arms crossed over his unbuttoned peacoat, feet splayed against the slight sway of the ship, studying the crippled deck crane above them. He'd found a pair of mirrored aviator sunglasses somewhere and was wearing them, which rendered his bronze face completely inscrutable except for the firm set of his jaw.

"Who're you?" the chief asked in a surprised way that made her think he might be wondering if he was so tired he was hallucinating.

She made the introductions, and Walker stuck out his hand, which Shandy shook assessingly.

"You weld?" the chief asked, with the hopeful voice of someone who'd been too oft disappointed.

"Yep," the lieutenant commander said, followed by something indecipherable about acetylene and load capacity.

"Well. There you go, Chief," Sam said, grateful for Walker's unexpected expertise. Maybe her decision to let him stay hadn't been so rash—or selfish—after all. "Bring Mr. Walker up to speed, then get below for some shut-eye," she ordered Shandy. "We'll be pushing hard for Nome, and I'd like you alert if we have engine issues." She glanced at Walker. "Thanks. I appreciate the help."

She didn't wait for a reply but hurried off to do her last-minute checks and get the crew moving. The tide was nearly at its zenith. Time to get this show on the road.

"Samantha," he called after her, bringing her to an abrupt halt halfway to the midstructure ladder that rose up to the poop deck, then up to the bridge.

She whirled and opened her mouth to rebuke him about calling her by her first name.

But he beat her to the punch. "Sorry, ma'am. I meant

Captain Richardson," he said with a transparently unrepentant grin.

"What is it, Mr. Walker?" she ground out, feeling disturbingly torn between irritation over the breach . . . and absurd pleasure at the way he was looking at her.

"Just wondered," he drawled, "if I'm smelling better this morning?"

4

Clint chuckled as Samantha—that is, Captain Richardson—snapped her mouth shut, turned about, and strode wordlessly away.

Not that he'd expected an answer. He'd just wanted to remind her of last night's implied invitation. Or rather, her straight-up invitation. There'd been nothing implied about it. And there was nothing he'd rather do than make good on that offer.

Just as soon as the ship was free of the harbor and any danger of Xing Guan's operators catching up to him was past. That was the only way he could even *think* about stepping outside his mission parameters.

On the one hand, he was frustrated being forced to make an unnecessary four-day detour . . . but on the other hand, Nome, Alaska, was in exactly the wrong direction, and therefore probably the last place on the planet his Chinese pursuers would think to look for him. With any luck the three assassins were still at the Dutch Harbor airport waiting for him to show up. When he didn't, hopefully they'd assume he'd managed to sneak onto a plane without them spotting him. And if he was really lucky, they'd be off on a wild-goose chase to D.C.

Thus giving him the next few days to let down his guard a bit and enjoy his ride on *Île de Cœur*, relatively worry free. And become better acquainted with its pretty captain. *Much* better acquainted.

"Nice try, but you're fishin' in the wrong waters, son," Chief Shandon said, interrupting his schemes with a wry tilt to his tired smile as they watched Samantha walk away.

"Yeah?" Clint asked, turning his attention back to the grizzled chief engineer. He squatted next to him and casually examined the neat piles of crane parts spread out around them.

"Better men than you have tried and failed miserably," the chief said.

"And why's that?" Clint asked, his curiosity piquing. He picked up a few of the parts, grabbed a wrench, and started assembling. Clint enjoyed tinkering, and this was the perfect spot on deck to keep an eye on comings and goings down on the dock. Not to mention when he climbed the crane to do the welding. No one was getting within spitting distance of *Île de Cœur* without him knowing about it.

The old man watched his swift, sure movements approvingly. "Hell. The skipper hasn't looked at anything in pants since that no-good husband of hers went off an' broke her heart."

Clint paused and glanced up at him. "She's married?" Damn. So much for his fantasies.

Ah, well. It was a bad idea anyway. He was on a mission. He shouldn't even be considering this—

"*Ex*-husband," the chief corrected, and muttered, "Pond scum."

That was all Clint needed to hear. "Well," he said, forgetting all about his rationalizations, "I'll keep that in mind."

Or not. It wasn't like he planned on going steady with the woman. A few stolen nights together on a ship a relationship did not make. Nor did he *want* a relationship. His fantasies of a family notwithstanding, Clint knew himself better than that. He was a loner. He liked being a loner. After his grandfather died, he'd grown up alone, spent most of his life alone, and no doubt it would continue that way.

He was too busy for a serious relationship. His job took him all over the world at a moment's notice. He could see *that* going over really well with a woman. Not. Nor did he know the first thing about maintaining a relationship. Besides, they seldom lasted, he'd observed, despite both parties' best intentions. Captain Richardson's failed marriage was one shining example of that. He was pretty sure she hadn't gone down the aisle thinking she'd get her heart broken.

No. A relationship was not something he was looking for.

Which wasn't to say he didn't love women, because he most definitely did. He adored them. Adored flirting with them. Adored being around them. And generally, they returned the sentiment.

Which was why he had every confidence that Samantha's invitation last night had not been an idle promise. And why a smile stayed on his lips as he suggested Chief Shandon go below for a nap, he could take care of the rest of the repairs on his own. Then he started the work to raise the crane back to its full erect height.

He stifled an ironic grin.

Talk about a fitting analogy.

A short time later, the ship's engines began to rumble. The deck vibrated softly beneath Clint's boots. After a few shouts between Samantha and their tugboat captain, the lines were cast off, and *Île de Cœur* eased away from the wharf, being pulled through the harbor by the tug assigned to ferry them out into the Bering Sea.

Clint breathed a sigh of relief.

There'd been no sign this morning of his pursuers. Once again, he'd slipped right out from under their noses, keep-

ing the data storage card with its critical intel safe for his
country.

Thank God. Now he could relax for a few days without
looking over his shoulder.

Playing 007 and running from bad guys had been his life
for over ten years, so he wasn't complaining. He'd chosen
his profession. He'd always gotten off on the adrenaline
rush and the constant change of scenery, the deadly battle
of wits and the importance of his work to the welfare and
security of his native land. He was good at his job. One of
the best.

But this past week had been a real ballbuster, every one
of his thirty-six years showing, in stark contrast to the
much younger fishermen he'd worked beside on the
trawler. Oh, he'd held his own. But it had been hard-won.
That had been a shocker to him. He'd always prided himself on his physical prowess, his old SEAL conditioning
making him a standout among the usual fat cats inside the
D.C. beltway.

He had to admit, after the past few weeks it would be
real nice just to kick back and let himself unwind a bit,
enjoy the brisk sea breeze in his hair and the sun on his face
as he worked on fixing the crane. And indulged in a few
more fantasies . . . about how and when he was going to get
the beautiful Captain Richardson alone and naked.

Something whooshed by just above his head and he
ducked instinctively, almost hitting the deck in a roll and
going for his weapon. Which, of course, he'd left in his
stateroom, under the mattress. He nearly rolled his eyes at
that clever hiding place. But he hadn't had time to come up
with anything better. He would. Later.

Meanwhile, he peered up at the heavy cargo net that
would have taken his head off had he been a foot or two
taller. It dangled at the end of the crane hook, sweeping
back and forth above the deck in a wide arc, making a
complete circuit with each wave the ship rolled over. The
tip of the crane arm was bent like an elbow that shouldn't
be there. Several of the lower sections of metal struts had

been removed for repair. The whole thing looked like a project made from an Erector Set with half the parts missing.

Until it got put together again, it was a disaster waiting to happen. Best get to work.

He gathered tools and eye protection, and a few of the sections that Shandy had assembled, and approached the base of the sturdy king post that supported the crane. To reach the crane's control cabin, you had to climb up using the round metal hand- and footholds that stuck out opposite sides of the king post, as on a giant telephone pole.

He surveyed the towering structure with distaste. He'd never been one for heights. Unless they were underwater. Mohawk he was definitely not.

Perhaps if he thought about the delectable Captain Richardson and how they might take a tour of the ship together, exploring the sensual possibilities of each different compartment, maybe he wouldn't notice how far above the deck he was.

Oh, yeah. That seemed to do the trick.

Before he knew it, several hours had gone by . . . and he'd played out quite a few tantalizing scenarios in his mind, each more enjoyable than the last.

The fog had disappeared, the midsummer sun was now high overhead, and the newly repaired crane soared up into a brilliant blue sky. He vaguely remembered asking some of the other men to help him ratchet the top section into place after he'd welded it. It was still a little crooked, but at least it was no longer in danger of falling off.

Clint was sitting up in the cab at the control console, trying to figure out which button and lever controlled which crane function—without releasing the steel mesh net from the claw-hook onto one of the crew members' heads below—when a feminine voice came through the cabin door.

"Wow. You're good." The captain climbed up into the small cabin with him. "And fast," she added with a shade of admiration.

He looked at her and blinked, his mind still steeped in the tempting fantasies he'd been indulging in. About her. And him. Together.

Good, yes. But fast? Hardly.

Then he realized with a start that she was talking about the crane.

He glanced out through the cab's expansive windows at the crane arm.

"Almost done," he said, getting up from the low operator's seat so she could sit. "I'm trying to figure out all these levers so I can position the crane so that damn net swings out over the side and not over the deck."

"Here, use this instead. It's easier." She picked up a portable device that resembled a complicated video game controller. He squatted down to look over her shoulder. She touched the center joystick. "This moves the crane around in any direction." She pointed at a green button on the side. "Just don't touch this one. It releases the net." She turned her face up to smile at him.

Damn, she was pretty. He just wished she'd take off that old hat. He wanted to put his nose in her hair and breathe in the scent of her.

"Go on. Try it," she said, and he had to physically stop himself from spinning that chair around and doing just that. The high cab was practically all glass windshield. Unless they got down on the floor, they could be seen from anywhere on two decks and the bridge.

Still, it was tempting.

Especially since he'd hunted down the medical supply closet after breakfast, and was delighted to find several boxes of assorted condoms. Some of which were even now burning a hole in his pocket.

He cleared his throat and wrangled his mind back on point. "All right." Bracketing his arms around her from behind, he took the controller in his hands. She watched as he manipulated the joystick, testing the crane arm. He made it go back and forth, up and down, then rotated it out over the water. "There. That's— Whoa!" The crane arm tilted abruptly down. He jerked the joystick, stopping its descent at an angle nearly parallel with the deck. "Still a few glitches I guess."

He set the controller down but didn't rise, and didn't move his arms away.

She touched the joystick with a finger, running it along the smooth plastic. "Hmm. But a whole lot better than it was before. I'm impressed, Walker."

He winked at her reflection in the windshield. "I aim to please, ma'am."

She tipped her head to one side and regarded him back. "Honestly," she said, "I never thought you'd get it up so quickly." Her expression was guileless.

Too guileless.

He smothered a smile. *Sassy.* "Trust me," he murmured, "getting it up has never been a problem for me."

She turned to slant a glance up at him from beneath the brim of her beat-up cap. Her full lips quirked. "But keeping it up seems to be."

He wanted to pull her into his arms and taste those impertinent lips. "Hell no," he drawled. "I just enjoy going down, too."

The barest tinge of pink washed her cheeks. Embarrassment? Or desire . . . ?

He decided to find out. Slowly, he spun the chair around so she faced him. He was still squatting, his knees spread. There was no mistaking what *he* was feeling.

Her tongue peeked out and swiped over her lower lip. He slowly started to lean in.

Somewhere nearby a loudspeaker abruptly crackled. "Captain Richardson to the bridge," a male voice boomed over the PA system. "Captain please report to the bridge."

Clint halted, halfway to kissing her. *Damn.*

Her eyes closed for a nanosecond, then opened. "Bolun," she said. "He needs to get a life."

Clint chuckled, banking his frustration. "He's just trying to protect you. He thinks I'm a stowaway of less than stellar character."

Her green eyes twinkled. "No. He thinks you're trying to seduce me."

He eased away with an answering smile. "Smart man."

For a long, sizzling moment their gazes locked. "I should probably go," she said at length.

"Yeah."

Neither of them moved.

"See what he wants."

Clint lifted a brow. "I'd say that's pretty obvious."

"Too bad for him." She gave Clint a Mona Lisa smile and stood to go. "You coming?"

Hell, yeah. "In a bit." He glanced out at the crane. "Have a few things to finish up first."

"Hmm." She grasped the doorframe and half turned, following the direction of his gaze. "Well, Mr. Walker, when you get it up for good, come and find me."

"That," he said with a lazy grin, "is a promise."

She disappeared down the ladder, and the smile spread slowly over his face.

Desire, he thought with satisfaction. *Definitely desire.*

5

///////////////

Clint came to find her later that afternoon.

Sam had been thinking about him all day. Going back and forth in her mind about what she had set in motion, alternately horrified with herself and impatient with his delay.

Good lord. Was she really going to do this?

She shouldn't.

She *really* shouldn't. Surely, it wasn't too late to put a stop to things.

Was it?

Even though she was wildly attracted to Lieutenant Commander Walker, a part of her was genuinely terrified. She hadn't been with a man since her ex-husband left over three years ago. Not even on a date, let alone . . .

It was a real shame she liked sex so much. Sex had been the one thing she and Jim had been good at. Really good. After fourteen years with a partner who knew her body better than she did, she missed it.

A lot.

During the last three years spent alone, she hadn't let

herself think about how much she'd missed it. That's why God had invented batteries, right?

But it just wasn't the same.

She loved the feel of a man's strong arms holding her. The hardness of his body pressed into hers. The rough scrape of his chest hair against her tender breasts. The hot, wet slide of his cock thrusting into her.

Damn.

She might not trust men anymore, but she was achingly, desperately, howl-at-the-moon lonely for the touch of a man.

This man.

"Hi," Clint's voice said behind her, snapping her out of her disconcerting thoughts.

She whirled, fumbling the pen in her hand. She'd been making notations on a clipboard, standing in one of the ship's cramped storage rooms on the orlop deck, where they kept their general supplies. "Oh! Hi."

He snatched the flying pen in midair and handed it back to her with a smile, glancing at the clipboard.

"Inventory," she said by way of explanation. Thankfully the transit supplies strapped onto massive metal shelves had been better secured than the cargo, so the storm hadn't created as big a mess in the storage areas. Johnny, Frank, and Spiros had straightened them all up this morning. Sam was now doing a careful inventory to see if anything needed to be replaced. She puffed out a sigh. "Ah, the glamour of a ship captain's job never fails to inspire awe."

His smile twisted. "Still, beats the hell out of being tortured in a Chinese prison."

Her eyes widened. Yikes. Where had that come from? Was he talking about himself? "You've been tortured?"

He lifted an easy shoulder. "Define 'torture.'"

She blinked. Jeez, what exactly did a Naval Intelligence officer *do*, anyway? "You're kidding, right?"

If he had been tortured, he didn't seem particularly upset by it. "Not on this mission. Thanks to you. Again, I appreciate you trusting me."

This mission? She seriously wondered if he was pulling her leg. "Not trust," she corrected. *"Believe—"*

He held up a hand with a chuckle. "Ah, yes. I remember. We have, I'm guessing, trust issues?"

"You have no idea," she said, meeting his gaze.

Okay. This was a pretty bizarre conversation. Especially if he'd come here with seduction on his mind. *Or maybe she'd just misinterpreted his signals . . .*

He propped a shoulder against the metal doorframe and watched her with casual interest. His stance was relaxed, his expression friendly. And yet she couldn't help noticing that his large body blocked her way. She wasn't getting out of the storage room without him moving to let her past.

A frisson shivered through her. *Or maybe she hadn't misinterpreted . . .*

"You're fairly young to be a ship's captain," he remarked, tilting his head.

"Yes, well," she began, her defenses coming up with a vengeance. *Not* the way to get into her good graces. Or her pants.

But he forestalled her tirade. "You must have worked your butt off. I know it's not easy for a woman to push her way up the ranks in this profession," he said, surprising her so much she just gaped at him for a few seconds.

"You could say that," she finally responded. Most people assumed . . . Well, never mind what most people assumed. It wasn't true.

He unpropped himself from the doorframe and took a step closer, nearly closing the short distance between them. "Especially a beautiful woman like you, I expect."

She felt her lips part and her cheeks warm. "I, um—"

Conflicting emotions swirled through her. Surprise. Desire. *Fear.* God, and earlier when they flirted she'd felt so . . . fearless.

He reached out and touched her cheek, running his knuckles down to brush along her jawline. "Most men wouldn't see beyond the delicate outside to the strength within."

And he did?

"Hardly delicate," she murmured. She was five eight and probably hadn't been a size two since she graduated from first grade.

His fingers trailed over her lips. "Delicate, confident, and lovely."

A spill of sizzling awareness washed through her. His fingertips were rough, but warm and supple. She imagined them on her body. . . . "Thank you," she whispered.

"And obviously great at what you do."

His compliment felt like warmth flooding her belly. It had been so long since anyone had actually respected, or even noticed, her abilities. Anyone that mattered.

"If this is that seduction you promised," she whispered, "you're doing a hell of a job."

His gentle smile made the corners of his eyes crinkle. "Glad to hear it."

She swallowed, and when his hand threaded through her hair, pulling her to him, she went willingly to meet his lips.

They were smooth and moist, tasting of temptation, and forbidden delight, and sweet love in front of a roaring fire. And persuasive male desire.

She didn't need to be persuaded.

The kiss went on and on, easing her hesitancy, filling her with a tumbling ache of need. His arms came around her and hers went around him, feeling the hard muscles of his biceps, the press of his fingers, the pounding of his heart against her breasts. Lord, the man could kiss!

When he finally lifted his mouth, they were both breathless.

He looked at her, his eyes half-lidded and lambent with desire. "I want you," he murmured.

Her pulse pounded. *This is it. The point of no return.*

She didn't want to stop. She wanted him, too. Like crazy.

"Did you bring protection?" she whispered shakily.

"What do you think?" His hand eased under her shirt.

She sucked in a breath as his thumb brushed her nipple.

"G-good," she managed, uncertain if she meant his pre-paredness . . . or the skill of his touch.

His hand stilled. "I want you to know," he said in a low rumble. "I don't usually do this sort of thing. I mean, under circumstances like—" He shook his head. "I don't want you to think—"

"I don't. And I don't, either," she choked out, wanting nothing more than for him to continue what he'd started. She took a deep breath. "But who can resist a man who barges into your bedroom in the dead of night at gunpoint?"

He nuzzled her hair, and murmured, "Or a woman who sneaks a good, long look at you in the shower?"

She put her lips to the base of his throat and kissed him, tasting the salt of the sea, smelling the tang of his male scent. "If only I'd dared," she admitted softly. "Might have saved me a sleepless night of regret."

Against her cheek, his lips curved. "I'll give you a do-over. We can go up to my stateroom right now." He grasped her jaw between his fingers and kissed her again, slow and hot. "Because this closet isn't the most romantic place I can think of for a seduction."

She agreed, but shook her head. "No, not there. The crew deck is too public. I don't really want to be seen. I—"

He cut her off with another kiss. "Hush. No need to ex-plain. I get it—the need to keep this just between us."

She broke the kiss and took his hand. "I have a better idea. Come on."

She quickly led him out of the storage areas, down the passageway, and past the mechanical spaces to a small, very well-hidden room, tucked into the very aft of the ship be-hind the engines, the entrance of which was disguised by a small forest of bulkhead-mounted equipment and instru-ments. She pulled him inside the room and tugged the door shut after them, cranking down the lever that locked it. It was completely dark inside.

"What is this place?" His voice echoed thinly against the metal bulkheads, muffled by the noise of the nearby engines and the rhythmic *whump* of the propellers. If you closed

your eyes and concentrated, you could just make out the
sound of churning water. The space smelled of salt, oil, and
rust, and the distinctive, comforting musty odor of an old
ship.

She loved it here.

"It's my secret place," she said into the darkness, feeling
oddly vulnerable. "Where I come to escape."

She felt him reach for her and tug, and she fell into his
arms again. Excitement rushed through her as he kissed his
way down the side of her throat, his hands seeking the
curves of her body. She let out a soft moan.

He started to unbutton her uniform shirt. "I hope to hell
there's a bed in here," he murmured between kisses.

"Better," she said, untangled herself, and groped along
the wall behind her for the light switch. She pressed it on.
A dim glow came from an ancient fixture in the ceiling,
throwing the small room into a jungle of shadows.

Clint grunted against the light, and at her urging turned
to look behind him. There, suspended between the two opposite bulkheads, was a large woven hammock, complete
with pillow and quilt.

He grinned.

"Ever slept in one?" she asked.

"Yep. You?"

"All the time."

"Ever made love in one?" he asked.

"Not yet."

His grin widened as he caught hold of her again. "Me,
neither."

"I'm game if you are," she murmured into his ear as he
walked her backward toward it.

"Every sailor should try it at least once," his gravelly
voice rumbled.

"At the very least," she agreed breathlessly.

The backs of her knees hit the hammock. He grabbed it,
shook it open, and they tumbled entwined into its depths.

They tried it.

More than once.

6

Making love in a hammock was different from anything Sam had ever experienced. It was closer. Deeper. More exciting.

Better.

Or maybe the hammock had nothing to do with it.

Maybe it was just Clint Walker that was better.

Because of the curve and fluidity of their hanging bed, conventional positions would not work. They had to try other, more imaginative ways of arranging their bodies to come together. More exhilarating. More stimulating and edgy.

Or maybe it was that Clint was a more exhilarating and edgy lover.

Except it wasn't just a matter of positions. There was something more, something different lurking behind the excitement and the edge he brought to their lovemaking. It was . . . a *feeling.* An added depth . . . and not just physical. A connection she had not felt with another human being, especially a man, for a very, very long time.

"*Mmm,*" Clint groaned as the hammock swung them

back and forth like babes in a cradle after their last explosive orgasm. Which, unlike the previous ones, they'd experienced in perfect unison. "Baby, that was truly spectacular."

She didn't have the strength to answer with more than a long moan of agreement. Her body unfurled from him on its own, her legs sliding down from his hips in a tangle of limbs as she let him wrap himself around her, almost protectively, face-to-face within the folds of the quilt. He pulled it around them, tucked the pillow under their heads, and tugged the edges of the hammock over them, creating their own dark, warm, and very private cocoon. She was surrounded by delicious male flesh and the arousing scent of their lovemaking. *Pure heaven.*

She couldn't ever remember feeling so relaxed, so replete. So at one with the world. Every cell of her body pulsed with pleasure and contentment. It felt wonderful.

"You good?" he asked in a low, contented purr.

"Amazing," she whispered in reply. God, she never wanted to move. She wanted to stay like this, exactly like this, for the rest of her life. If she died right now, she'd die a very, very happy woman.

He eased out a deep hum. "Yeah. Me, too."

"This was a great idea."

"Ya think?"

They chuckled and cuddled. Such a novelty. Jim had never wanted to cuddle after sex. Or even on the couch watching TV. She wondered why. It was so nice.

She knew she shouldn't, but she let herself drift off, dozing skin to skin in Clint's strong arms. The gentle pitch and roll of the ship as it coursed through the waves rocked the hammock like the hand of a loving mother. The steady beat of Clint's heart and his slow, even breathing hinted that he had already given in to sleep.

She'd stay here with him for a few more minutes. She couldn't bear to break the blissful spell just yet. Cold reality would intrude soon enough. This was so . . . *Mmm.*

She had no idea how long they slept. It could have been minutes or hours. It felt so comfortable. So . . . right.

When she finally awoke, it was to the hot, delicious push of his cock between her thighs. She didn't open her eyes, but with a smile she opened her legs and accepted him into her body. He grunted, and the hammock shifted under her as he adjusted his position to thrust deep.

She let out a throaty moan as he scythed into her, her body already slick and ready for him. He had been a generous lover earlier, giving her several inventive climaxes to his two. His first had been at her insistence, by her tongue, the second, the last mindless, pounding monkey sex that had brought them both to a panting, roaring, simultaneous explosion of pleasure. She was frankly surprised he now had the appetite for one more for the road, but was more than happy to oblige him.

She lost herself in the hard delight of his possession. In the way he hungered for her. In the way they fit together so perfectly.

This is the way it should be with a man, always.

Too bad that wasn't possible. Men didn't do "always." Men got bored and moved on. Didn't keep their vows. Didn't care if a good, loving woman was devastated in the process.

Just one of the many hard lessons the men in Sam's life had taught her.

Trust issues? Yeah, you could say that.

But for right now, this was good. Clint was good. *Very* good. Besides, she wasn't looking for forever. Or even next week. Hell, no. She would take what he gave and not ask for more. Not expect any more. She would not give him her trust. And she sure as hell would not give him her heart. She'd made that mistake once too often.

But her body she would gladly give him. For the short time they'd have together.

So she did. She gave herself. Fully, and eagerly.

He took what she offered, and offered her the same in return. *Touch. Smell. Sound. Taste.*

And the sight of his profound enjoyment etched starkly on his handsome bronze face.

She cried out in a torrent of physical pleasure, riding on the thrilling edge of fulfillment, and gave herself over to the moment . . . and to the man.

It was good. He was good. They were good together.

For right now.

And for right now, that was all she wanted.

"We should probably get back to work," Sam said reluctantly, after they'd recovered their breath and floated back from oblivion. "Lord knows what time it is. I'm sure it's late."

"You don't wear a watch?" Clint asked, extracting his arm from the quilt.

She twisted her lips. "Yeah, but when we're underway I leave it in my stateroom. It keeps getting caught on things when I work." And it wasn't like she had a busy social calendar on board to keep up with.

He made a noise in his throat and winced when he glanced at his wristwatch. "You probably don't want to know the time anyway."

She groaned. "That bad?" The one disadvantage of being in the bowels of the ship was no portholes to the outside. No indication of passing time. How would she ever explain her absence—their absence together—all afternoon? She just hoped they hadn't missed supper. Their empty chairs would be like a flashing neon sign announcing their guilty assignation.

"Hopefully there's enough time to grab a quick shower before people send out a search party," he said.

She didn't have the energy to worry about consequences. She felt too good. "You were reading my mind. Come with me."

As they tipped out of the hammock and gathered up their clothes, he glanced around her hideaway. It was pretty minimalist. About all she'd done was to install her hammock and cover the floor with heavy-duty Astroturf to keep the Arctic chill and the sea damp from her feet. She didn't need anything else. She only came down here when she wanted to decompress.

"Does the crew know you have this clever hideaway?" he asked, probably worried they'd come knocking any minute.

She shook her head. "Nope. One of the former owners of *Île de Cœur* had a problem with thievery among the crew, so he had this room installed for a secret guard to keep an eye on the supplies. I'm the only one who knows about it."

"That's handy."

She led him to a door on one side of the room and opened it to reveal a primitive bathroom, complete with an ancient, rusty shower. "There's no water heater, but the tank is right next to the engines so it gets pretty hot."

"Believe me, this is the lap of luxury compared to some places I've been," he returned.

She cut him a glance. "Like that Chinese prison?"

He just smiled mysteriously and kissed the end of her nose. "Sorry. Classified."

She snorted and turned on the shower. She wondered if he was really that security conscious, or just trying to intrigue her.

It was working.

"Watch out, the water can be a little nasty at first," she warned.

Despite the increasing lateness, once it ran clear, neither could resist taking their time in the shower. As Sam smoothed her soapy hands over Clint's body, scenarios danced in her head about how he'd acquired the scatter of scars in various sizes and shapes dotting his dusky copper skin. She didn't bother to ask, already knowing he wouldn't answer. She concentrated instead on the exquisite geography of his broad, muscle-ripped chest and his powerful, corded arms.

"Nice tattoos," she said, running her fingers over the eagle clutching a navy anchor that graced his left pec, then smoothed suds over the wolf on his bicep. "Why a wolf?" she asked.

He hesitated, then said, "My clan name is Wolf Walker."

She smiled. "Clint Wolf Walker. I like it. It suits you."

One black brow went up. "Thanks. I think."

She took in his features. Firm, square jaw. Sharp, high cheekbones. The midnight black hair, straight and a little short for her taste. His dark eyes had lusciously long lashes and a slight exotic tilt to them. Not the features of an Inuit, the most common native tribe in these parts.

"What nation are you?" she asked curiously.

His soapy hands were tracing the curves of her waist and hips. He paused and searched her face. Apparently deciding she was sincere, he answered, "Kind of a mix. Arapaho mostly. Some Apache and Cree. And a dash of *wasichu* of course." He winked. "That's Indian for 'gringo.'"

She laughed. "And a very nice mix it is." She pulled his face toward her for a long kiss.

"What about you?" he asked. "Who are your people?"

She was tempted to say she didn't have any people. Because she *didn't* have any people. Not anymore. Jim was gone, her mother had died several years ago, and her father . . . well, he was her father. But her family or lack of it was the last thing she wanted to talk about at the moment. "Oh, the usual Heinz 57, I expect," she evaded. "Now, hand me that soap, Lieutenant Commander."

His smile broadened. "Yes, ma'am."

Long minutes later, showered and dressed, they reluctantly headed for the stairs—or ladder as most stairs were called on a ship—that would take them to the upper decks, back to the real world. He checked his watch. "Just in time for dinner," he said ruefully.

"Be prepared for the Spanish Inquisition," she drawled, pulling on her cap. "I suppose it'll be useless to deny we were—"

Suddenly, a loud *rat-a-tat-tat* echoed down from the deck above, stopping them in their tracks.

"What the hell was *that*?" Suddenly, she realized it was far too quiet out there, on a broader level. "My God. The engines have stopped."

He looked at her sharply, listened, and swore.

She took a step, preparing to launch into a sprint up the narrow stairway to the weather deck.

His firm grip on her arm yanked her to a halt. "Stop," he ordered. His face, his entire body had changed, as though an internal switch had been flipped. He was all hard angles now, and tight muscles and frowns. Gone was the tender lover. This man was all business, and scary as hell.

"What?" she demanded, trying to pry him loose from her.

He held on like a limpet. "Slow down. You're not going anywhere."

"What the hell? Let me go!" She needed to find out what was happening up there.

Another report blasted through the space, sending her pulse into the stratosphere. His grip on her arm tightened even more.

"Sorry. I can't let you do that."

An insidious, cold fear clawed through her belly as a rapid series of horrible thoughts streaked through her mind.

What was going on?

Why wouldn't he let go of her arm?

And worst of all . . . just how badly had she misjudged this man?

Was he a terrorist, after all? Sent as an advance soldier to distract the captain? And, once he'd seen the captain was a woman, to use his considerable skills at seduction to keep her occupied elsewhere . . . while his comrades hijacked her ship?

Because one thing was for damned certain.

The *rat-a-tat-tat*? That was the unmistakable sound of *machine gun fire*.

7

\\\\\\\\\//////

Sonofabitch!

Clint's whole body went on high alert. *Automatic weapons fire?* What in God's name was happening up there on deck?

Samantha continued to struggle against him. "Stop!" he repeated tightly, pulling her up against him to prevent her from wriggling away. "Let me listen, for godsake!" He couldn't believe he'd missed the engines being shut off. How distracted had he *been*?

He could feel her gaze bore holes in his face. He ignored her and strained to hear something in the eerie mechanical silence, anything that would clue him in to the situation topside.

Not that there was a whole lot of doubt.

The shrill of a high-pitched scream stabbed down from above, confirming his worst fears.

Samantha jerked at him again. "That was Ginger!" she exclaimed, the pitch of her voice urgent but thankfully hushed. Drawing attention to themselves was *not* a good idea. "I need to go—"

He cut her off. "I said you're not going anywhere." He scanned around for a hiding place where they could hear and observe, but not be seen. "Not until I figure out what the hell is going on."

"I think it's fairly obvious what's going on," she hissed, her angry expression filled with accusation.

He did a double take. And suddenly it dawned on him exactly what she must be thinking.

"Really?" he asked, instantly furious and . . . yeah, and hurt. "We just fucked each other's brains out for five hours! And you think I'm *part of this*?"

"Charming," she said between clamped teeth, but at least had the grace to look uncomfortable. For a split second, anyway. But suspicion came roaring back over her face as he pulled her toward an open door behind the steep metal companionway stairs. "It's a pretty damn big coincidence, don't you think?" she continued under her breath. "You sneak aboard in the middle of the night, seduce me, and suddenly the ship is hijacked by pirates?"

"*Seduce*?" He glared at her. "As I recall, *you* were the one to suggest this little interlude."

She sputtered. But because they both knew it was true, she had no comeback.

"Besides," he bit out, a sizeable lance of guilt piercing through his anger, "you don't know it's pirates."

Though he hoped to God it *was* pirates. The alternative was potentially far more dangerous. Pirates were motivated by greed. Greed they—he—could deal with. Political zealots and stone-cold assassination squads were far more difficult.

"Oh, right," she said, slapping her forehead. "What was I thinking? It's just the Coast Guard paying us a visit and firing off their guns in anticipation of the Fourth of July."

He shoved her through the door into a dark, narrow space, and dove in after her. "You're avoiding the issue."

"No *you're* avoiding the issue." She narrowed her eyes, peering up at him in the dark. "*Are* you part of this?"

He hung on to his temper. He allowed that she had every

right, and good reason, to ask. "I am not a pirate," he said meeting her eyes levelly. "Or any other kind of criminal. I am employed by U.S. Naval Intelligence. I work to *prevent* terrorist acts against American ships, not participate in them."

She digested his denial for a long, skeptical moment. Thankfully she didn't examine his careful wording too closely.

Part of it? No. But he may well be the catalyst. *Interpretation.*

"All right," she said at length. "I'll choose to continue to believe you. For now." She pushed out a breath. "Now please, let me go. I need to get up there and find out—"

"What part of *no fucking way* don't you get?" he said vehemently. "I am *not* letting you go up there. You stay here. *I'll*—"

"Excuse me? *I* am the goddamn captain of this ship!" she declared. She went up on her toes, putting her face right into his. The brim of her old yachting cap poked at his forehead. "And last time I checked, *captain* trumps *lieutenant commander*." For emphasis, she jabbed her forefinger at his chest with each syllable. "Which means *you*, sir, will follow *my* orders!"

Seriously?

First she accused him, and now she was pulling rank on him?

Anger simmered through his veins. "And what, exactly," he queried softly, "are those orders, ma'am?"

She backed down a fraction, relief minutely easing her tight muscles. He couldn't believe she actually thought he'd ceded command to her. He clamped his jaw and let her keep her fantasy for now.

"I need to go up and see for certain what's happening." She took a step back from him, banding her arms over her midriff. "We have a cargo hold packed with fireworks. Literally. What we heard may just have been some of those going off by accident. Or even a practical joke. Some of the crew are real wiseacres."

He jerked a nod. It was solid reasoning. Except for the part where it was Samantha who went up to check on things. There was not a chance he'd let her put herself in danger like that.

"If it is pirates," she continued as though she honestly believed he'd go along with this, "I need to get to the radio on the bridge. To set off the DSC, and contact the authorities."

Which was exactly what Clint planned to do. The DSC—short for digital select calling—was the automated distress signal transmitter required on all ships. Press the button and help would arrive. Eventually.

But he didn't relish rushing the bridge without a weapon. Silently he cursed his bad judgment in leaving the SIG hidden under the mattress in his stateroom. A rookie move, no doubt caused by diminished brain capacity resulting from his bad case of rampaging hormones.

Hell of a time to be stranded bare-assed, without even his gun. What he wouldn't give for the bag of gear he'd been forced to leave behind last week on that damn Russian submarine. That was where he'd started out this joyride—going undercover on an international scientific expedition hosted by the Russians, in order to acquire the stolen Chinese data card that had been hidden on the submarine. Things had not gone exactly as planned.

"Does anyone on board have a satellite phone?" he asked.

She made a frustrated face. "Don't think so. Just regular cell phones. We're generally not out of range long enough to justify the expense."

Great. "Any chance of cell reception?"

She grimaced. "Not this far out to sea. Sometimes you can get a bar if the weather's just right, but it's rare."

"What about a computer?"

She jetted out a breath, not looking any more hopeful. "There's a desktop in the main salon, and I have a laptop in my cabin. But there's no wireless out here, not without a satellite connection. When we're at sea, we rely on the ship-to-shore radio for communication."

"On the bridge."

She nodded unhappily.

The bridge, the command center for the entire ship, was the first place any competent pirate would secure. Or anyone else taking over a vessel for whatever reason . . .

"And I'm guessing the engine room has not been retrofitted as a safe room." On most newer ships, the engine room was built so that during a hostile attack, the entire crew could withdraw and barricade themselves inside, shut down the ship's engines, cut off the bridge controls remotely so the hijackers couldn't turn them back on, trigger the DSC distress transmission, and simply drift until the ship was rescued or the pirates gave up and left.

"God forbid the company actually spend good money on security," she muttered in response.

He wondered briefly at the bitter note in her words, but now was not the time to ask.

He put a hand to her shoulder. "Okay. Here's what's going to happen. I'll go up top and do a reconnaissance. Then—"

She cut him with a death ray look. "What part of *I'm the fucking captain* don't *you* get? You have absolutely no authori—"

Suddenly there was a loud clattering of boots on the metal stairs of the companionway. Angry shouts ricocheted across the ro-ro deck above.

Instantly, Clint clapped a hand over Samantha's mouth, cutting off her rant, trying to discern the language of the shouts as he dragged her back behind the solid door of the storage room they'd taken refuge in.

It sounded like Chinese. Though, admittedly, he was no Asian language expert. It could be Korean. Or even some flavor of Indonesian. The Indonesians were big in the pirate business. Although not usually in the Bering Sea.

How many? Clint silently counted. *One, two, three* individuals were now clomping down toward the lower deck. There had to be at minimum two more up on the weather or crew decks guarding the captured crew. Therefore an enemy force of at least five pirates.

Or Chinese operatives.

Samantha was right. The chances of this takeover being a coincidence on the day after he came on board were slim to none. Clint did not believe in coincidence any more than she apparently did.

He gathered himself, preparing for battle. For once, she didn't fight him as they stood there, barely breathing, hiding behind the open door to the closet-sized storage room. It was pitch-dark inside, but overhead lights from the staircase painted the surrounding bulkhead with irregular shadows, providing a bit of camouflage. With luck, the hijackers wouldn't spot the opening.

Or them.

There was louder clattering on the stairs.

"I'm telling you, I *am* Captain Sam Richardson!" a voice protested loudly. The voice was male. American. "You won't find anyone else down here!"

Clint realized someone from the crew was pretending to be the captain. Someone too brave for his own good.

Clint moved his head slightly to look at Samantha. Even in the relative dark he could see she'd gone pale. She opened her mouth, and he could tell she was about to protest, to step out and reveal herself. He swiftly covered her mouth again and banded an arm around her so she couldn't do anything stupid.

"You lie!" shouted another male voice, this one with a heavy Asian accent. The sound of flesh being struck cracked through the air. "Tell me where the passenger is!"

"I'm not lying," the fake Captain Richardson said after a grunt of pain. "I'm the captain, and there's no one else on board. I swear."

Another whack resounded. "You *not* captain! Stripes on uniform not correct!" The Asian interrogator sounded older. And completely unsympathetic. Clint's heart sank. Was he about to meet the infamous Xing Guan in person?

"Maybe for the military," the American said with another grunt of pain. "But this ship is owned by a private company. The uniforms are different. Just ask the crew."

"I will find man you hide from me!" the interrogator gritted out. "Then you both die!"

Samantha had started to tremble. She looked at Clint imploringly. He eased his hand from her mouth but shook his head somberly and kept his arm wrapped firmly around her shoulders.

"Who else on ship? How many?" the interrogator demanded.

"There are seven crew members," the imposter captain said. "Everyone's on deck but me. I'm telling you, there's no one else."

"Seven not enough. You lie!"

"No! Only"—the American gave a sharp *oof* of pain—"seven!"

The interrogator barked out orders to the other two tangos and they sprang to obey, beginning a thorough search of the orlop.

The two went methodically through the engineering spaces and storage areas, room by room with guns in hand. Clint could feel Samantha's body jump each time a metal door banged open. He listened with growing trepidation as the hurried footfalls and shouted progress of the searchers got closer and closer to their hiding place.

They were so screwed.

Samantha's wide eyes latched onto him and held. The dawning panic in them made his resolve harden to stone.

Okay. Clint may be screwed, and possibly the crewman impersonating the captain. But Samantha didn't have to be.

If Clint gave himself up, they'd take him prisoner and stop the search. Whether the hijackers were pirates looking for the ship's real captain, or Xing Guan's assassination squad hunting the spy in possession of their stolen technology, capturing Clint would satisfy either objective. He looked down at the gold stripes on his shirt and then at Samantha's. Okay, maybe not the captain, but he'd think of something.

And as they dragged him away, he'd drop the precious data card somewhere on *Île de Cœur* where the navy could find it.

He'd be dead. But Samantha and her crew would be safe.

He let her go and scooted past, intending to step out from behind the door. She grabbed his arm and shook her head vigorously. "No!" she silently mouthed.

"Yes," he mouthed back, his mind made up. "Stay here. You'll be okay."

One of the searchers smacked a door open just down the passageway. It banged like a gunshot. Sam's fingers dug into him.

Clint grimly set his jaw and peeled them from his arm. But before he could step away, she grasped the heavy metal door and pulled it tight against them so they were crushed between it and the bulkhead. The gap was so narrow he had to quickly turn his head for fear his nose would be squashed flat.

He glared down at her. She ignored him.

In a deft maneuver, she reached for the rod used to secure the open door in rough seas, and clipped the end hook into the matching eye in the bulkhead next to him, effectively locking them in place like two sardines in a can.

Loud footsteps pounded along the passageway, bearing quickly down on them.

Damn it! If he moved now, he'd give her away, too.

Angrily, he froze in place, and they both held their breath as the tango clomped into their closet. The overhead light snapped on. Samantha's eyes squeezed shut, and Clint could feel her body tremble against his side. He moved his hand infinitesimally, caught her fingers in his, and gave them a squeeze.

The tango let out a furious growl, and suddenly cans and containers were swept from metal shelves so hard they crashed against the bulkhead and peppered to the floor like a hailstorm. Clint turned his head to see better, scraping his nose on rough metal.

A set of blunt fingers curled around the edge of the door and jerked it. The hook rattled loudly, but held.

Clint coiled his muscles, preparing to launch into a fight for his life. *For Samantha's life.*

She squeezed his hand in a death grip.

The door jerked again.

Then the fingers disappeared. The tango shouted something to the head honcho as, miraculously, his footsteps pounded out of the room, joining the other searchers as they climbed down into the cargo holds below the orlop.

The whole time the leader continued to harangue, interrogate, and abuse the crew member claiming to be Captain Sam Richardson. With every blow, Samantha grew more and more upset. Her pretty green eyes had long since filled with liquid rage. She didn't look as much like she wanted to burst into tears as like she wanted to burst out of their hiding place and kill the hijackers with her bare hands.

He got that. No worse punishment existed than being forced to stand by helpless, watching as a friend was brutalized.

Finally the tangos finished their search of the cargo holds. The commander barked at his underlings, his irate voice making it clear he was not happy that no one else had been found. Clint wouldn't want to be the imposter captain, who was sure to take the brunt of the brute's anger.

The question was, would he take the abuse and remain mute?

Or would he break, and throw Clint to the dragon . . . ?

8

〰〰〰〰〰

"I have to do something!" Sam said shakily after the pirates were well out of earshot. "Now!"

She battled the trembling in her voice and limbs, struggling to appear just as strong as the muscle-bound caveman standing next to her who seemed intent on preventing her from doing her job.

She and Clint were still hiding in the storage room but had quietly shut the door so they could talk. Well, argue. She might be terrified down to her toes, but she'd be damned if she'd let those bastard pirates hurt her crew or take her ship!

Damn it! She didn't *need* this happening right now! What she needed was a speedy transit to Nome with her crew unhurt and her cargo intact. She didn't even want to *think* about the shit that would come hurtling at her from all sides if she failed to bring in this shipment on time. Let alone if the crew was harmed. Or the ship was lost completely.

Oh, hell.

"Samantha." Clint took hold of her shoulders with steely

fingers. His black eyes drilled into hers. "Listen to me. I know you feel you must act—"

"That's *my* crew up there. God knows what those bastards are doing to them!"

"I understand." Clint's tone held barely leashed rage. Well, join the club! "But I'm trained to deal with this kind of situation. You aren't."

She was sick of going around and around; it was getting them nowhere. She threw up her hands. "Fine. Whatever." To be honest, she had no earthly clue how to wrest back control of her ship from the hijackers. If Clint did, so much the better. "But I'm coming with you."

The stubborn look in her eyes must have convinced him she would not take no for an answer. He jetted out a breath. "Okay. But you've got to do exactly as I say."

She shook her head. "My ship. We decide together."

She could tell he wanted to strangle her. "God, you are stubborn!" he said between his teeth.

She just said back at him through *her* teeth, "Deal with it."

His jaw worked, but he finally accepted the compromise—grudgingly. "We need to do a recon," he said tightly. "Get on deck and scope things out. Make sure the crew isn't in immediate danger."

She nodded in agreement. "And see if there's any way to reach the radio and DSC on the bridge."

"Right." He turned aside and started rooting through the things on the shelves and the supplies scattered on the deck. "But first we need weapons. I'd rather not face five tangos armed with only my wits."

"Tangos?"

"Bad guys." With a curse he turned away from the shelves empty-handed. "Where's your gun?"

"In the wall safe in my cabin."

"And my SIG is under my mattress," he murmured disgustedly.

She hiked her brows, and he made a pained face. "Don't start with me. I thought the crew would get suspicious if someone caught me sporting a shoulder holster and a loaded pistol." He made a move for the door. "We'd better try and retrieve them. How can we get to the staterooms?"

She followed. "There are two ventilation chutes built into the cofferdams—the double walls between the cargo holds—that go up vertically through the decks. They both lead to the outside to bring in fresh air, and are secured with a scuttle hatch. They're shaped kinda like a narrow elevator shaft without the elevator. One goes all the way up through the midstructure and opens onto a small balcony behind the bridge. The other one is shorter, and ends on the main weather deck by the deck crane."

He turned to look at her. "And this helps us how?"

"They both have emergency ladders going up the sides."

His brows dipped thoughtfully. "How do you get into the shafts from here?"

"There are small latched hatches that open at each deck. They can be opened from both sides, including the outside scuttles. Unless, of course, a hijacker is standing on top of it." She bit her lip, only half kidding.

"That works. The one that goes to the staterooms, you said it opens up outside behind the bridge?"

She nodded. "Yeah."

"Let's check that out first," he said, grasping the door handle. "You never know. We could get lucky and there won't be a guard."

"Okay." She hoped to hell he was right.

"Follow my lead, and don't take *any* chances."

She nodded, and he put a finger to his lips, eased open the storage room door a fraction, and peeked out. "It's clear."

Swiftly, they made their way to the midstructure ventilation shaft. Its heavy, hobbit-sized hatch opened with a squeal that made Sam's pulse skyrocket. Clint urged her to grab the ladder and climb, then spit on the hinge before following her in and easing the hatch closed after them.

The small, square shaft plunged straight upward into stygian darkness. The safety lights were off, and they didn't dare switch them on. Inside, it smelled stale and salty, the taste of the cold air acrid on her tongue. She clung precariously to the ladder for a long moment, getting her bearings and adjusting to the roll of the ship from this unfamiliar position.

"Just pretend you're climbing the mast of an old sailing ship," he suggested.

"Oh, that helps a lot," she muttered, feeling even dizzier with *that* visual in her head. God, she hated heights.

She fumbled her way up a few rungs. She knew the ladder went straight up the side of the shaft, but she couldn't see a damned thing. Thank God the seas were relatively calm today. She didn't relish the thought of swinging up the ladder like a monkey, dodging waves.

Clint stood a few rungs down, waiting patiently for her to move. His body was behind hers, his head about waist level and his arms fluidly bracketing her legs against the vessel's pitch. If she slipped, he would catch her. At least until she started climbing.

"Still time to change your mind," he said softly. "I can go on my own."

She sucked down a steadying breath. "No way."

The metal rungs were freezing cold and grimy. But they felt fairly solid. She hoped they really were. She hadn't ever actually been inside either of these ventilation chutes before. That would teach her not to know every inch of her vessel. With a prayer that she could hang on if a big wave hit, she swallowed her fear and started up in earnest.

It probably only took a few minutes to reach the top, where a scuttle opened on a small balcony behind the bridge, but it seemed as though climbing up the claustrophobic chute took forever. Her heart was pounding like an Arctic storm and they hadn't even gotten to the dangerous part yet. She held her breath as Clint climbed up behind her and groped up past her shoulder for the scuttle hatch. He carefully unlatched it and opened it just a crack. Closing her eyes against the bright light that streamed in, she hoped the metal hinge wouldn't squeak.

It didn't, but Clint pulled the hatch immediately closed. "Yep. There's a man guarding the bridge."

"Damn." In the darkness, they clung to the ladder, not surprised but still disappointed.

Swaying with the roll of the passing swells, Clint's body pressed rhythmically against her back, reminding her of earlier, when they'd made love. It felt good. But, lord, how quickly things changed.

Still, she knew instinctively she wouldn't want to be in this situation with anyone else on earth.

He jetted out a breath. "All right. Let's try for our weapons in the staterooms."

Right. Weapons.

"Wait," she said. Why hadn't she thought of this sooner? "There's a gun safe in the wardroom. We should go for that instead."

He came to attention. "How many weapons?"

"Three rifles. Five or six handguns."

She felt his sharp inhale. "Is the gun safe hidden? Or in full view?"

"It's in a locked cupboard."

His warm breath soughed past her ear. "Then with any luck they haven't found it yet. Where's the wardroom?"

"Quarterdeck, just below us, at the stern end of the passageway where it tees at the back of the ship."

They descended the several rungs down the ladder to the deck below. Sam halted and felt for the hatch. Clint stood behind her and gently muscled the lever open. The hatch creaked in protest when he opened it, making them both freeze. They quickly peered around the door. To their relief, no guard was posted in the passageway to hear it.

"I'm going to have to start carrying a friggin' oil can," Clint muttered under his breath as they both nervously exhaled. He pushed the door open.

She started to duck out through it. He caught her arm.

"No. You stay here—" he began, but halted when she turned and glared at him. His jaw tightened but he didn't complete the thought.

He was learning.

They eased out and swiftly ran down the passageway to the junction where another short corridor intersected it in a *T*. They peeked around to check it was clear, then slid around the corner and flattened themselves to the wall.

"Which door?" he asked.

There were three doors opening off each arm of the *T*. To the left of the intersection, a crew lounge overlooked the smallish poop deck that ran crosswise along the stern of the ship; on the interior side was a media room and a tiny library. Off the right arm of the tee, where they stood now, one door led to the interior galley, and opposite that, also overlooking the outside deck, was the large dining area. The third door farther down opened to their objective—the wardroom, or officers' lounge.

She pointed at that one.

Clint looked grim. Not only did they have to pass by two doors that stood wide open, but then they must risk opening the one door that was closed. And hope like hell no one was inside.

Her heart pounded in her throat as they glided silently past the open rooms and approached the wardroom. Clint cautiously put his ear to the door, but she knew it was a useless exercise. The thing was made of solid steel, specifically designed to allow the officers inside to hold private conversations without fear of being overheard by curious crew members.

He put a hand to the door handle, but she stopped him. Something just didn't feel right.

She shook her head and indicated the dining room door they'd passed. If they went through that way and out onto the poop deck, they could sneak around and take a peek through the windows to see if anyone was in the lounge.

He seemed to understand immediately, but stopped her when she led the way back to the door. He grabbed her arm and forcibly moved her behind him as he pressed himself to the doorframe, ducked a head around, then melted into the mess hall like a wraith.

No one was inside.

But she was impressed with the move nonetheless. She'd heard about First Nation hunters who could become one with their environment and disappear at will, but she'd always chalked it up as being the fanciful stuff of New Age woo-woo legend. But damn if he hadn't done exactly that.

Wolf Walker? More like Ghost Walker.

He materialized at her side just as she stepped through the doorway. She had to stifle a gasp.

"How did you do that?" she whispered, heart pounding.

"Do what?" he asked, still concentrating, his gaze taking in every detail of their surroundings. In an unconscious movement, he handed her a baguette of French bread.

"What's this?"

"What?"

She shook her head instead of rolling her eyes. "Never mind. Let's go." She crouch-ran between the tables, heading for the double doors leading to the deck, with Clint at her heels. Again he stopped her as she reached for the handle.

Okay, so maybe he *wasn't* learning. She was getting pretty tired of his bossiness.

"There's no sense in both of us getting caught," he preempted her protest. "Your crew needs to know you're free and working on a rescue. It gives them hope."

She wasn't so sure about that, but the idea made her hesitate just long enough for him to glide past her and out onto the deck. She tore off a hunk of bread with her teeth in annoyance, wondering if it were his exotic good looks and imposing body that gave him such a sense of entitlement over her—and no doubt every other woman on the planet— or if he was just naturally a domineering chauvinist.

Yet another reason she would never get involved with the man, even if she could. Not that she was remotely in the market for any kind of involvement, other than the kind they already shared.

By the time she'd gotten her pique under control, he'd returned, wearing a scowl.

"Someone's in there," he said in a low voice. "And all the lockers have been thrown open, things tossed everywhere." A muscle jumped in his cheek.

She swore softly. "So they've found the gun safe. Is that open, too?"

He shook his head. "No. But there's no way to get to it now."

Frustration welled up alongside the knife edge of fear that never stopped whittling away at her. She felt so helpless.

"Shall we try for our weapons in the staterooms?" he suggested. He didn't sound optimistic.

Her stomach rumbled softly. She'd already eaten the French bread baguette and wished she'd thought to pick up another on the way out. They hadn't eaten dinner. Well, if going hungry was the worst that happened to them tonight, she'd be grateful. She ignored her stomach.

The staterooms. "Yeah. Let's go."

But when they got there, they realized it would be impossible. The staterooms were located at the other end of the passageway, and a guard was posted just a few yards away on the landing of the main companionway. He was leaning against the railing in a bored slouch, but he had one of those big, ugly machine guns slung by its strap over one shoulder. Thank God his back was turned so he didn't see the hatch open, then swiftly shut again.

"Any ideas?" Clint murmured after letting out a low string of curses.

"A diversion?" she suggested, clearing her throat. At least she wasn't the only one feeling the pressure.

She felt his head shake. "Anything unusual happens, and they'll know someone else is on board."

Right. That wouldn't be good. And they were all armed to the teeth.

"What will we do?" she asked. "We can't fight them with our bare hands."

"As long as they don't know we're here, we've still got a shot at retrieving the guns, either our own or the ones in the wardroom. Hopefully sooner than later."

She prayed it would be sooner.

"Come on. We should go and see what the situation is with the crew. The other ventilation shaft lets out on the weather deck, right?"

"Yeah."

It took them several minutes to climb back down to the lowest deck, the orlop, where they'd started out. It was still and quiet down there, other than a low hum of machinery and the muted suck of the sea against the hull. The engines were silent, which probably meant the hijackers didn't intend to take the ship, or they'd already be steaming off to parts unknown. Sam wondered what they did want . . .

She and Clint carefully made their way forward to the other chute. They slipped into the dark confines of the enclosure, but this time Clint left the hatch a few inches ajar. Unfortunately, the small wedge of light it let in barely registered.

Even so, by now she was used to the darkness and barely noticed it. But the sea had grown rougher, and she had to hang on to each rung for dear life as she climbed, fearful of losing her grip. Her calves and thighs had started to burn from all the climbing, and her palms felt like they had big blisters. Thank goodness Clint was right behind her.

Every pitch of the boat had their bodies swinging back and forth precariously. By the time they reached the top of the chute, she'd broken out in a clammy sweat. Clint climbed up behind her, stopping on the rung below so their heads were even. After he'd let her catch her ragged breath for a few moments, he helped her climb up and sit on a perilously narrow ledge that formed a lip going around the inside of the access chute. There was barely enough room for their butts to perch on, and they had to bend over to keep from hitting their heads on the scuttle.

Then he reached up and lifted the small round deck hatch a fraction of an inch. Hanging on to the jagged edge, they both peered out through the narrow crack for a quick check.

Thankfully, the hijackers were not standing anywhere

close. But she could hear one of them yelling. Her pulse quickened. What was happening with her crew?

Clint raised the scuttle another few inches, gradually letting their eyes get used to the glare from the midsummer sun. It was late, probably eight or nine o'clock by now, but the sun would be up all night. Anxious to actually see the crew, she stretched up as high as she could and swiveled around to look.

A big wave hit and she swallowed a gasp. She clung to Clint's arm as he grabbed her and they rolled with the motion of the ship.

"Steady on," he whispered. "You okay?"

She nodded. But her heart was beating triple-time. She didn't know what terrified her more, the thought of being discovered by the pirates and shot, or slipping off the ledge and falling with a big, bloody splat at the bottom of the three-story shaft.

She took a fortifying breath and they lifted their heads again to look out, this time really taking in what was happening on deck.

All thoughts of her own safety fled.

The seven members of her crew had been shoved into a line in front of the tall midship structure that housed the crew deck, quarterdeck, and the bridge. The two women were huddled at the center of the hostage line; Carin's arm was around Ginger, who was weeping. The second mate, Lars Bolun, stood at one end, his shoulders slumped inward and his arms banded across his stomach as though against intense pain. Sam could see dark blotches of blood on his face.

Her own stomach clenched, and guilt stabbed through her. Bolun had told the pirates he was *Île de Cœur*'s captain, taking the punishment intended for Sam. *It should be her out there bleeding.* Clint was undoubtedly correct in assuming the second mate had done it to give her and Clint a fighting chance to rescue the crew.

She couldn't let them down.

Her people were surrounded by three hijackers carrying

nasty-looking machine guns. They were dressed head to toe in black, like some kind of damn ninjas.

A fourth man paced up and down the line yelling at the captives, occasionally shoving one roughly into the bulkhead. She couldn't hear his words, but it was obvious he didn't like their responses. Or rather, the lack thereof.

When no one answered his increasingly loud and impatient questions, the pirate raised the stock of his machine gun and bashed Johnny Dorn hard on the side of the head. The crack of his skull reverberated sickeningly through the air.

Johnny sank to his knees, crying out. At that, Ginger started to sob even louder.

Sam clapped a hand over her own mouth to stifle the cry that bubbled up. The *bastard*! She white-knuckled the rim of the hatch with her other hand, swallowing down waves of rage.

Clint wasn't watching the brutality. His narrowed eyes had fastened on something off to starboard. Even so, he looked as furious as she'd ever seen him. She followed his gaze and saw another ship, much smaller than *Île de Cœur*, moored about a football field away. A fishing trawler. Undoubtedly the vessel the pirates had arrived on. The name "Eliza Jane" was lettered across the rear escutcheon, and she was flying the Australian flag.

Outrage swept through her. If these pirates were Aussies, she was from Mongolia!

But her attention was once again grabbed by the brutal scene unfolding next to the midstructure. This time Frank received the blow from the pirate leader. It was even harder than the first. Sam could barely breathe for her fury.

Clint's hand cupped her chin and forced her face around to look at him. His expression was deadly. His molten eyes held hers as he shook his head in firm warning. She made herself take a deep, steadying breath so she wouldn't launch herself out of their hiding place to defend her crew. In her head she knew there was nothing she could do that wouldn't result in disaster for all concerned. But her heart hurt like it had been caught in a vise and squeezed till it bled.

She fought back the despair flooding through her. For all her earlier bravado, she felt utterly useless now, too terrified and emotional to think straight, let alone help the situation.

That had to change. Her crew was counting on her.

She told herself she must work to be cool and professional, despite her anger. Like Clint. It was obvious he was seething inside, yet she could see his concentration and almost hear the cogs in his head turning, coming up with a solution to this terrible situation.

She'd barely bolstered her inner resolve when the scumbag pirate leader stopped in front of Shandy and stared malevolently into his kind, leathery face.

Oh, no.

Sam felt herself totally losing it.

Clint's arm caught her around her middle, as though he knew nothing in the world would stop her from jumping up to save the old man. But she never got the chance.

Because when the pirate leader raised his rifle to deliver the blow to Shandy's head, it wasn't the stock he aimed at the old man. It was the muzzle.

Then he pulled the trigger.

9

////////////////

A shower of crimson erupted from the chief engineer's head as he crumpled to the deck.

Dead.

For a moment Clint froze, unable to move.

Jesus God!

No way had he been expecting the violence to escalate this quickly—no matter who the hijackers were.

His stomach twisted. But he should have guessed.

The likelihood that these tangos were ordinary pirates was now virtually nil. They were focused, organized, carried Chinese regulation Type-85 submachine guns, and were not afraid to use them. No, these thugs had every attribute of a Chinese military special ops death squad. And the leader's behavior matched exactly the reputation of the infamous Xing Guan. Clearly, he meant business.

And if Clint was right, the business was him.

Jolting out of his frozen suspension, he grabbed Samantha before she could do something really stupid. He dragged her off the ledge onto the ladder, fighting her the whole way down as her shock dissolved into quivers of fury.

She flailed, not wanting to go, but he didn't loosen his hold, so she had no choice but to continue climbing to the bottom. Her whole body vibrated with anger under his iron grip. He could feel she'd be back topside in a shot if he didn't mercilessly control her movements. It was a damn miracle they made it down to the orlop without her plunging them both to their deaths.

They made their way hastily back to engineering, narrowly missing being spotted by the guard that had been posted at the engine room.

When they finally reached the hideaway, he firmly shut and latched the door behind them, then drilled a hand through his short hair and tugged, feeling it spike up between his fingers.

Since the engines still weren't running, they'd have to talk quietly or the guard might hear them.

"You need to calm down," he clipped out as she paced like a caged tiger, tears streaming down her face. Now that they were safely hidden, the bottled-up fear was slipping through her bravado.

"Calm down? I want to *kill* them," she muttered, a soft sob choking past her control. "No. Killing is too *good* for them. I want to feed them to the sharks! Bit by bloody bit!"

He couldn't deny he shared the sentiment.

But though he doubted she could actually bring herself to take a life, he also knew that if she did kill one of Xing Guan's apes, she'd probably be charged with murder, regardless of how justified the act. Despite public belief to the contrary, a civilian vessel and its crew had no legal recourse to use force against armed hijackers, even if the attackers clearly had deadly intent.

Piracy was against the laws of every country on the planet, with stiff penalties, but there was no international justice system to enforce those laws or to mete out punishment even if the lawbreakers were served up to local authorities on a silver platter unless the attack was committed in territorial waters. If a ship's crew fought back when attacked on the high seas, especially if they killed one of the aggressors, the crew members responsible as well as the ship's captain would be brought up on professional charges. Because unlike the international legal system, the world's marine shipping authorities embraced a clear-cut set of rules. At the very least, the defending crew would be stripped of their merchant marine papers, unable to work on any decent ship again. And depending on the country, they could also be formally charged in court with any crimes committed. In the United States, the letter of the law tended to win out over logic and moral justice.

It was an outdated, lopsided system, one that badly needed revising—and enforcing—to reflect the brutal realities of the modern seafaring world. But that didn't help them today.

Luckily, Clint had no such qualms or restrictions on his own responses. He was a soldier under orders and would do whatever necessary to protect his country and the information he carried.

Yeah, and Samantha.

He grasped her by the shoulders and urged her onto the hammock. She was shaking so badly he was afraid her legs would give out. She teetered, sitting on the edge, wrapping her arms around her middle in agitated despair, clutching that stupid hat in her white-knuckled fingers.

"I can't believe they killed Shandy," she said hoarsely, slumping as the adrenaline in her bloodstream crashed.

"I can't either." If this was an official Chinese military mission they'd just violated every international convention in existence.

Clint thought furiously, debating what the hell to do about this newest disaster. It was happening fast, and he needed to get a handle on the situation and his options for fighting it.

"Why would they do this?" she demanded tearfully. "What did they hope to accomplish by killing an innocent old man?"

Clint pushed out a breath, wishing he didn't know the answer firsthand. "Terror," he enlightened her. "After this, the crew will follow any orders, do anything the hijackers want."

She looked up at him in even deeper dismay. "Like what? They've seized the ship and the cargo. What else can they possibly want?"

Yeah. A total mystery.

Not.

He couldn't meet her gaze he felt so guilty. The muscle in his cheek felt like a Mexican jumping bean.

Suddenly her watery eyes widened, and she practically tumbled out of the hammock, landing on wobbly feet and staring at him in horror.

Shit. The woman was too smart for her own good.

"*You!*"

Shit shit shit.

She stalked over to him, grabbed the front of his borrowed uniform shirt in shaking fingers, and bunched it in her fists. "My God. Please tell me my ship isn't being held hostage and my chief engineer dead because I had the bad judgment to let *you* on board!" Her green eyes burned like an Alaskan forest on fire.

His heart felt like an animal caught in the blaze.

"I can't," he admitted, keeping his voice and his temper under control. Not to mention the floodgates of guilt. He'd been on plenty of life-threatening ops before, but he wasn't in the habit of dragging unwitting civilians into the fray. This time he hadn't had a choice. He really hadn't.

But that didn't mean he felt less awful about what was happening.

"God*damn* it!" she seethed, letting his shirt go with another sob. "When will I *ever* learn never to trust a man?"

He frowned. Where had *that* come from?

"Samantha . . ." He knew better than to reach for her. "Please, I—"

"Don't 'Samantha' me," she spat out. "While we were busy fucking each other's brains out, as you so succinctly put it, my ship was taken over by madmen. Madmen who are out to kill *you*. Oh, don't try to deny it. But it's my crew who are dying for my mistake! Oh, God, this is all my fault!"

"Don't." He rubbed a hand over his hair in frustration. "That's not fair. To you *or* me. Neither of us had any way of—"

"Fair?" She paced away from him, swiping the tears from her face. "*Fair?* Tell that to Bert Shandon!"

Mentally, Clint counted to ten. Make that twenty. Hell, he didn't blame her for feeling this way. She couldn't know how vital his mission was to the security of their country, and he couldn't tell her. Not without putting her in even more danger. If the worst happened and Xing Guan got his hands on her . . .

He didn't even want to think about that possibility. He'd do everything in his power to make sure it didn't happen.

Everything short of surrendering the microcard.

He desperately needed a way out of this untenable situation. But he couldn't put on a wetsuit, jump overboard, and swim to shore as he had from the Russian submarine where he'd acquired the SD card a week ago. *Île de Cœur* was too far out to sea. Besides, he wouldn't leave Samantha and her crew to suffer an uncertain fate. Which he'd brought on them.

Nor could he hope to win this battle alone.

What he needed was the cavalry to come riding over the horizon. In the form of a U.S. Coast Guard cutter. Or better yet, a U.S. Navy destroyer.

He straightened, a glimmer of hope going through him. "Where is this ship registered?" he asked.

Samantha spun and glared at him. She must know why he was asking, but judging by the look on her face, he wouldn't be getting the answer he'd hoped for.

She gave her head a curt shake. "Liberia."

Hell. His brief hope deflated.

Within a country's territorial waters, or if a country's own flagged vessel was threatened on the open seas, that country's military was allowed to intervene and deal with the culprits. Of course, that almost never happened. Most

pirates were smart enough to wait until a ship was in international waters to strike and to pick ships registered in
countries far from the attack site and with no inclination to
rescue. Which effectively rendered the targeted ship helpless.

A different sort of anger flashed across her face, like a
bad taste. "I've tried to get my father to change all his ships
to U.S. registry, but he refuses to listen. All he cares about
is the goddamn bottom line."

Clint stared, momentarily taken aback. To fly the American flag, a ship must be owned and crewed by Americans,
making it subject to U.S. labor laws, including minimum
wage, which discouraged most ship owners from doing so.
But it was the *other* thing she'd let slip that had snagged his
attention. "Your *father*?"

Her lips thinned. "Richardson Shipping?" she said.
"Sound familiar?"

Captain Sam—

Jesus.

Samantha Richardson?

Another important detail he'd missed last night in his
exhausted stupor.

She was the daughter of none other than shipping mag-
nate Jason Richardson, the last of a dying breed of American shipping line owners. An old-school renegade and a
ruthless shark in business, if the stories about him were
true.

She shuttered at his shocked expression. "Yeah. *That*
Richardson."

Fucking hell. No wonder she was being so damn protective of the ship and crew!

On second thought, no. Daddy's company or not, this
captain would be protective of her crew, regardless. He
hadn't known her for very long, but he already knew that
much about Samantha Richardson.

This put a whole different angle on things. Several
things.

"Does the company have a plan in place to deal with this

sort of incident?" he asked briskly, setting aside the whole other ball of wax for now.

"Not to my knowledge. Piracy isn't a big problem in the Arctic," she said dryly. "In fact, I can't remember the last time a ship was hijacked in the Bering Sea, if ever. Trust me, we're on our own out here."

They'd see about that. "We've got to alert the authorities," he said.

She seemed to make an effort to gather herself. "Not that I disagree, but how do you propose we do that?"

At least she was still speaking to him.

"We have to get to the DSC."

"I told you, the radio is on the bridge," she reminded him. "How are we supposed to get past the guard they've posted?"

Yeah. That would be tricky.

In addition to the five tangos Clint had counted on deck, one of whom was now in engineering, plus the men on the bridge and the wardroom, he'd spotted two others on the trawler moored off their port side. So, eight tangos in all. Unless there were even more of them lurking somewhere else, hidden from view.

Eight against one. Well, two. Okay, one and a half.

Either way, not great odds.

There was really only one viable option that he could see.

"*Eliza Jane*," he said. "The fishing trawler they arrived on. Every vessel at sea must be equipped with a radio and a DSC transmitter."

She made a dismissive gesture. "You've got to be kidding. That trawler's anchored at least three hundred feet away. And even if she were lashed alongside, you really think you could just leap over there without anyone seeing you?"

"Not leap. Swim. Three hundred feet is nothing."

"*Swim?*" She looked at him as though he'd completely lost his mind. "Are you freaking *insane*? That water's freezing! Literally."

He was pretty sure those were the exact words CIA officer Julie Severin had uttered last week when he'd suggested he don a wetsuit and brave twenty miles of frigid Bering Sea to reach Attu Island from the sinking Russian sub they'd both been trapped on. It was a swim that would have killed most people. But he wasn't most people. He'd endured far worse in his SEAL days. Even so, the thought of doing it again made him shudder.

Yeah. He was *definitely* too old for this shit.

But it was either jump into the icy depths or be captured and shot by Xing Guan's hit squad. And there was not a chance in hell he was going through *that*. Not a week ago. Not now. Not ever.

He cleared his throat. Hell, it was only a few hundred yards over to the trawler. Not twenty miles. He'd barely get wet.

"I assume you have an Arctic-weight wetsuit on board?" he asked.

Her mouth dropped open. "You're serious."

"As a bullet in the head."

She cringed visibly. But he wasn't about to mince words. They really had to do something, fast, or Shandy wouldn't be the only one suffering that fate. Xing Guan wasn't known for his patience or his mercy.

"Yeah," she said. "We've got full Arctic dive equipment on board in case we need to make emergency repairs at sea."

"Well. There you go. We're all set." He started for the door.

"There's just one slight problem," she said unhappily. "Over and above the craziness factor."

He turned, a sinking feeling in his gut. "What's that?"

"Well, two problems, actually."

"What?" he repeated, more vehemently.

"First, there's only one wetsuit." She eyed him up and down. "And it's for someone a lot smaller than you are. I doubt it'll fit."

He almost groaned. Fabulous. There was nothing better

than a wetsuit that crammed your balls up to your Adam's apple and restricted the movement of your limbs. "I'll make do," he said, determined to do just that. "And second?"

She made a noise of frustration. "It's in the uniform closet. On the crew deck. Next to the officers' staterooms."

Fucking hell.

Right where the guard was posted.

10

////\\\\\\/\////\

"This is ridiculous," Samantha muttered, though softly, so even Clint had trouble hearing the words. But he could read the look on her face without a problem. It was a wellspring of frustration. As was his, no doubt.

"He's got to turn away at some point," Clint responded in an equally low whisper, watching the guard take another slug from a supersize plastic soda bottle. He'd been drinking steadily for the past quarter hour as they'd observed him, hoping to catch a window and sneak past to the uniform closet. The bottle was nearly empty. "Or take a pee break."

Clint and Samantha were making like snipers on the ro-ro deck below the main companionway, lying side by side as they peered up at the guard from their hiding place beneath a big yellow earthmover, part of the ship's cargo. Other vehicles and equipment filled the width of the deck, helping to shield them—Chinese versions of John Deeres and Caterpillars, plus a dozen or two Japanese snowmobiles. The overhead lights had been left on, but as long as no one was looking for them, they should be fine. They kept their sparse conversation barely audible, only daring to speak because the sound of their voices was swallowed in the creaks and groans of the bulky cargo.

"I need a pee break, too," Samantha grumbled. "Just watching him drinking all that tea, or whatever it is, is making my bladder hurt."

Clint shot her a grin. "Should have brought the adult diapers, I guess," he whispered.

"Ha ha," she mouthed, and rolled her eyes, then went silent for a beat. "But that's not what I meant was ridiculous."

"No?" Inwardly, he fought his irritation. He'd been waiting for an argument from her. Up until now, their need to keep quiet had prevented it.

"This whole idea. It's insane," she said.

"Which part?" he asked with guarded patience.

"*Every* part! Trying to sneak by this guard. You swimming in that ice-cold ocean. Possibly getting shot for your trouble." Her voice strangled a little on that last bit.

Out of respect for Shandy, he tempered his response. "I told you, I was a SEAL. This is what I do." He grimaced. "Did."

"And how long ago was that?" she challenged, zeroing in on the last word.

He tried not to be insulted. "I'm not *that* old." He allowed a knowing glance and raked it over her, memories of their passion flooding through him. "You certainly weren't complaining about my stamina this afternoon."

Her answering withering look was belied by a twitch of her lips. Their eyes held, and for a moment they were both back in that hammock, locked in each other's arms. Had it really been just hours ago he'd held her naked body under his, experiencing more pleasure than he'd ever felt in his life?

Her cheeks went rosy, and his body quickened. Hell of a time to get a hard-on.

She tore her gaze away. "Okay, let's pretend you don't freeze your ass solid in that water. There are still two bad guys on that trawler. How are you going to get past them to the radio?"

He shifted on his elbows. *Details.* "I'll deal with that when I get there." He was trained to think on his feet. "But whatever happens to me, you need to stay safe. Promise me you'll stay hidden no matter what."

"I'll do what I have to do," she said, her tone uncompromising. Gone were the weakness and despair of the woman in the hideaway.

As was the palpable heat of their connection seconds ago.

He bit back a curse. "Why are you like this? Why do you have to fight me every fucking inch of the way, every fucking minute of the day?"

She blinked at his rebuke. But to his mild surprise, she didn't give him a knee-jerk retort. She sighed and remained mute for several moments. At length, she said, "I don't like when men try to steamroll over me. You said it yourself, it happens all too often. Especially in my profession. Men think because I'm a woman, and blond, that I'm a brainless idiot."

"I don't think that," he returned evenly.

"Maybe not. But you do have a bad habit of issuing me orders. I know you're the terrorist expert here, but it's *me* who's captain of this ship. I'm the one ultimately responsible for everything that happens on board."

He swallowed back his own knee-jerk response. He wasn't about to get into a debate on military versus civilian rank and whose orders took precedence in a situation like this. "We both want the best possible outcome for the ship and the crew," he said reasonably. "If achieving that means I, as the expert, have to give you orders, so be it." But he decided a concession wouldn't go amiss, and added, "However, I'll try to include you more in the decisions."

For a brief second her lips thinned. She said, "That's all I ask."

They went back to staking out the guard, and Clint's respect for Samantha inched up a notch. This couldn't be easy on her. She must be torn up inside and champing at the bit to do something to defend her crew, let alone save her father's ship. She was handling herself well, considering. Okay. He really would try to dial down on the commands.

It was probably a mistake, but he leaned over and pressed a kiss to the frown lines between her brows.

Her eyes sought his warily. "What was that for?"

He didn't answer, just winked, and turned his attention back on task. Mostly because he wasn't sure why he'd done it. Hell, he didn't want to know.

When *Île de Cœur* left Dutch Harbor this morning, he was convinced he'd shaken off his dogged pursuers—at least until they reached their next port of call.

That had been his first mistake.

Despite being in the middle of a critical op, he'd then made the inappropriate decision to shift into civilian mode . . . and succumb to the temptation of an affair with Samantha. Sure, he'd thought he would have four days without a goddamn death squad nipping at his heels. Four days to finally let down his guard a little and enjoy the rare physical chemistry that had instantly blossomed between him and Samantha. Four stress-free days where the only difficult decision he'd have to make was how many times they could sneak away to be alone together.

He fucking should have known better.

How quickly the situation had changed. He'd now been hurled back into full combat mode, and instead of making love, they were engaged in a deadly battle with a ruthless enemy.

In combat, the rules were very different. There wasn't time for personal issues. Not when lives were on the line. Clint knew as well as he knew his own name that mixing business with pleasure in his profession was never a good idea. It always ended badly.

Too bad he hadn't listened to the warning bells in his

mind last night as he'd fantasized about getting the pretty captain alone and slowly stripping her naked. Or this afternoon when he'd made fantasy into reality.

The worst was, now that they'd been intimate, he found he couldn't reclaim the distance he so desperately needed between them. Couldn't get back to that cool, professional space he should occupy in their personal interactions. Couldn't, because he'd been deep inside her, and enjoyed a passion with the woman he hadn't felt in more years than he could count. He couldn't separate himself from that no matter how much he wanted to. Or how dangerous it was not to.

However unwillingly, he felt a bone-deep connection with Samantha Richardson. And as foolish as it was, he wished down to the marrow that she felt the same way.

Most of all, he wanted her to trust him.

But it was clear she didn't. Not on any level.

Hell, he wasn't even sure she *liked* him. She definitely didn't like the way he automatically took charge of a situation. Issuing orders, she called it. He called it expediency. And leadership.

Damn it, he was just trying to *protect* her. What kind of woman didn't want that from a man? Especially the man she was sleeping with? Clint wanted Samantha to feel safe with him. Wanted her to feel safe *because* of him. But he always seemed to have the exact opposite effect on her.

Definitely something going on there in her head. Some kind of armor she'd built up against him. What had she said earlier about not trusting men? Was it *all* men she didn't trust? Or just him in particular, because of his tendency to take charge . . . ?

Unconsciously, he shook his head, wondering what had brought such an outwardly confident woman to such a cynical place inside.

On second thought, no. He didn't want to know. Knowing stuff like that would only bring them closer, and right now he needed distance.

Like about a thousand miles.

Thankfully, he was jerked from his uncomfortable musings when the guard suddenly tossed aside the plastic bottle with a hollow *thunk* and stretched his arms, glancing down the passageway toward the staterooms.

"This could be it," Clint whispered.

They watched alertly as the guard did a thorough 360° scan of the crew deck, his gaze pausing at the nearest stateroom doors. He strolled to the stairs leading up to the quarterdeck and bridge, checked it, then turned and peered down the narrower metal stairs that went past the main deck level to the ro-ro deck—and right at them. They held perfectly still.

"Get ready," Clint murmured when the guard was finally satisfied he was alone, and turned back toward the staterooms. "You remember what to do, right?"

To her credit, she just gritted her teeth and said, "Yes, Clint. I remember."

They'd only gone over the plan a dozen times as they waited.

He coiled his muscles, preparing to spring into action the instant the guard strolled into a stateroom to do his business.

He *really* didn't want to take Samantha along on this sortie to the uniform closet. But he didn't see a way around it. He'd have maybe forty-five seconds, maybe a minute, to grab the wetsuit, boots, gloves, snorkel, and mask. Without Samantha along to show him exactly where they were stored, he'd surely waste half that time just looking for the damn things.

This was not an idle exercise. Without the Arctic gear, he wouldn't survive a swim in four-degree water. Not for more than a few minutes. But if the guard returned from the head before they got clear of the passageway, they were both dead meat.

They both held their breath as the man turned and ambled toward the nearest stateroom.

Clint really, *really* wished he could leave her behind.

"You're not going to try and be a fucking cowboy, right?" he pressed.

She just smiled. His stomach sank.

The guard opened the stateroom door and disappeared through it.

"Go!" Clint vaulted up, sprinting noiselessly for the stairs and the uniform closet.

And right behind him, he swore he heard Samantha murmur, "Yippee kayay, baby."

11

``\\\\\\\\\\\//////////``

Sam didn't miss Clint's questioning look as they hit the crew deck running. *What?* Hey, she could do Bruce Willis when she wasn't having a nervous breakdown. It helped to have a mission and a role model.

She was breathing hard when they reached the closet and wasted precious seconds fumbling with the bolt until she finally managed to unlatch it and swing the door open.

They surged in. God knew how many—or few—seconds they had to find the gear. Her heart was pounding out of control, but she forced herself to stop in the dimly lit space and point out the cupboard containing the wetsuit to Clint. Then she spun around to the shelves on the opposite wall. The regulator, snorkel, mask, and other things should be stored somewhere among the clutter of equipment they contained. *Should* be.

Groping along the shelves in the murky darkness, she came up empty. Her pulse skyrocketed. *Where the hell are they?* Finally, way in the very back, her fingers touched the stiff neoprene of the dive boots. She shuddered out a sigh of relief. *Thank God!*

"Got them," she whispered. "You?"

"Yep." She heard a grunt and the click of a weight belt.

Swiftly gathering the other things from the shelf, her hand brushed over a knife in a sheath. Her pulse leapt and she grabbed that, too. "I found a dive knife."

He made a sound of approval. "Excellent. Keep it in your hand. We may need it. Ready?"

"Yeah."

He cracked the door, checking the passageway for any sign of the guard, who'd be returning any second. A thin sliver of light spilled over them. She knew from experience that the extra thick wetsuit was super heavy and unwieldy to carry. But somehow Clint had managed to roll it up and tuck it under one arm. The weight belt was around his waist and the fins dangled from his other hand.

"We're good. Let's go," he ordered.

She didn't dare look over her shoulder, just made a mad dash for the stairs back down to the ro-ro deck. But she stumbled at the landing, and Clint knocked into her, dropping one of the fins in his effort to keep them both from falling down the stairs.

The fin hit the metal steps like a shot and clattered down the two flights like a string of firecrackers, sending Sam's pulse straight into hyperspace. She gasped and started to freeze, but Clint grabbed her arm.

"Keep moving!"

They flew down the stairs as fast as they could. Above, the stateroom door banged open and rapid bootfalls thudded down the passageway. They hit the deck and rolled back under the earthmover just as the guard loomed over the landing rail. Cowering behind the Caterpillar treads, Sam was shaking so hard she had to clap both hands over her mouth to stop her teeth from chattering.

That's when she saw the fin.

Lying on the deck, right next to the stairs.

In plain sight.

Oh, God!

She shot Clint a desperate look. But his attention was

lasered in on the guard, who had moved to the top of the stairs and was gripping his machine gun in his stubby hands, head swiveling slowly back and forth as he scrutinized the cargo for whatever had made the noise.

A lump of fear wedged in her throat, throbbing painfully. There was no way he could miss seeing the fin. As soon as he turned his head this way—

Oh, God. It was all over. They were going to die.

All at once, Clint shot from their hiding place in a roll. *What the—?*

In terrified disbelief she watched him dart out fast as a snake's tongue to grab the fin, then dart back under cover—less than a nanosecond before the guard turned back in their direction. He halted next to her, clutching the fin to his broad chest, a grim but satisfied look on his face.

The most irrational thought burst through her. She suddenly wanted to be that fin, held so tight and secure in his strong arms. Rescued from disaster. Safe from harm. She swallowed.

His dark eyes captured hers, steady and unflappable. Telling her it would be okay.

But would it?

The guard's heavy boots clomped down the metal treads, one by one, coming closer and closer. As the sound grew louder, Clint carefully set the fin aside and plucked the dive knife from her hand. He slid his other hand over hers, cool and confident, lacing their fingers together. *How could he be so calm?* She squeezed her eyes shut, as she'd done as a kid at the scary parts of movies. Okay, she still did that.

It didn't help. This was no Hollywood film, and it would not be okay. It could never be okay. Shandy was not going to jump up and shake off the fake blood when some director called "Cut!" And the bad things that would happen to her and Clint if that guard found them hiding here were all too sickeningly real.

Time ground to a halt, suspended on the numbing crest of fear.

She wanted to scream, but managed to hold it together

thanks to the comforting feel of Clint's hand on hers. God, she was being such a wuss!

Maybe her father was right. Maybe she really did belong in an office, not in command of a multimillion-dollar vessel and valuable cargo. And other people's precious lives.

As if reading her thoughts, Clint tightened his grip and gave her hand a squeeze. She took a steadying breath.

A nanosecond later, the guard stepped off the stairs onto the hard deck. Clint let go of her, silently slid the sheath from the knife, and eased his body up into a spring-coiled crouch, deadly and still. He looked like a panther ready to take down its prey. She shivered involuntarily, very glad he was on her side.

The guard's footsteps paused on the other side of the earthmover's bandolier tread, practically on top of them. The man was so close she could smell the acrid odor of sweat and gun grease and the cloying scent of Cherry Coke that clung to him. If she extended her fingers through one of the gaps between the big metal treads, she could have traced the seams of his black ninja pants.

He hung there, poised in a mute vigil, his head slowly rotating, searching for any movement among the vehicles, his gun raised in readiness.

She didn't move a muscle. Not even an eyelash. Nor did Clint.

They waited. And waited. Clint crouched there like a spring-loaded statue, ready to attack. She just did her best not to let her teeth chatter, or cramp up and give them away.

After torturously long moments that dragged like hours, the guard turned and padded away, still listening attentively as he inched up the stairs, silent as a shark.

Sam's heart was still pounding painfully fifteen minutes later. But at least she could breathe again.

The minute the guard had reached the crew deck and turned his back, they'd scrambled out from their hiding place and fled back to the hideout. Well, she'd fled anyway.

Clint had more like stalked. The look on his face . . . Let's just say he looked angry. Sam was glad they hadn't run into the guard in engineering, for more reasons than one.

She glanced uneasily between him and the pile of diving gear as he started stripping out of his clothes. So different from when she'd watched him undress this afternoon . . . There was nothing remotely sexual about his movements this time. He hadn't even glanced her way.

The man was all business. Determination bled from his pores.

She tamped down a growing sense of doom. "So you're really going to do this?"

He tossed his uniform shirt onto the hammock. "I really am," he responded, unbuckling his pants. The broad expanse of his chest gleamed bronze in the dim overhead light. She made a vain attempt to distract herself from thinking about what he intended to do, by following the ripple and play of the tattoo on his impressive muscles as he grabbed the wetsuit's Farmer John and held it up to his front, measuring the size against his body. But it was no use, even the sight of his powerful body couldn't distract her. It only made her worry more, imagining what might happen to it—to him—if he went through with this.

"There's nothing I can say to talk you out of this insanity?" she pleaded.

He looked up, lips thin. "Sure. You can tell me a better plan."

Their eyes held, and she could sense he wasn't thrilled with the present one but was determined to see it through. Her heart sank. She felt as though she had been put through a meat grinder since waking up this morning, but no doubt the coming hours would be even worse on her frazzled nerves. Clint would be risking his life to get to the radio and send a distress signal, and the odds of him succeeding weren't great. She'd be stuck down here belowdecks, unable to see where he was, whether he was alive or dead, or even what he was doing over on that trawler.

Assuming he made it that far.

And, yeah, if she obeyed his orders and actually stayed put. Which wasn't at all a certainty. What if he needed her, and she wasn't there to help? How could she cower and hide when he was putting his very life on the line?

Her dismal thoughts must have shown on her face. With a sigh, his harsh expression softened and he put the wetsuit aside and pulled her into his arms. "It'll be okay," he said.

"Please don't go," she whispered, sinking into the momentary comfort of his embrace. With him there to support her, the shakes came back, and she had to close her eyes against a painful rocket of fear. "What if they've smashed the radio, and you can't—"

"It's a chance I have to take. There's no other way."

"I don't know what I'd do if anything happened to—"

"It won't," he assured her, and tilted her chin up. "And even if it does," he said, "you'll be fine. If these bastards are who I think they are, I'm the one they want. If I'm dead or captured, they've got no reason to stay on board."

Dead. A burst of dismay went through her. She clutched him tighter. "Don't even say that. I won't—"

"Shhh," he murmured. He searched her face for a moment, then bent and kissed her. It was a sweet, tender kiss. Filled with all the poignancy of an uncertain future. And totally at odds with the desperate situation.

"Clint . . ." she began when their lips parted.

He put a finger to her mouth, brushed another kiss over her temple, and said, "Come on. Help me get into this thing," then let her go to reach for the wetsuit again.

Though bursting with reluctance, she didn't argue, but held the stiff, heavy wetsuit overalls up for him as he struggled into them. Thankfully the size was a bit larger and stretchier than she'd remembered, but it was still a tight squeeze. And about four inches too short.

He frowned down at his exposed ankles, tugged at the material where it clamped around his thighs, then gave up and fiddled with the shoulder straps. "Damn, you weren't kidding about it being too small."

He'd definitely never get the Velcro ends to meet over

his broad expanse of shoulders. Not without castrating himself in the process.

She glanced around, and her gaze fastened on the hammock, still hanging between the bulkheads. She scooped up the dive knife and walked over to it. Ignoring the depressing symbolism that streaked through her mind, she sliced through its leader ropes. The end of the hammock fell to the floor in a big tangle, the other end swaying limply from side to side. Focusing determinedly on her task, she cut two lengths from the dangling ropes, each a couple of feet long.

She brought them to Clint, who was still wrestling with the wetsuit. "I'll slice holes in the straps where they meet and you can extend them with these."

His gaze followed her as she made a pair of oversized buttonholes, threaded the ropes through them, and tied the ends securely over his shoulders.

"Probably won't be all that comfortable," she observed, yanking at the knots to make sure they were tight.

"I'll live," he said, then grimaced and added, "With any luck."

She opened her mouth to protest.

But before she could get a word out, he said, "Kidding," and his lips pressed once again against hers. He gave her another long kiss, and she could feel the heightened urgency in the way his fingers held her, the way his blood pulsed so close to the surface where she touched him.

When he lifted his mouth, she was breathless. Mostly from her growing fear for him, but despite everything, also because of the way she felt whenever he kissed her. She watched in growing trepidation as he tugged on the wetsuit jacket and with some difficulty zipped it up.

This was so damned unfair. She'd lost her ship, her crew, would no doubt lose her job if she made it through this alive, and now she was about to lose Clint, too—a man who somehow, in a few short hours, had come to mean the world to her.

Everything about this situation sucked.

After pulling on the pair of dive boots she handed him,

he turned away to gather up the snorkel and other gear. The feel of hard steel in her hand suddenly reminded her of the knife she was still clutching. A too-ugly symbol of reality. She tried jerkily to slide it back into its plastic sheath, but missed. She tried again.

"Don't forget this," she said. "You'll need a—" She cursed as her second attempt missed, too. Finally on the third try, she succeeded. She looked up and saw him shaking his head.

"No, you keep it. You've got nothing else to defend—"

"Are you kidding me?" She pushed it into his hand. "You are *not* going over there unarmed."

He still didn't take the knife. "No, I—"

"That's an order, LC." She let go and stuck her hands under her armpits so he had no choice but to catch it. "They've got guns, Clint. And I'm not Crocodile Dundee."

Finally he relented with a tight smile. "Fine."

If she'd expected another lecture on staying hidden while he was gone, he didn't deliver. Instead, he gave her a look that was so penetrating it made her heart stall in her throat.

"I'm sorry," he said. "I'm sorry I brought this on you and your ship. And I'm sorry as hell about Shandy." A slow fuse of bone-deep rage burned through his eyes. "I'm going to take down these bastards if it's the last thing I do. That is a goddamn promise."

She was torn between sadness and alarm at his solemn declaration. "I'm sorry, too," she said. "But please, don't be a hero. Just get to the DSC radio and send that signal, nothing else."

She took a step toward him, nearly overcome with the urge to grab his arms and hang on with all her might. Not let him go on this insane errand. "Just come back safe. That's all that matters."

He didn't respond, but he didn't have to. She could see the unspeakable knowledge lurking there in his molten dark eyes—the knowledge that he might not be coming back at all, let alone safe.

"Please, Clint," she whispered hoarsely.

She would have felt the same way regardless of who was about to brave the icy sea and two brutal hijackers, she told herself. It didn't matter that she'd made love to this near-stranger just hours ago. She'd only just met him, for god-sake. She didn't know him at all. Had little basis on which to mourn him if he died. Hell, she didn't even know whom to notify of his death. But her heart hurt so much at the thought of it that she nearly doubled over.

His jaw muscles moved. "Samantha . . ." he began, his voice an uneven blade of iron. But his lips compressed, and he shook his head. He glanced down at his wrist, paused for a millisecond, then grasped the brown leather thong tied around it. With a swift jerk he snapped it off.

She gasped, knowing how much the totem meant to him. After they'd made love, she'd asked about the unusual totem bracelet, and he'd told her about his grandfather and how he'd sent Clint on his first vision quest where he'd also killed his first deer with a bow and arrow. He'd had to use every bit of the animal for something useful, and this was one of the many things he'd made. The only thing he hadn't given away. Later, he'd added a claw from the first—and only—bear he'd killed.

"What are you—"

He held it out to her. The ivory bear claw hanging from it was pale and lustrous against his bronze skin. "Keep it for me."

"But—"

"I've got to go." He went to the door and cracked it, checked the passageway, then swung it open. He looked at her one last time, and gave the lecture she'd been expecting. "Stay here. Stay hidden. Do not even think about sneaking up on deck." His expression, even sterner than usual, if that was possible, willed her to obey.

She nodded, though she knew at once she wouldn't. Couldn't. Not while he was in danger.

Her heart lurched as he stepped through the door into the passageway. The ivory totem was still warm between her fingers. *Warm from his body.* "Clint?" she called after him, her breath oddly strangled.

His head came around, eyes indecipherable. "Yeah."

Suddenly she had no idea what she wanted to say. There was too much. Too many bewildering emotions. Too little time to sort it all out. *Too little time . . .* The ivory claw stabbed into her flesh as her fingers curled tight around it. She swallowed. "When you broke into my stateroom last night," she managed past a thick lump of confusion, "I . . . I lied to you."

A guarded expression flicked over his face. "Yeah?"

"Yeah." She swallowed again, wishing . . . "I said you smelled like a bilge rat."

His eyebrows hiked.

. . . wishing they'd just had more time together.

She took another halting step. "That wasn't true."

He stared down at her, and all the air squeezed from her lungs.

Oh, God. What would she do if she lost this man, too?

"It wasn't?" The query came out low and rumbling, like the sound of a ship's engine deep in its belly.

Her vision swam as a deep regret washed through her. Regret for dreams that were already lost. But more for the ones she'd never get to dream.

"No," she whispered. "You smelled like week-old chum."

12

〜〜〜〜〜〜〜〜

Week-old chum.

A reluctant smile sifted through Clint as he crept stiffly around the fringes of the pitch-black ro-ro deck. The lights had been turned off, and he was feeling his way along the bulkhead in the dark. His fins were tucked under one arm, his mask and snorkel hanging from his neck, the dive knife strapped to his right thigh, and a coiled-up rope circled his chest like a bandolier.

"Feeling" being the operative word.

What had Samantha really been trying to say? Because it sure as hell wasn't anything about the way he smelled. His wry smile quickly faded. He didn't feel good about leaving her on her own. In point of fact, he was downright worried. The woman he'd left behind in that hideaway was not the same dauntless, in-your-face fighter he'd gotten to know since sneaking on board *Île de Cœur*. This woman had been scared witless—which, admittedly, was only natural. Then again, he was grateful for her fear. Nothing like abject terror to keep a body hidden and safe.

Unfortunately, he didn't think it would last very long.

Samantha Richardson just wasn't the type to cower in fear
on the sidelines, letting someone else relieve her of what
she saw as her own responsibility. Especially not a man.
She definitely had issues with men controlling her.

Five minutes alone and she'd be itching to spring her jail
cell. Talking herself into doing something stupid. Something
really stupid. Like try to get to those guns in the officer's
lounge. Or rescue her crew single-handedly. Or hell, even
try to rescue *him* if and when the bullets started flying.

His heart clenched. Yeah, that was what he feared the
most she'd do.

Because there had been something else in her expression, something in the way she'd looked at him as he'd
turned and walked away from her after that chum remark.
Something that tied his stomach in knots.

Speaking of which . . . Letting out an uneven breath, he
pressed close into the hulking black bulk of a large cargo
vehicle to adjust his wetsuit. Already the makeshift Farmer
John suspenders were cutting into his shoulders, and the
thick strangle of the rubbery fabric was binding him in
places that made him fear for the fate of his future grandkids.

He tightened his jaw. The irony of *that* concern did not
escape him. When had the idea of grandkids even entered
his consciousness? Let alone make him fret about not having them?

Blame it on Samantha. The woman had a talent for
bringing out totally unfamiliar and vaguely disturbing sides
of him. Sides that apparently wanted grandkids.

Jesus.

With a grimace, he continued picking his way along the
bulkhead. Hell, maybe he was just feeling his mortality.

Not that he was worried about those two goons on *Eliza
Jane*, as Samantha seemed to be. But making a jump into
mile-deep water with nothing but blue for two hundred
miles in every direction tended to make a body contemplate
its limitations. He'd done it with his former team too many
times to count, but he'd felt a healthy respect for the situa-

tion every single time. Unlike some of the guys, he'd never been a danger junkie.

His fingertips told him he'd finally reached the triple cargo bay that rolled up like a giant garage door, opening up to the outside, usually to a pier where the ship's wheeled cargo was loaded on and off. He was on the port side. There was also a matching set on the starboard. Samantha had told him there were regular-sized doors, as well, for easy access to the outside by the crew when the big ones were closed.

That was where he planned to make his splash-out.

Adrenaline started to pump as he swiftly felt his way along the giant bay and found the small crew door at the far side. It felt more like a watertight door on a submarine, with a wheeled locking mechanism and all. Thankfully, he'd listened to his own advice and picked up a can of gear oil when he'd stopped for the rope, to keep any metal hinges from squeaking.

Using his hands as eyes, he located and squirted oil on the wheel and lock as well as the rusty side hinges, and prayed they wouldn't squeal like stuck pigs when he opened the door.

He glanced aft down the length of the ship, and upward. The guard was still posted at the top of the main companionway two decks up, prowling around the small, visible square of light, the strap of his Type-85 submachine gun still slung over one shoulder. Clint mentally gauged the distance between them. Far enough away for the guard not to hear the metallic scrape of the hatch opening, or notice when a sliver of sunlight suddenly cut through it into the dark deck. *Probably.*

But Clint didn't have a lot of choice. This was the only practical way out. He'd have to risk it.

He took his time, gingerly finessing the rusty bolt, stopping dead when the beginnings of a metallic protest threatened to betray him. He splashed more oil on and eased the door open another fraction of an inch. Splashed and eased. Splashed and eased. Until finally there was a crack large enough to see through to the outside.

The sun was still high in the robin's-egg blue sky, and he squinted against the razor's edge of light that hit his eye as he peered across the frigid expanse of the Bering Sea. A slice of the cold July wind cut into his face, but no storm clouds hovered overhead.

And there was the Australian trawler, just where it was supposed to be, bobbing on the sparkling silver waves about two hundred yards off their starboard side.

The pewter gray span of water that lay between *Île de Cœur* and the other vessel looked as cold as it surely was, but unlike on his marathon swim to escape the Russian sub last week, there wasn't an iceberg in sight. Summer hit fast and hard in the far north; temperatures sometimes soared into the fifties.

He glanced down, calculating the distance to the waves from where he stood. About thirty feet or so. The coil of thin nylon rope he'd picked up from the storage closet on his way here was at least that long and strong enough to secure a two-ton tractor. He'd have no trouble going over the side and rappelling down to where he could slip unobtrusively into the sea—without risking two broken legs.

Or a hailstorm of machine gun fire.

All in all, the swim was going to be a piece of cake. Seriously. When he and his former SEAL team had stopped off in Iceland for a few days of R&R on the way back from a particularly weird mission in the North Sea, they'd seen goddamn *tourists* diving in colder water than this, in some unpronounceable lake formed by an ancient volcano.

Of course, no one had been shooting at them. And they did have drysuits that fit.

Details.

Everyone knew bullets didn't penetrate any farther than six inches when shot into water, no matter how hard Hollywood tried to convince moviegoers otherwise. He'd be fine. At least until he got to the trawler. That's where the diceyness factor would kick in.

The bad news was that the trawler was not one of the big, modern kinds with a U-shaped fantail at the stern where the

Gilson-winch was mounted for casting off the fishing nets.
If it had been, he could have swum right up the slot and
climbed aboard practically at the back of the wheelhouse.
That would have been convenient. Still, although the trawler's back end was flat as a pancake, the good news was that
one of the tow warps lay in a disorderly pile on the very back
edge of the afterdeck. Even from here he could see several
cables and lines snaking over the transom gunwale, with
their ends trailing in the water.

No, he'd have no problem climbing aboard the enemy
vessel.

However, doing so without getting caught was an entirely different matter.

He scanned the length of the trawler, immediately spotting
a tango standing splay-legged on the forward deck, smoking
a cigarette. Could be worse. At least the man was facing forward.

Clint grimaced and studied the boat, looking for the second man he'd seen earlier. There was no sign of him. Not
on deck. Not in the pilothouse. Not among the jumble of
warps and lines, or the scatter of fishing equipment that
packed the aft working deck. Well, there was one more
thing he had to do before he splashed out, anyway.

For several minutes he searched for the perfect hiding
place for the SD card. It made him nervous as hell to have it
anywhere but on his person. He didn't want to have to go
back for it if he needed to make a fast getaway. On the other
hand, a fast getaway seemed highly unlikely under the circumstances. Plus, he didn't want to take any chances on his
swim, in case the small dry-bag he was taking with him
leaked and the card was ruined. Or he didn't make it back
alive. This way his boss at least had a shot at finding it.

A few yards away was an orange snowplow. He crept
under the plow and looked up at the mechanicals in the undercarriage. A small in-line fuse box was right above him.
He pried open the plastic top and tucked the data card inside,
then closed the lid and pressed his thumbprint clearly onto it.

That should do it.

Clint went back to the hatch and checked the trawler for Tango Two. Still not visible. He stood and watched for a few more minutes, but that was as long as he dared. He couldn't wait any longer. He'd just have to go in blind.

The more time it took to get to that radio and call in the Coast Guard, the more shit could rain down on the situation. One good man had already been killed because of him. He wasn't about to let the body count go any higher. He could handle whatever those two threw at him. He just hoped it wouldn't come to that.

Over and back. Send the signal. Quick and dirty. That was the order of the day.

And if he had the devil's own luck, he'd even live to tell the tale.

Sam felt like she was going to pass out. She halted her pacing, bent over at the waist, and took a deep breath. Probably lack of oxygen from being cooped up in this damn room. She was slowly going stir-crazy down here.

Up until today, this secret hideaway had been her private sanctuary. A place she could come to be alone with her thoughts. A place she could contemplate her life and reach important decisions. And mere hours ago, a place where she'd been happier and more content than she'd been in a long, long time.

She grasped the leather bracelet in her fist and squeezed her eyes shut.

But now . . . Now being here felt claustrophobic. Like she was enduring a horrible punishment of solitary confinement in prison. The last thing Sam wanted was to be alone. Or to be forced to listen to the witches' brew of thoughts roiling around in her head.

Thoughts of her crew and what might be happening to them.

Thoughts of the man who just this afternoon had left her breathless with his passion and his tenderness.

Thoughts of the incredible danger he was in right now,

this very moment. While she was down here hiding like a coward.

No.

She opened her fist, looked at the cherished bear claw, and let out a mewl of anguish. Then a growl of anger. And came to the most important decision of her life.

This was not acceptable.

She had to do something.

She needed to get to someplace she could watch what was happening and be prepared to go to him, to jump in and help him if he needed her. Like with a hand, or an extra pair of eyes, or a timely distraction, if he needed it to get safely back on board.

Lieutenant Commander Walker might be prepared to die to save her and the crew. But she was not prepared to let him.

No. Damn. Way.

Taking a deep breath, she tucked the bracelet into her bra, next to her heart, straightened, and marched to the door. She pretended she didn't feel how her hand was shaking as she reached for the latch and lifted it. Determinedly, she squared her jaw, swung open the door, and quickly stepped through it.

Before she could chicken out and change her mind.

13

,,,,,,,\\/////

Holy *shit*, the water was cold.

The Arctic-weight wetsuit was decent and kept Clint from feeling the very worst of it, but because of the small size, he was shivering by the time he'd swum the relatively short distance to the trawler. Where the edges of the wetsuit, boots, and gloves barely met at his ankles and wrists, his skin stung with icy shards of pain. Thankfully, the full-face hood covered him well, so his face didn't burn too badly from the cold.

Once he'd rappelled down into the water, it had only taken him a short time to reach the other vessel, swimming as deep as he could, and only coming to the surface for quick snatches of breath through the snorkel.

He bobbed up on the far side of the trawler, where he'd be hidden from *Île de Cœur* and prying eyes. But to get on board, he'd have to swim around to the transom and climb up the stern, since that part of the trawler's deck dipped closest to the water. Swimming to the corner of the boat's backside, he listened carefully for any movement on the afterdeck. Under the salty smell of the sea, a faint drift of cigarette smoke teased his nose. But not strong enough for the guy to be smoking anywhere close by. Good. Still no sign of the other man. Hopefully he'd stay put wherever he was.

Clint raised his mask and peered across the choppy waves to *Île de Cœur*, assessing the likelihood of being spotted by someone on the larger ship during the few moments he'd be open and exposed as he climbed aboard the trawler.

Not surprisingly, the hostages had been moved off the deck. He wondered briefly where they'd been taken and hoped they were unharmed. A flare of fury made him clench his jaw when he saw the bloody body of Shandy, still sprawled where he had fallen. *The fucking bastards.* Couldn't they at least put a damned sheet over the man?

He shifted his gaze and saw that three of the hijackers were standing on deck having a heated discussion. He recognized the fireplug shape of the head honcho, whom he assumed was Xing Guan, and as usual the fucker was not a happy camper. The good news was the trio was paying no attention to anything else around them. And no one else was on deck.

Effectively camouflaged by a huge black shadow cast by the cargo ship in the late evening sun against the smaller vessel, he swam around to the flat of the trawler's transom, grabbed one of the dangling lines, and gingerly gave it a tug. Instantly, he felt the fishing net attached to it start to slide across the afterdeck. He dropped the line at once. He definitely didn't want the whole damn mess to slide off and topple into the sea. Nothing like attracting unwanted attention.

He swam a couple more feet and caught up another line. Same result. The third did the same. *Hell.*

His last two attempts went no better.

Suddenly, a corner of the fishing net broke loose from the pile and slithered under the taffrail, nearly landing on his shoulders before the rest caught on something that halted its progress.

Crap.

He dove back under the frigid water, half expecting excited shouts and bullets to follow. He held his breath, controlling the chattering of his teeth with an iron jaw.

But the silence was not broken—other than from the surge of blood in his ears.

Damn it anyway. This was not working. He needed a different plan.

Cautiously he surfaced and scoped out the flat span of transom more closely. The back of the trawler lay low in the water, but not low enough for him to reach the deck without help. He needed a way up. But there was nothing. No swim step. No chock. No anchor cable. Not even a damn propeller he could hoist himself up from. Where was his grappling hook when he needed it? Oh, yeah, on that Russian sub at the bottom of the sea.

He cursed inwardly, eyeing the corner of net that was dangling over the gunwale. He'd just have to secure it somehow, so it could support his weight without sliding into the sea. His gaze landed on a sturdy deck cleat a foot or two in from the edge, and he pushed out a breath. Not great, but it would have to do.

It took him several harrowing minutes of concentration, grabbing the corner of the net and flicking it up in a rippling motion to inch it over to the cleat, praying fervently each time that the rest of the net stayed put on deck—and that the two goons didn't hear him doing it. By the time the heavy webbing finally caught on the cleat and fastened securely, sweat was trickling down his temples beneath his hood . . . and his ankles were all but numb from being in the cold water for so long.

Which of course made climbing the net one-handed—because his fins were clutched in the other—nearly impossible. It was only with the help of the dive knife to cut occasional slits in the mess for footholds that he managed to haul himself up, no doubt looking far more like a crab than a SEAL.

Definitely time to retire from fieldwork, he thought disgustedly as he rolled himself onto the afterdeck, scooting tight up against the base of the capstan. Again he held his breath, waiting for shouts of discovery. But once again, none came.

Amazingly, his luck was holding.

Of course, this had been the easy part.

He lay very still and gave himself a minute of rest as he peeled off his mask and snorkel. His ankles were thawing so his feet throbbed like twin bastards. Pain shot up his legs all the way to his squashed, smarting crotch.

He ground his teeth and tugged in irritation at the wetsuit. This was *so* not how he'd fantasized that *particular* bit of anatomy would be feeling tonight.

Damn. He closed his eyes as a hot jumble of emotions and sweet memories of the afternoon tangled up inside him. Unbidden thoughts of Samantha coursed through his blood. Of how good they'd been together. And how brave she'd turned out to be. Brave and determined to do the right thing, no matter how scared she was. The woman was one in a million.

His raw emotions turned to steely resolve to get her out of this, come hell or high water. And to see that the Chinese memory card with its vital information made it safely into the hands of the navy. The *U.S.* Navy.

There was only one way to accomplish either of those things. He had to get moving and reach the bridge to send that distress signal.

Ignoring the pain in his body and the heaviness in his heart, he rose to a crouch and skimmed his gaze over the deck around him, looking for a place to stash his fins and mask. Somewhere they'd be handy if he had to make an emergency exit. He decided to tie them on the end of a line and suspend them over the side. Another dangling line would never be noticed, and the gear would be at water level should he not have time to do more than jump in. He left his hood on but pulled it down around his neck, and stashed his gloves inside the zippered jacket.

He made a quick foray to the rail, lowered the gear line

into the water, then scurried back to the shelter of the capstan.

Looking around, he took in every detail of the trawler visible to him, then glanced over to *Île de Cœur*—noting that the three tangos were still arguing—then back again.

Tango One remained out of Clint's line of vision on the trawler's forward deck in front of the pilothouse. Still no sign of Tango Two. For now, his path to the bridge was clear.

He started across the afterdeck in a crouching lope, heading for the side door to the wheelhouse, and cast one last glance across to *Île de Cœur* just to be sure he wasn't spotted.

What he saw nearly made him trip and fall flat on his face. He jerked to a halt, letting out a string of mental curses, then realized his vulnerable position and leapt to the back wall of the wheelhouse, cramming his body against it, directly under a rectangular window.

He whipped his gaze back to the cargo ship, praying what he'd seen had been an optical illusion. No such luck. As he watched with growing vexation, sure enough, the scuttle atop the forward ventilation shaft slowly inched up.

Samantha!

Sonofabitch! He'd *ordered* her to stay put below! And she'd *promised* . . .

Anger at the infuriating woman twisted his gut in equal measure with a wrenching fear.

The scuttle rose another inch.

He had to physically stop from launching himself after her. What the hell was she *doing*?

He wanted to jump up and shout at her. Wave his arms and scream at her to get her goddamn butt back down to the hideaway. He wanted to swim back over there at breakneck speed and shake her until her goddamn teeth rattled. Until she learned to do as she was goddamn *told*!

He hissed out a breath between clenched teeth. Just *wait* until he got his hands on her.

The scuttle stopped moving and, thank God, didn't rise any higher. He shot a quick glance at the three hijackers standing not forty feet away from her. The argument had devolved, and the head honcho, Xing Guan, was now haranguing the other two men, striding back and forth, and—*God*. Right in the direction of the partially open scuttle!

Urgency caught Clint by the throat with claws of fear. What if they saw her? What if they caught her? *What if they*—

God*damn* it. He had to get back there. *Now!*

He shot up, and almost took a running step before he again stopped himself with a curse.

No. He *couldn't* go yet. Not until he'd hit that DSC button.

A surge of helpless frustration iced through his veins. Never before had he been so torn, forced to choose between his head and his heart.

Except there *was* no choice.

And *this*, he told himself angrily, was why it was *always* a mistake to let yourself get distracted while on a mission. A monumental error not to maintain that laser focus, regardless of the tempting diversions thrown in your path. And the worst mistake of all was to become emotionally involved with that distraction, so you couldn't think straight and do what needed doing, without a second's hesitation.

Ruthlessly, he shoved away his present distraction and ripped his gaze from the hatch. Samantha was a big girl, captain of her own ship, for fuck sake, and responsible for her own foolish decisions. This one included. She would just have to deal with the consequences on her own, too.

At least until he'd done his job over here. When he got back he intended to kill her himself.

Nevertheless his stomach clenched, and the quintessentially male part of him that desperately needed to protect her, with or without her permission, gave a low growl as he turned his back on her. Determinedly, he emptied his mind of thoughts of her and forced himself back on task.

After taking a calming moment, he straightened up just enough to peer over the bottom sill of the pilothouse window he'd been crouched under. As he'd hoped, the window looked into the rear of the bridge, positioned just above the map table.

The bridge was empty.

He scanned the pilot's station, and his jaw tightened. There was a dark red, irregular stain on the captain's chair, with matching dark streaks on the floor beneath. On the navigational console below the windshield, a few of the instruments had been destroyed, their screens smashed.

Including the compass and GPS.

A rough expletive almost made it through his clenched teeth. Both at the implications of the blood and because a distress call sent without the ship's position was as good as useless. Even giving his best estimate of where they were, locating them in the vast Bering Sea would be like finding a bomb somewhere in the Sahara.

He spotted a pair of headphones hanging within reach of the stained chair. The radio was bracketed above it. He nearly groaned. The aging metal housing and huge dials spoke eloquently of a bygone era. Not quite vacuum tubes, but almost. Which meant the DSC had to be an external add-on, not built-in. He looked around but didn't see the unit. Surely, the trawler hadn't put out to sea without a DSC transmitter. That would be crazy, not to mention illegal.

He examined the radio again. And noticed several stripped wires sticking out from the back panel like bad spiked hair—as though something had been violently ripped from them. He let out another string of mental curses. One guess what that was.

God*damn* it.

He briefly closed his eyes. *Okay.* Could be worse, he told himself. The bastards could have smashed the radio, too. As long as the radio worked, he still had a chance.

Knowing this was likely the last chance he'd get, he pushed aside his physical pain and let instinct take over. His pounding pulse slowed, his senses opened, and his body became a vortex of concentration.

Calm and steady now, he melted around the wheelhouse corner and slipped through the door, easing it closed behind him. Turning, he went to reach for the earphones.

And came face-to-face with the barrel of a gun.

14

///////////

Sam's heart stopped in her chest, then hurtled into double time as she watched Clint go through the wheelhouse door. *No! Oh, God, no!*

From her perch on the ledge atop *Île de Cœur*'s access chute, Sam had seen exactly when Clint's searching gaze had stumbled onto her peeking out from under the scuttle. Seen his immediate, furious reaction—and how he'd had to crouch under the pilothouse window to calm down, shooting her dagger looks she could feel all the way across the water.

Moments later, she'd watched in consternation as one of the hijackers, with hideously bad timing, suddenly appeared in the narrow companionway leading from the lower deck to inside the bridge—just as Clint came sneaking in through the side door.

And then she saw the guard's gun.

She gasped in shock, nearly tumbling backward down the chute. She grabbed hold of the ledge, a scream of warning leaping to her lips. She slapped a hand over her mouth and bit back the sound, helplessly watching the terrifying drama unfold across the water.

Clint stuck his hands in the air.

Oh, sweet Jesus. No! A mewl of dismay slipped past Sam's fingers. *Please, God, don't let him be—*

All at once the gun jerked, and there was a blur of clashing bodies. Both men vanished below the window.

Sam froze in sheer panic, pressing her hand to her mouth so hard she tasted blood. Holding an agonized breath, she prayed for Clint to reappear.

He didn't.

Desperation blossomed in her heart. Had he been shot?

Paralyzed with fear for him, she replayed the scene in her mind. The telltale jerk of the gun was unmistakable.

Ohgod, ohgod. He *had* been shot!

The world swam out of focus as tears sprang to her eyes. *No!*

She swiped at them, determined not to lose it . . . or hope. *Okay. Okay. People survived gunshots every day, right?* He couldn't be dead! He *couldn't*.

But the memory of Shandy's bloody death ravaged through her, sending a ragged shudder of pain straight to her heart.

Her arms turned to jelly, and she had to let the scuttle drop, slumping down to hug herself in the all-encompassing darkness. She didn't *want* to believe it. She fought like hell against the awful truth . . . but there was no use denying what she'd seen.

She'd lost him.

She'd lost him before she ever really had him.

Hunched over beneath the heavy metal scuttle hatch, she rocked herself back and forth on the narrow ledge, oblivious to the three-story drop to the bottom of the pitch-black shaft.

An emptiness filled her, so vast it nearly swallowed her whole. An emptiness tinged with profound regret.

Just this morning Clint had been so . . . alive. So vibrant, and intense. So tender and thoughtful. A stranger, and yet so easily able to read her every nuance. A man of honor, willing to make the ultimate sacrifice without a thought for himself.

How could such goodness be snuffed out in an instant?

She thought about the last words she'd said to him. That inane nonsense about smelling like chum. How stupid was that?

Sure, she'd had her doubts about him, at first. What sane person wouldn't, under the circumstances? But any doubts about what side he was playing for were long gone, quickly replaced by a growing respect for the man and his selfless deeds . . . along with a combustible chemistry that had ignited between them like firecrackers whenever their eyes met, or their bodies touched.

And now he was dead, or bleeding and about to be dead, and would never, could never—

She swallowed, tasting bitter regret. If only she'd told him how she felt! Told him how hard she was falling for him . . . and asked for a chance to explore those dazzling, unexpected feelings that bubbled up whenever she was with him. To see if there might, against all odds, have been something real and lasting between them. Something that would rekindle her trust in men and her ability to read them.

And possibly even . . . make her believe in love again.

But no, she hadn't told him. Instead, fear had congealed the scary words in her throat. And stupidity had emerged in their place.

Not that her blossoming feelings would have made any difference to his fate today. But she would have liked him to know, to have seen the look in his dark, expressive eyes as she told him, just once, before he . . .

A tear trickled down her cheek. Now she would never get the chance.

If only she hadn't been such a damn coward.

She touched the bear claw totem pressed to her heart. "Oh, Clint Wolf Walker," she whispered, her voice cracking in sorrow. "I'm so very sorry."

The body of his enemy went easily over the side, feetfirst, sliding into the slate gray sea with a tiny splash. It sank

beneath the waves, disappearing in seconds courtesy of a
metal winch handle lashed to its ankles.

Clint let go of the line he'd used to lower the corpse,
tossed it in after, followed by the bound and weighted knot
of bloody rags he'd found to mop up the bridge floor with.
Of course, there was already so much blood on the bridge
that a little more hardly showed.

As soon as the bundle went under, he returned to the
obscuring shadow of the wheelhouse wall and stood very
still, listening intently.

This part of the deck was hidden from *Île de Cœur*, but
he could still smell cigarette smoke wafting back from the
trawler's forward deck, just half a boat length away.

All remained quiet. He eased out a long, even breath.

It had been unbelievably risky to dispose of the body and
rags like that, but even more risky not to. At least now
there'd be momentary confusion and uncertainty about the
dead man's fate. Finding a body with a gaping stab wound
and broken neck would have left no doubt. It would also
have confirmed Clint's presence somewhere on board the
two vessels, and result in a full-scale search of both. There
was no question, the enemy would not give up until they'd
found him.

Getting rid of the evidence might just buy enough time
for the Coast Guard to arrive before that happened.

Assuming Clint could somehow send that distress call.

Making a move for the wheelhouse door, he flinched,
and glanced down at his arm. Blood oozed from a long
slash in his wetsuit—the price of stopping his attacker's
gun from going off. As he had lunged for it, the man had
grabbed his knife hand and nearly succeeded in forcing the
blade to Clint's throat. He'd managed to knock the gun to
the floor, then swing his arm up to block the knife, saving
his life . . . but taking a nasty slice in the process.

Hell, at least he was alive. And on an even more positive
note, he now had a loaded gun zipped under his jacket.
Things were looking up.

Snagging another clean rag from a deck locker, he

wound it around his bleeding cut, tied it with his teeth, and slid quietly back onto the bridge. He paused just inside the door for a millisecond, half expecting Tango One to appear out of nowhere as his buddy had done. But the man was still clearly visible through the forward windshield, standing at the bow rail idly studying *Île de Cœur*'s deck.

Oh, shit.

Clint whipped his gaze to the other ship. A spurt of relief zinged through him when he saw the scuttle was now battened down tight. Thank God Samantha had come to her senses and gone back down below.

He wondered briefly if she'd seen what had happened on the bridge. She must have. Probably that was what finally got through her stubborn head and drove her back into hiding. It was dangerous on deck. These bastards were not fooling around.

Small favors. At least now he wouldn't have to worry about her.

Making himself small, he padded quietly to the pilot's station to assess the damaged instruments. The engine controls seemed to have been spared, so the boat could still be started and driven—which made sense since the hijackers had arrived on it—though they must have been running without navigation. Of course, any spec ops unit on the planet, even an assassination squad, would be carrying its own GPS equipment.

More evidence he was right about the hijackers being Chinese agents.

He glanced back at the murdering bastard in the bow, and with a short moment of satisfaction considered killing him, too, then cranking up *Eliza Jane* and racing to get help in person . . . instead of trying to convince a skeptical Coastie radio dispatcher to send valuable resources to a possible hoax at an unknown position.

So damn tempting. But he dismissed the idea. Even if he was willing to leave Samantha on her own—*which he wasn't*—fishing trawlers did not race. Besides, it may *look* like the engines had not been disabled, but he could be wrong about that.

And totally screwed if he was.

He peered up at the radio and the stripped wires hanging from its back, dimly hoping they hadn't really been attached to the DSC unit. But they had, and a quick visual of the bridge did not reveal the unit itself tossed in a corner. Probably long since thrown overboard—the first thing *he* would have done in their place.

He flicked his eyes back to the radio. It was mounted right under the overhead. But he sure as hell didn't dare try removing the monstrosity from its corroded bracket. God knew what mechanical disaster that would bring down on him. Literally.

Damn, this was going to be a royal bitch. In order to reach the radio dials he'd have to actually sit in the blood-soaked captain's chair. . . .

In front of the panoramic windshield, in full view of anyone looking in.

Sam's heart was slamming against her chest so hard she was positive the beats must be echoing off the ro-ro cargo, bouncing from tractor to Caterpillar like pinballs. Giving away her position.

Frankly, she didn't give a damn.

She was mad. *Really* mad.

These assholes thought they could go around hijacking ships and shooting innocent people? Well, she had news for them. They were *not* going to get away with it. Not *her* ship. Not *her* crew. And *definitely* not her—

She squelched the thought before it could form. *Clint might be gone.* But Bolun, Matty, Frank and Johnny, and the others . . . her faithful crew, *they* were still alive. Somewhere on this ship. Counting on her to save them.

She intended to do just that.

All she needed was a weapon. And she knew just where to find one.

She straightened her spine against the cold metal earthmover at her back, steeling her nerve. She ducked her head around a giant tread and peeked up at the crew deck two flights above.

Just as before, there was a guard positioned on the weather deck landing of the central companionway. But this was a new guy. And not as vigilant, it appeared. He was pacing back and forth impatiently, casting resentful looks up toward the quarterdeck level.

She almost sympathized. Even way down here, her nose was twitching at the hint of delicious smells wafting out from the galley and mess, where the hijackers must be having a midnight supper of the night's meal for her crew. Ginger's lasagna and garlic bread. Sam would know those heavenly smells anywhere.

She expected stomach growls to join the pinball game with her pulse any second. She hadn't eaten anything since lunchtime, nearly twelve hours ago, other than the small loaf of French bread Clint had pressed on her.

At the thought of him, once again she had to shut her eyes and squeeze them fiercely not to tear up again.

Stop!

Crying was not going to help anyone, least of all Clint.

Lieutenant Commander Walker would not want her to fall apart; not now, not on his account. For reasons she'd never fathom, from their very first meeting Clint had trusted in her skills and abilities—despite his admittedly overprotective tendencies. Now that he wasn't here to protect her, he'd want her to step up and be that brave leader he'd believed she was. The take-charge commander she had worked so hard to become. The rightful captain her father so steadfastly refused to approve of.

A shimmer of hurt went through her, knowing that nothing she did would ever be good enough for Jason Richardson. This hijacking? It would only confirm her father's low opinion of her competence. Losing control of the ship was not her fault, but that wouldn't matter. He'd still lay the blame squarely on her.

Her job was as good as gone. Even if she somehow managed to save the ship and the crew, it would be too late to deliver the cargo. She'd never get the fireworks to Nome in time for the mayor's Fourth of July celebration. Neither the egotistical mayor nor her father would give a damn that she had moved heaven and earth in Japan to fulfill the all but impossible, last-minute order. If she didn't get it to Nome before noon on the Fourth—two days and two hundred fifty miles away—it was all for naught.

Which made her even angrier.

Fuck them. She was a good captain. She'd show her father what she was capable of. She'd show them all.

You bet she would.

With eye-stinging determination, she hunkered down to wait for the guard's patience to run out and go for the lasagna.

She'd get that gun from her cabin. And while she was at it, she'd get rid of this nice white uniform. Put on something more appropriate for some down and dirty guerilla warfare.

Then they'd see what she was really made of.

Yippee kayay, assholes.

Oh yeah.

The war was definitely on.

15

\\\\\\\\\\\\////////

Keeping a close eye on Tango One's back, Clint lifted the pair of earphones from the clip next to the pilot's chair and slid them over his ears. Grimacing, he ignored the squelch of blood beneath his wetsuit backside as he reached up to plug in the earphones, for once glad he was wearing the damned thing.

A red light on the front of the radio told him it was already powered up. No surprise there. Every ship the world over was required to maintain a listening watch on channel 16, the universal emergency voice channel.

Except the radio wasn't tuned to channel 16. Instead it was on 70—the DSC distress transmissions channel. At that realization, Clint's hand paused on the dial. Had the captain of the ill-fated crew of *Eliza Jane* in his last moments tried to signal for help—Clint's gaze dropped to the crimson stains on the chair—and died for his trouble . . . ?

Swallowing down a surge of renewed anger, he spun the dial to 16.

Now came the tricky part. He had to speak loudly enough

to be heard by the receiver, but not loud enough to reach Tango One's ears. And he had to avoid saying anything over channel 16 that would alert the hijackers on *Île de Cœur*. There might be no one stationed on the bridge over there, but undoubtedly one of them was monitoring the radio in the wardroom for any activity in the Bering Sea that might threaten their takeover—or help their mission to find and kill him.

With an inhale, he keyed the mike and put it close to his lips. He tried to sound casual and a little drunk for good measure, to throw off anyone listening. "Coast Guard, Coast Guard, Coast Guard, this is motor vessel *Sea Wolf*, number one-zero-four-two one-zero-niner-niner. Reality check, over."

The ship name was a decoy, and the smart-ass reality check request just close enough to a radio check to give the receiver pause—and the fishing crews out there a good chuckle. The ship's call number he'd given was actually Alaska state trooper ten-code for "Emergency" and "Armed and Dangerous." He was fairly certain, anyway. He hoped he remembered them right. It would be just his luck if his secret message to the Coast Guard was "Mental case" and "Going for donuts."

On any other day he might have smiled. The hail's wording and attitude were designed to get him hustled off channel 16 pronto.

His SEAL team had regularly worked with the Coasties, so he was pretty sure it would do the trick. How they'd react when he relayed *Île de Cœur*'s situation was a different story. This kind of thing could be a jurisdictional nightmare, taking time to sort out. Time he didn't have.

He listened for a response, automatically checking the dive watch he wasn't wearing because he'd traded it for a ride in a leaky outboard from Attu Station to Kiska, and of course he had left the cheap drugstore watch he'd picked up in Dutch back on *Île de Cœur*, then slashed a hand impatiently through his hair.

Damn, he'd already spent too much time on the trawler. He'd given himself a target of five minutes max. But disposing of the dead body had already put him at more than ten, if his internal clock was to be trusted.

More seconds ticked by, and still no answering call. He tweaked up the volume a bit and repeated the hail.

Finally the radio gave a crackle. "*Sea Wolf, Sea Wolf*, this is Coast Guard Station Kodiak," an efficient female voice answered at last. "Please go to channel two-three-alpha."

Thank God.

"*Sea Wolf* switching to channel two-three-alpha, over," he returned.

The tingle of relief he'd felt was short-lived. He still had eyes on Tango One. As he reached for the dial to switch over, the other man came alert at the rail and stared down at the water below.

Clint froze, ready to bolt and hit the afterdeck running.

Could it be the body? Had it somehow come loose from the weight he'd attached and floated up to the surface? He scanned the waves and saw a familiar black fin cut through the water. Two black fins. Three.

Sharks. He cringed.

Jesus. That hadn't taken long. He didn't know whether to be horrified or grateful.

Unaware of the grisly implications, Tango One tapped another cigarette from his pack and lit up, his impassive gaze watching the creatures make a few more darting passes, then disappear into the deep.

Clint's shoulders notched down, but his pulse continued to drum a fast beat in his throat as he returned his attention to the radio—and tried not to think about the swim back.

He spun the dial to the other channel, hoping the hijackers on *Île de Cœur* wouldn't get curious about the tipsy tourist and do the same. If they heard what he was about to say, the swim wouldn't matter, he'd be shark bait anyway.

"Station Kodiak, this is *Sea Wolf* on two-three-alpha," he said, pitching his voice just above a whisper, which was as loud as he dared. "Do you read, over?"

"*Sea Wolf*, Kodiak. Please restate your—"

"Mayday, mayday, mayday," he interrupted, his tone urgent. "*Sea Wolf* was a decoy, repeat, a decoy. This is commercial vessel *Île de Cœur*, *Île de Cœur*, *Île de Cœur*." As he recited the cargo ship's call number, Clint slid from the chair and crouched down below window-level, to better shield the sound of his voice. "Mayday *Île de Cœur*. Code E, code E for echo, code E. Over."

That code he *was* sure of. In Coastie speak, it meant "armed assault." If that didn't get their attention, nothing would.

There was a short pause on the other end of the line before the Coastie came back. "Vessel *Île de Cœur*, please state your position and the nature of your emergency." She sounded irritated and suspicious.

He bit back the impulse to snap at her—*What part of armed assault don't you get, lady?*—took a breath, and said with forced calm, "Kodiak, *Île de Cœur*. My position is approximately 200 miles northeast of Dutch Harbor. The ship has been attacked and seized. Eight assailants, possibly PRC nationals, armed and dangerous. Seven captives alive, one dead, myself and Captain Richardson evading capture so far." He went on rapidly, wanting to get out as much information as he could. Just in case. "Also seized is Australian stern trawler *Eliza Jane*; crew gone, fate unknown. Request immediate assistance. Repeat, immediate assistance. Proceed with extreme caution, over."

He winced against a burst of static in his ears.

"PRC? Vessel *Île de Cœur*," she said crisply, "are you aware of the penalty for fraudulent distress calls?"

He leashed his temper and growled, "Ma'am, I am Lieutenant Commander Clint Walker, U.S. Navy. To get to this radio I had to swim in freezing water in a—" He ground his teeth. "As we speak one of the *eight* men trying to catch and kill me is standing thirty feet away. If he hears me talking, I'm a dead man. Do you think I give a crap about any goddamn penalties? I *need help*."

In the thirty seconds of total silence that followed, he

leaned his back against the instrument panel, feeling like a spring-loaded pretzel. He tried to stretch his legs, easing the unrelenting grip of the wetsuit. Without success. His goddamn knees hurt, his goddamn wound throbbed, and the circulation to his goddamn limbs was at a dead frickin' stop. Not to mention his goddamn blue balls, which would probably never recover.

Though most likely he wouldn't live long enough to care.

He slammed his eyes shut and groaned inwardly. *Jesus.* Was he actually *whining*?

Hell.

He was being a goddamn wuss. And he shouldn't have cussed at the woman. She was only doing her job, filtering out the nut jobs.

As if sensing his chagrin, she came back at last. "Roger that, LC," she said, crispness intact. "I'll need a complete sitrep."

He allowed himself to hope. And apologized for cursing.

Clint did not get a chance to give his sitrep. He'd basically just repeated the information he'd already given and made a request for the Coast Guard to apprise his boss at Naval Intelligence in Washington of the situation, when a loud squawk blasted through the bridge.

He vaulted away from the console in a crouch, whirling to see where the sound had come from. His eyes snagged on a black backpack sitting in the corner that he hadn't noticed before. The backpack squawked again, and this time a spate of indecipherable Chinese tumbled out after.

Walkie-talkie.

Oh, shit.

"Gotta go," he gritted into the radio mike as he stuck his head up a few inches and saw Tango One flick his cigarette into the sea and start toward the wheelhouse.

In a single motion, Clint racked the mike, ripped off the earphones and threw them onto the clip, yanked the plug, and gave the radio dial a spin to change the channel.

The walkie-talkie squawked a third time. The harsh Chinese verbiage grew more impatient.

Tango One was nearly at the wheelhouse.

Clint's blood went cold.

Too late. He was trapped.

No way would he make it out the door unseen.

16

///////////////

Sam didn't think she'd ever run this fast in her life. Not even the day she'd left the lawyer's office after divorcing her cheating bastard of a husband—though that was probably a close second. She was feeling just about as gutted. And twice as determined.

She flew up the steps of the central companionway like greased lightning, screeching to a halt just below the landing for a heart-pounding nanosecond. She wanted to make sure the guard was striding up the stairs to the quarterdeck and the mess hall.

She was not about to miss this rare window of opportunity to get to her stateroom. If the guard looked down over his shoulder or changed his mind and turned around before she made it inside, she'd be toast.

But she was well past caring.

She had to move quickly. The bastard in charge might order the guard right back to his post or send someone else there in his place. In which case she'd be stuck. For a while, anyway. Or, hell, she might just shoot her way out.

She ran down the passageway close to the wall, keeping

her body compact and her steps light. She'd left her shoes tucked under the earthmover, unperturbed by a fleeting thought of Bruce Willis's bare feet in *Die Hard*. He'd done okay, hadn't he? Besides, there weren't many glass windows on a cargo ship, and they'd cleaned up the broken beer bottles in the hold.

She made it to the stateroom seconds after the guard disappeared onto the quarterdeck. She grabbed the door handle, alarmed when it nearly came off in her hand. It was bent at an acute angle, the lock cracked open and its cylinder spilling out. They must have broken in during their search for the ship's captain . . . or for Clint, if he'd been right about his role in all this.

She hurried in and eased the door shut behind her. The lock didn't catch, but it stayed closed.

She'd made it!

If adrenaline hadn't been streaking through her veins, she'd probably have passed out from sheer relief.

Her hands shook a little as she pulled a flashlight from her pocket. She flicked it on, careful to point the beam away from the door.

Whoa.

She stiffened in shock. All her belongings had been dumped out and scattered on the floor. She stared at the mess wide-eyed. What the heck?

As she took it in, a realization slowly dawned.

This did not look like the hijackers hunting for a person. This looked like they were searching for something. Something a whole lot smaller.

But what? She sifted through the possibilities.

Money? If so, they'd been sorely disappointed.

But somehow she didn't think it was money these brutes were after. Not according to Clint, anyway.

He'd never told her exactly why the men chasing him wanted to kill him. Or who they were, either. *Classified*, he'd said. *A matter of national security.* Then he'd clammed up about it.

She wasn't sure she'd truly believed him at the time,

even given his legit navy credentials. Though she hadn't really pushed him for a better explanation. Blame *that* on starry eyes and begging hormones. Even now, after all that had happened, it was difficult to believe Clint was . . . had been . . . a real, live spy.

But if he was telling the truth . . . did that mean the hijackers were spies, too? Foreign agents? Spectre to his James Bond?

She wanted to scoff at the notion . . . but their unpredictable and violent behavior seemed to support that conclusion. They hadn't seized the cargo or taken the ship to a questionable port to cash it in. When they'd interrogated Lars Bolun and the crew, they hadn't spouted political garbage, or demanded blood money, or called Richardson Shipping for ransom—that she'd heard, at least. Their main concerns had been about the captain and whether or not the ship had picked up a passenger or stowaway.

Clint?

That's what he thought.

Had thought, she mentally corrected herself with another twinge of pain in her heart.

She poked with a toe at the pile of her belongings on the floor and dusted over the scatter with the flashlight. They'd ruined her pretty zippered bag of toiletries, her hair products and tubes of makeup emptied and tossed aside. Some of her clothes had even been ripped open at the seams.

What a freaking mess.

One thing seemed painfully clear. Clint must have taken something of theirs, and they wanted it back. Something small. Something really important, to make them search with this degree of thoroughness, let alone kill for it.

A microdot?

Did they even do microdots anymore? Wasn't that old school?

She frowned, and bent to pick up a pair of black sweatpants, shaking them free of debris. These would do. She started to strip off her white uniform pants.

More likely it was a computer storage device of some

sort they were looking for, like a CD, or a thumb drive. God only knew what vital information was on it that was worth killing for. Or giving your life for.

She shivered. She didn't really *want* to know. She, like most other Americans, had a vague awareness that things went on at a national security level that the public was never told about. Bad things. Like terrorist threats, and foiled biological pandemic plots, and electrical grid sabotage, or financial cyberattacks.

And she knew that people like Clint were covertly fighting them. Defending the nation against all those terrible things and more, so everyday citizens could go about their daily lives feeling safe and secure, blissfully unaware that Clint—and no doubt many others—had died in defense of their freedom.

She swallowed the sudden lump in her throat and picked up a black Henley, knowing with certainty that, despite dearly wishing she could go back to being clueless, she would never again be so naïve and blind.

The Henley had a ripped sleeve, so she tossed it back and picked up a dark blue sweatshirt instead. Her watch lay next to it on the floor. She hesitated, then picked it up and strapped it to her wrist.

As she exchanged her top, she felt Clint's bear claw, hidden close to her heart. What had Clint done with this thing, whatever he'd taken from the hijackers—the foreign agents, or operatives? Whatever you called them. Had he hidden it somewhere on the ship? Or dropped it in the sea, maybe? Or had his killer found it on his body . . . ?

She thought about that. If they'd gotten it back, wouldn't they desert *Île de Cœur* like the rats they were and leave the crew in peace, as Clint guessed they would?

She truly hoped he was right, then at least a little good would come of losing him.

But one thing worried her. If they did leave, would they let the crew live? Or would they kill them all first . . . ?

A shiver tore through her flesh. They'd already murdered two people in cold blood. Why not seven more?

Her stomach clenched, acid clawing through it.

No.

Not my ship. Not my crew.

That couldn't happen. She would make sure it didn't happen. Or it would be *eight* more dead bodies on the deck.

She swung the flashlight toward the wall safe where she'd stowed her Glock 23. *Oh, no.*

The safe stood wide open, its contents strewn on the floor beneath, as though a hand had swept the shelves clean.

Her heart sank.

Her gun was gone.

It was the same story when she tiptoed two doors down and slipped into the stateroom Clint had slept in last night. The place wasn't a mess like hers, but only because he hadn't brought a duffel or backpack aboard with him, so there hadn't been much to throw around.

Nevertheless, the hijackers had obviously searched the place. She set down the small gym bag that held her small laptop computer plus a few items of clothing and toiletries she'd packed before leaving her own stateroom, and went straight for the mattress where Clint had told her he'd hidden his big silver semiautomatic pistol.

Also gone.

Damn. Damn. Damn.

If their two guns had been taken, the weapons locker in the officers' lounge had surely been ransacked and emptied, too.

So much for plan A.

Not that she had a clue what she'd do with guns if she had them. In fact, she was almost relieved. She might be the ship's captain, and was definitely determined to rescue her crew, but she was only one person. She sure as hell didn't relish a Butch and Sundance ending to this whole thing.

Even so, she'd feel a lot better about her chances of survival with a loaded gun in her hand.

Or not. Didn't the cops at the range always tell her you

should never point a gun at another person if you weren't willing to pull the trigger? After today, she was pretty sure she could do that . . . but . . . not one hundred percent sure. When it came right down to it, could she really take a person's life?

Which was *such* a stupid question. Because if anyone deserved to die, it was the soulless scumbags who'd killed Shandy and Clint.

Taking a breath, she glanced around the stateroom for anything else that might come in handy in the coming battle to get her crew back. Save her own gym bag by the door, it was all but bare.

She glanced at the tiny bathroom and saw the shower cubicle. For a second her heart stopped beating, then started up with a squeeze. Memories flooded through her . . . of both last night's heated fantasies and this afternoon's sensual reality.

Oh, Clint.

He must have washed his clothes in the sink, because his T-shirt and jeans hung over the top of the shower stall. They drew her in like a magnet. Without conscious thought, some primal instinct made her reach for the T-shirt and bring it to her nose. She closed her eyes.

It felt damp and cold against her skin.

But, oh, it still smelled of Clint.

Yes, and Ivory soap and the lingering hint of fish and saltwater . . . but mostly of Clint. His familiar earthy masculine scent filled her senses. And brought a fresh ache to her middle.

She fought it back. She couldn't do this. As much as she longed to lie down on his bunk, wrap herself in his sheets, and have a good cry, she didn't have time to grieve.

Later she would allow herself to mourn him. Right now she had to think of the living.

But her fingers refused to relinquish his shirt. She swallowed. Okay. She'd give herself that much. She grabbed her gym bag, stuffed the damp T-shirt into it, and went to the door.

If she was going to rescue her crew, the first order of business was to find out exactly where the filthy scum were holding them prisoner.

Then she had to come up with a plan of action. Something smart. Something bold. Something brave.

Something Bruce Willis would do.

Or someone like Clint.

17

///////////////////

Clint melted into the shadows of the trawler's lower deck, behind the bulkhead separating the galley from the ghostly dark main salon. He flexed and coiled his muscles, readying them for action, his stance absorbing the motion of the boat with practiced ease. Tango Two's confiscated pistol was a reassuring weight in his hand, dull, black, and reassuringly deadly. *An assassin's gun.* Been there, done that. Yeah, he could do assassin.

In the pilothouse just above his head, clipped footsteps made tight turns back and forth. They sounded agitated. So did the staccato starts and stops of Chinese conversation that drifted down the companionway.

Good. Let them fight each other. Maybe they'd forget about him for a while. Long enough to get the hell off this banana boat and back to *Île de Cœur*.

But first he wanted to do a quick look-see, hopefully scavenge a few supplies. He'd brought along a small dry-bag just for that purpose.

He didn't have a flashlight, and the only hint of the mid-night sun that penetrated the lower deck was a dim glow on

the curtains blocking the portholes. But he had excellent
night vision, and his eyes were already adjusting. Silhouettes of furnishings and features began to emerge from the
black void of the salon.

The galley came into focus, tidy and spotless, evidence
of a fastidious cook on the former crew. The larger salon
area, not so much. Every horizontal surface was littered
with the everyday detritus of a rough-and-ready crew of
fishermen. Men who worked hard and relaxed harder, who
after a twenty-hour day hauling nets and sorting fish, didn't
give a damn about how a room looked as long as it was
comfortable and the contents entertaining. It almost made
him nostalgic for last week.

Not.

Thankfully, he saw no black stains of blood. He hoped
to God the others had survived.

Deserting his cover of shadows, he stole down the aft
passageway to the crew quarters, moving swiftly but cautiously. He'd only spotted two tangos on the trawler earlier,
but that didn't mean there weren't more. Though he didn't
think so. It was quiet as a tomb down here, the only sound
the lapping and sucking of the waves against the hull. He
sensed no other movement than the deck beneath his feet.

Four staterooms and a head opened off the stygian passageway. Four of the five doors yawned open. He approached the first, paused, and whipped in using a standard
close quarters entrance. No one home. He searched the
space, found nothing of interest, then did the same to the
head and the two other open staterooms.

Damn. He'd hoped to find a few more weapons. Auto-
matics, or better yet, machine guns. No such luck. Only the
sparse, disorderly belongings of the original crew remained.
If Xing Guan and his goons had ever been in the staterooms, they'd left no trace.

He did, however, stumble across a couple of chocolate
bars hidden in one of the stateroom lockers. He suddenly
realized he was starving.

"Don't mind if I do," he murmured under his breath, and

grabbed them. Thinking of Samantha, he pulled the dry-bag from inside his jacket and stuck one of the bars into it. As he approached the last door, he scarfed down the other.

Wiping melted chocolate from his fingers, he cocked an ear back toward the companionway. Up on the bridge, the walkie-talkie conversation was getting louder. He figured he was safe for now.

Turning to the fifth and last door, he raised his gun, eased the handle down, and finessed it open a crack. All remained quiet. He peered in.

Three olive green mobile military cases took up most of the floor space. *Bingo.*

He cracked the door wider. And froze.

Someone was lying on the bunk.

Or . . . no, some*thing*. Tall and dark, it was the same height as a man . . . but skinnier. With no arms or legs.

Quickly he slipped inside and approached the object on the bunk. "What have we here?" he muttered warily.

He couldn't see shit in this light. He spotted a reading light at the head of the bunk and snapped it on.

A breath hissed between his teeth. He was staring down at the business end of a PF98 120mm antitank rocket launcher.

Make that *two* PF98s.

He narrowed his eyes in grim recognition. Oh, yeah, he'd seen these two ATs before, a week ago, on the other end of a periscope sight. Just before they'd blown holes in *Ostrov*, the Russian submarine where he'd started off this unlucky mission.

Gooseflesh crawled across his scalp. *Jesus. Île de Cœur*'s hijackers must be the same black-ops team that took down the sub. In which case, unlucky was about to morph into a clusterfuck.

Last week, in a showpiece of classic Sun Tzu strategy, a Chinese Shang-class submarine using its three UUVs as carrots had double-teamed with a spec ops unit on the surface using the AT rocket launchers as a big stick; together they'd set a deadly trap for *Ostrov*. It had been devastat-

ingly successful. The Russian sub now lay at the bottom of
the Bering Sea. It was a miracle Clint had been able to escape with his life—and the SD card.

He let out a long, tense breath. *Fucking hell.*

Was that why the hijackers hadn't moved the ship? They
were waiting to rendezvous with their pals on the Chinese
boomer?

Surely, the navy had long since chased the Shang-class
submarine out of the Bering Sea, back to the Atlantic where
it belonged . . . ? Or at least were keeping a close eye on it
so it didn't cross into U.S. waters . . .

Of course, there was no law the hijackers had to be
teamed with the same enemy sub as before. There were
plenty more vessels where that one came from. Smaller
ones. And quieter.

Or even UUVs being controlled from outside U.S. territorial limits—using the gen-1 version of the cutting-edge
long-range UUV guidance system contained on the stolen
data card.

Shit.

How do you fight that kind of threat with fireworks,
cookies, and earthmovers? His gaze whipped to the military
cases. *Please, God, let there be weapons.* One of them must
contain the antitank rockets, at least. He dropped down in
front of the nearest case and started flipping locks.

Abruptly, he stilled, his ears prickling. Something on the
trawler had changed.

The walkie-talkie conversation in the wheelhouse had
ceased.

He sprang to his feet, snapped off the reading light, and
shot to the door to listen.

Tango One yelled something short and irritated down
through the companionway hatch. Calling to wake up the
dead guy? Good luck with that.

Damn. Time was up.

Clint darted a glance back at the rocket launchers. He
ground his jaw. As much as he'd like to, no way was he
getting them off the trawler to *Île de Cœur*.

Somehow, he had to disable them.

He started back to the bunk but instantly halted as another shout bellowed down from the upper deck, even louder this time. It sounded angry and impatient.

Clint's pulse kicked up, and he felt a surge of frustration. Any second, Tango One would come barreling down the steps, mad as a hornet that the dead guy was ignoring his summons.

And find Clint instead.

He wavered in indecision. He could just shoot the fucker and dump the whole damn mess into the sea—cases, ATs, dead guy number two, and all. But then they'd be back to the problematic scenario of the rest of the Chinese operators knowing a saboteur was on board. They'd hunt Clint down and eliminate him, and with all likelihood Samantha, too. Or they'd start killing the hostages one by one until he surrendered—which he would—and then eliminate him *and* them.

Neither option was acceptable.

If he were on his own he could deal with dying; that was part of the job description. But without his help, Samantha and her crew were also as good as dead—*not* something he could live with . . . or die knowing.

Fight or flee. His pride chafed at having to make the coward's choice.

Again, he didn't get the chance. The sudden sound of boots clomping down the companionway made the decision for him.

Getting caught with the weapons would mean instant death, so he flew across the passageway, dove through the door to the head, and shut it. Just in time.

18

////////\\\\\\\\

The guard had not returned to his post on the crew deck when Sam peeked out of Clint's stateroom door to check. When she'd sprinted down to the orlop, the engine room guard had also vanished, making her quick trip back to the hideaway to stow her gear blessedly unharrowing.

She wondered about the lack of guards. The hijackers were either being extremely careless, or they'd decided that Clint and the phantom captain were not lurking belowdecks after all, and no longer felt armed guards were needed. Her money was on the latter. These creeps didn't strike her as the careless type.

But they were definitely not being as vigilant. She'd heard their loud voices all the way down the passageway as she'd scooted out from the stateroom. The smell of lasagna and fresh bread still lingered in the air. They were obviously still in the mess hall eating—or rather, arguing. And if the hijackers were there, the hostages were surely close by. Her best guess? Locked in one of the lounges.

She wanted to see them. Make sure they were okay.

Since there were no guards posted inside the ship, she

slipped cautiously up to the weather deck. No guards out here, either. She darted noiselessly up the outside ladder past the crew deck and quarterdeck above.

She sneaked her way aft along the gangway—the narrow strip of deck between the bulkhead and the rail that went the length of the ship and led to the small poop deck in back.

As she ran, a light wind bit into her cheeks. She tugged her cap low and pulled her sweatshirt tight around her midriff to keep the worst chill off. The night air was cold and crisp, the sky above a blueberry vanilla swirl. All around, the muted light of the midnight sun shone down upon the rolling sea, shattering into shards of deep indigo and silver. It was a night that would usually inspire awe, but tonight she couldn't begin to appreciate the beauty.

She checked her watch. Just after 1:00 a.m.

No wonder she was exhausted. She'd been up since five this morning, over twenty hours—if you didn't count the catnap this afternoon in the hammock with Clint, which wasn't as much rest as recovery.

She had to take a deep breath when the memories hit her all over again. The sight of the windows lining the poop deck brought back even more, of how she and Clint had been together just inside them earlier in their quest for weapons.

Had it really been mere hours ago all that had happened?

Raised voices brought her abruptly back to the present. She pressed herself against the freezing bulkhead of the back side of the quarterdeck and held her breath.

The mess, crew lounge, and officers' wardroom all had windows and doors opening onto the poop deck. But just as she'd guessed, the voices were coming from the mess hall.

She shut her eyes tight and fought a sudden stab of fear. Her plan was to creep under the windows and steal a quick peek between the curtains, as Clint had done this morning.

Clint had made it seem so easy. Hell, she'd even been angry at him for making her stay behind.

Where was her courage now?

She gathered it up and told herself not to be a damn coward. Without giving herself time to think, she bent over and crept to the wardroom window, then raised her head just high enough to look inside.

Her heart leapt in excitement, then squeezed.

Yes! Her crew was here, huddled together on the two couches. A hooded-eyed guard stood splay-legged in front of the door, cradling an ugly machine gun in his arms.

The crew's wrists and ankles had all been duct-taped, and the men had been gagged. Johnny and Frank had their heads tipped back on the couch, eyes closed. Ginger was curled up in one corner looking fetal, Spiros sat brooding at the other end. Carin dozed fitfully with her head against Lars Bolun's broad chest, his arm curved protectively around her shoulders. Even asleep she looked terrified. The two kids, Matty and Jeeter, did, too.

Hell, they all looked haggard and frightened but at least they were unhurt. Well, except for the second mate. She could only see the side of Bolun's face, but it was blotched with livid purple bruises; a nasty open cut bisected one temple.

As though he sensed her presence, Lars turned his head a fraction, and his gaze collided with hers. He blinked, and a flash of raw emotion streaked through his eyes but was gone in an instant. His impassive expression didn't alter.

She wanted to say something he could read on her lips, something encouraging, to tell him help was on the way, that everything would turn out fine.

But the words wouldn't form. She'd never been good at prevarication. She knew damn well there wasn't going to be any rescue. Clint hadn't even made it to the radio before being cut down. And she was suddenly terrified she wouldn't be able to do a goddamn thing to save them.

Again the second mate seemed to read her mind. His gaze softened and filled with understanding and forgiveness. The ghost of a smile played over his mouth for the barest moment. "It's okay," his expression seemed to be saying. "We know you did your best."

It didn't help. It made her feel ten times worse.

She glanced over at the guard, who stared straight ahead with cold, dead eyes, as though the captives were invisible, of no consequence whatsoever.

And at that moment, she knew with paralyzing certainty, her worst fears were going to come true. Men like these would never let their hostages live. The bastards were going to kill them all. God knew what they'd do with the ship. She didn't even want to think about what her own fate might be.

A choking fury swept through her and was just the mental kick in the ass she needed to reclaim her courage. In spades.

She could do this.

She *would* do this.

She clenched her jaw and looked back at Bolun. "Don't give up," she mouthed. "I'm getting you out of there."

With iron resolve, she left Bolun staring after her, and made her way deep into the bowels of the ship. Past the orlop, all the way to the bottommost deck, down, down, to the cargo holds.

She went straight to one of the cargo hatches and pulled it open. She knew exactly which one she needed.

Cargo hold three.

The one with the fireworks.

Hiding in the cramped head, Clint listened as Tango One stormed through the salon, spewing a torrent of shouts and exclamations, heading for the crew quarters.

Holding his breath, he eased the lock home. Not that it mattered. This was his Alamo, and Clint knew it. Damned if he ran, damned if he stayed. Damned if he shot the bastard, damned if he didn't.

Tango One marched along the passageway slamming open stateroom doors. When he got to the head and found it locked, he pounded on the door with his fist.

Okay, then. *Shoot the bastard it is.*

Oddly calmed by the resolution, Clint's body went instinctively into a fighting stance. He raised his gun for the killing shot.

Tango One's barked order was followed by another fist bang.

Clint coiled his muscles in readiness, which made the chocolate bar in his gut twinge. . . .

Suddenly an idea blossomed.

What the hell. He splayed his free hand over his mouth and let out a low, pathetic moan.

Tango One growled something and pounded again with his fist. Significantly, the door handle did not wiggle.

A good sign? Clint drew in a breath and made a very rude sound using his lips and tongue, then moaned again. He flushed the head for good measure.

Tango One was silent for a long moment.

Seriously?

On a roll, Clint made himself burp, let out another nasty noise, and mumbled some muted Arapaho words behind his hand that he hoped to hell at least remotely resembled garbled Chinese.

After a huffed expletive, Tango One barked another order at the door then stomped off.

Unbelievable. Clint let out the mental breath he'd been holding and slowly lowered the gun as Tango One clomped back up to the pilothouse. Yeah, this may be a temporary reprieve, but he'd take it.

If nothing else, it would give him time to deal with those rocket launchers.

He checked the passageway and started back across, but another sound caught his attention. He halted in the darkness. A soft clicking noise ticked down from the bridge. He frowned. It sounded like . . .

Like switches being flipped and settings being keyed in on the helm controls.

His back went arrow straight as he spun toward the dim square of light at the top of the companionway. *What the—*

Suddenly, the trawler's engines wheezed, farted twice,

and fired to life with a powerful rumble that made the whole boat vibrate—and Clint's blood chill.

Ah, hell.

Before he could pry himself back into action, the engines geared up and *Eliza Jane* began to move.

Okay. This was not good.

He sprinted forward to the salon and shifted aside a porthole curtain to see what direction they were headed in. The boat was chugging in a slow, wide circle. She seemed to be aligning herself to come alongside *Île de Cœur*.

Not a total surprise, but at this hour? It must be well after midnight by now.

He frowned. Maybe a change of guard? Team meeting? Abandoning ship? If so, which ship . . . ?

The good news was, whatever was happening, this would save him one seriously uncomfortable swim—with a bleeding open wound and a ripped wetsuit. Oh, yeah, and dodging hungry sharks.

He grimaced. Of course, jumping across from the trawler to *Île de Cœur* without being seen—or shot—wasn't going to be a picnic, either.

But first he needed to do something about those ATs.

He sprinted back to the stateroom with the weapons, flicked on the reading light, and examined the rocket launchers lying on the bunk, all gleaming tubes, LED screens, and electronic controls. Fertile fields for sabotage.

But experience had taught him that the simplest idea was usually the best, so on that principle, he shook a pillowcase off one of the bunk pillows, wadded it up, and stuffed it into the rear of one of the launch tubes. After latching the back lock, it looked completely normal. With any luck, when fired, the trapped gasses would blow the bastard pulling the trigger sky-high.

He considered the second AT. If the first one blew, they'd be looking for similar sabotage in the second. What could he do instead? Removing the firing pin was always good, but for that he'd need the pin extractor, or at least a screwdriver.

Maybe the tool kit was in one of the military cases. He
needed to go through them anyway.

Quickly, he knelt and opened the nearest one. It was
completely empty. Well, hell. He'd hoped for guns and
knives, at least.

He tried the next case. *Damn.* They must be using them
strictly for transport. Only a few things remained: a gun
cleaning kit, a half dozen ammo clips, two dozen or so
boxes of cartridges—a few of which he happily slipped into
his dry-bag, and—

Hello.

His hand hovered above a box with a familiar drawing
on the lid.

Detonators.

He regarded them grimly, letting the unthinkable implications sink in. On the back of his neck, the fine hairs tingled.

In a flash, he ripped open every other box in the case,
searching for Semtex, or C-4, or some other explosive
that would need a detonator to set it off. He found nothing.

Had they taken it on board *Île de Cœur* with them?

That could only mean one thing, and it wasn't good.

Silently cursing a blue streak, he shook the detonators
into order in the box. Several were missing.

He thought of Samantha and felt his heart race. What
would happen to her if he never made it back? If the Coast
Guard didn't find them in time? If he couldn't figure out a
way to take down these conscienceless bastards before the
same fate befell *Île de Cœur* as had *Ostrov* . . . ?

Every cell in his body urged him to get his ass up on
deck.

Holy fuck. They were going to blow up *Île de Cœur.*

He had to get back to Samantha!

19

〟〟〟〟〟〟〟

Sam knew she had to free the crew. One person alone couldn't fight the whole vicious pack of enemy operatives and win—not *her* anyway—but eight people working together at least had a chance.

She had no weapons. But she did have fireworks—lots and lots of fireworks. Enough to make the bastards think the entire U.S. Coast Guard was attacking them. She'd set them off in the wee hours, and before they figured out what was really going on, she could get past the—hopefully—distracted guard to cut Bolun's bonds. Lars would help her set the rest free.

The plan wasn't perfect. Not even close. The likelihood of failure was all too real. But without a gun, and without Clint's expert help, it was all she had.

She'd rather try, and die with her crew, than stand by and do nothing and have to live with the guilt.

Grabbing the box cutter from the cargo manifest clipboard, she sliced through the plastic around the pallet and ripped open a dozen boxes of fireworks. She couldn't read the Japanese labels and had no idea what any of them were, so she chose the box with the biggest mothers of all. They looked like frickin' mortar rounds. The explosion should be spectacular.

They were big, but not heavy. She set two boxes of them aside, ripped open a dozen more of different kinds, and put together a nice selection of the nastiest looking.

After putting the pallet back together, she crumpled the matching page of the manifest and dropped it behind the pallet so the hijackers couldn't discover her secret if they came looking.

After careful consideration, she decided to set off the explosion under the old Malaysian trolley car bound for San Francisco. It was up on the weather deck and highly visible, lashed down next to the railroad containers. The trolley was ornately decorated on the outside, but the car itself was built like a tank. The echoes and ricochets of the fireworks between the deck and the solid metal of the trolley's undercarriage should amplify the noise to epic proportions. She might even put a few inside to blow out the windows.

If she could figure out how to tie the fuses together to make one long fuse, that should give her enough time to run up and take position outside the wardroom before the explosion went off. Even if the man guarding the crew didn't charge out to the deck with the others, he should at least duck out to see what was going on. She fingered the box cutter in her pocket. That was all the time she'd need to free Bolun.

It took her two trips up and down the four flights of stairs to lug the boxes up to the weather deck. By the time she plopped down behind one of the railroad containers to recover, her legs were like jellyfish and her head was spinning like a dervish. She really needed to find something to eat.

Later.

After a brief respite, she rose and picked up one of the boxes. It slipped through her fingers, crashing back to the deck. She froze, pulse zooming, but no one came running to investigate the noise. *Thank God.*

She was about to drag the box over to the trolley, when suddenly she shot up straight. Her mouth dropped open. *Ohmigod!* Why hadn't she thought of this sooner?

She whirled and looked up at the bridge. *No guard.* Her pulse leapt off the charts. She could get to the radio!

In less than a minute she was standing at the helm, out of breath. And staring down at the smashed remains of the radio transmitter. She wanted to weep. Even if she knew how to fix it, there would be no possibility. It was that ruined.

She should have known. She really should have. It had been pure folly to hope these ruthless, efficient killers would have left a single thing to chance. A functioning radio? No way.

Even so, bitter disappointment stung through her.

With a sigh, she looked out over the vastness of the sea around her, trying to draw strength from its endless power. The deep water was calm now, but when angered . . .

She needed to be like the sea. Strong. Tireless. Relentless.

It was so hard to do. Especially alone.

She'd deliberately avoided looking at the fishing trawler. She didn't want to relive those awful moments, watching Clint be taken down.

But she couldn't help herself. She missed him so much! Against her will, her gaze was pulled toward *Eliza Jane*.

But it was no longer there. It was—

She sucked in a startled breath. The trawler had moved!

Hell, was *still* moving! Cruising in a half circle, on a course to come alongside *Île de Cœur*.

What was going on?

A cold shiver of fear spilled over her. Were the hijackers about to leave?

Oh, God. Was she too late?

Was the crew already—

No! She had just checked on them. She would have heard shots.

She rushed back down to the trolley, crawled on her

stomach under it, and began working feverishly to set up the fireworks distraction.

She could actually hear the trawler's engine now, getting closer and closer.

This could be a *good* thing, she told herself optimistically. Once she'd freed the crew, they could all storm the trawler and take control of it. There were only two guards. Eight against two. That was a fight they could win!

She started to tie fuses together with a vengeance.

Especially if their lives depended on it.

As long as Tango One stayed on the wheelhouse, Clint knew it would be impossible to get past him and off the trawler.

He forced himself to be patient, and reached for the third green military case. Last one. It had to contain the rockets for the PF98s.

And sure enough, there they were, packed in like pointy, green sardines. He counted six. And two empty slots. He pressed his lips into a thin line, remembering the havoc those two missing shells had wrecked upon *Ostrov*. The smoke and the fire and the panic that had enveloped everyone on board the submarine, and the bone-chilling sensation of icy seawater slowly creeping up one's ankles. It was not an experience a man would ever forget.

Fuckers.

Unfortunately, there was no way to sabotage the sealed-up waterproof rockets, other than removing the caps to disarm the things. But that would be too obvious, and unlikely to do any damage anyway. Not like rockets in the old days, when one rough juggle could set them off.

Instead, he went back to rifle through the gun-cleaning kit for a screwdriver. He'd just crouched down when the trawler jolted violently. The squeal of metal against metal ripped down the port side. He lost his balance and went flying against the bunk. The two ships must be scraping hulls.

He put out a hand to grab the bunk frame, but missed. His palm landed hard on the deck and slid under it into a low, empty recess that had once held a drawer.

The engine geared down and the vessel stuttered to a jerky stop, bouncing against the larger ship with another crash before rocking away. Clearly, Tango One was not a navy man.

Clint winced and gingerly pulled his hand from under the bunk. Coming out, his fingers brushed against a hard, rectangular object, knocking it farther under.

Curious, he groped for it, but couldn't quite reach. He bent his head and peered into the black recess, barely making out a boxy black shape. But there was something about it . . .

His pulse kicked up in disbelief. *No way.*

He couldn't get so lucky . . . could he?

He narrowed his eyes. That sure as hell *looked* like the distinctive bump of . . .

He flattened himself on the floor and stretched as far under the bunk as he could reach.

And pulled out a sat phone.

Sam let out a muffled *"Oof!"* as her stomach squashed against the deck.

She muttered a soft expletive at the idiot driving *Eliza Jane*. The trawler might be less than half the size as *Île de Cœur*, but still packed quite a punch.

She wiped the grit from her hands and started to lift back up.

All at once a door slammed open on the quarterdeck far above her, and a spate of foreign curses cut through the sudden silence when the trawler's engines cut off. Boots clattered on the stairs, rushing down from the poop to the main deck. Many boots.

Sam's heart raced. *Crap.*

She scooted farther back under the trolley car, so they wouldn't see her. An involuntary tremble went through her

as she watched five black-clad men beeline for the rail.
They weren't tall, but they were solid, muscular, and looked
mean as barracuda. Two split off to grab mooring lines and
toss them down; the other three stood yelling at the guy on
the trawler, who'd come out of the pilothouse steaming
mad. Alone, he sprinted to toss the fenders over the side and
catch the lines to tie her up before she drifted too far. Where
was the other guy? Hadn't Clint said there were two on
Eliza Jane?

Sam did a double take at the five men and counted again.
Yep, five.

Not seven. Not yet, anyway.

Excitement shot through her. The plan could still work!
And she didn't even need the fireworks.

She had to hurry, though. She started to scoot out from
under the trolley.

But something caught her eye down on the trawler. A
glimpse of something that didn't belong, a flash of movement.

She crept farther forward and peered down at the other
vessel's stern as it whipped away from *Île de Cœur*'s hull
and back again. *Île de Cœur* was small for a cargo ship in
this day and age—very small—but *Eliza Jane* was much
smaller. Her weather deck lay at about the same height as
the ro-ro deck on *Île de Cœur*. It all but disappeared from
her view as the lines were pulled taut and the two ships
were lashed together amid more loud yelling. She'd have to
get to the rail for a better look.

A sudden gust of wind blew up out of nowhere, whipping her hair into her face and knocking the brim of her cap
up so quickly she didn't have time to catch it. She watched
in distress as her favorite old hat that had been with her
through thick and thin for years was ripped from her head
and blown into the sea. She stared after it in despair, nearly
bursting into tears. God, was *everything* to be taken from
her today?

She shook her bare head, feeling oddly naked and vulnerable, and started to turn away again, but something

made her hesitate. She hung suspended in indecision. She looked down again to where her beloved cap had vanished. Was it trying to tell her something . . . lead her somewhere? Such as . . . *Eliza Jane*.

Talk about crazy. Crazy to hope. Insane to even *think*, but . . .

The cap floated toward the trawler.

She bit her lip.

What if, somehow, Clint had survived?

What if he was hidden somewhere over on *Eliza Jane*, wounded and dying? Desperately needing her help?

Oh, God.

She swallowed a spurt of panic. She had to find out.

But . . .

She glanced up at the quarterdeck, torn as never before. She'd lose this golden chance to free the crew.

But she still had the fireworks, she told herself. She could go back to the original plan. Later.

This couldn't wait.

She crept out from under the trolley and darted behind the nearest railroad container. Using the other giant containers for cover, she made her way as close to the rail as she could.

Six feet of open space lay between her and the gunwale.

The five muscle-bound hijackers stood twenty, maybe thirty feet away. They were all leaning over the rail, and the leader was yelling furiously. The guy on the trawler was making short, angry gestures and shouting back. Everyone's attention was riveted.

She dropped to her stomach and took a deep breath to still the shakes, then inched forward to the edge of the deck.

Heart slamming, she peered over at the trawler.

Long, dark shadows cast by the waxing midnight sun raked over *Eliza Jane*'s rolling deck, looking like the evil fingers of a malevolent sea god. Sam shivered and watched anxiously for another flash, a movement, for any hint at all that Clint might be there.

Nothing.

She cursed his ghost walker's gift for disappearing into his surroundings. How could she be certain he wasn't there if she couldn't see him?

She ignored the inherent contradiction of that and squeezed her eyes shut in bitter disappointment. *Damn.* She'd known it was a long shot. She'd seen the gun. She'd seen when it fired, and how he'd fallen.

This had been wishful thinking, pure and simple.

Pushing out a breath, she opened her eyes.

Wait. Had that shadow moved? Just a little? She peered closer.

And blinked. Now her eyes were definitely playing tricks on her. Two spots of light made it seem . . . almost like the shadow was . . .

Staring back.

She blinked again, swallowing a soft gasp.

And then the shadow smiled.

20

//////\//////

Clint couldn't help himself. He grinned like an idiot.

Yeah, he was smack in the middle of a situation here, death staring him in the face if one of those goons at the rail spotted him. But *damn*.

He was just so fucking glad to see Samantha.

He was crouched in a deeply shadowed corner of the trawler's afterdeck with a panoramic view of the larger ship's entire starboard hull, bow to stern and up to the rail. Which was how he'd spotted her.

Her pretty green eyes went wide as saucers when they met his, and her sweet-sexy mouth parted in surprise. Then damn if her face didn't light up like it was the Fourth of July and he was the best fireworks show in town.

Made a man feel good clear to his toes, and all parts in between. He just *had* to grin.

Then the goons spoiled the moment by stealing her attention away. Which gave him a chance to really notice her precarious position—and almost have a heart attack.

He could only see her face looking down at him, but he knew the layout of that deck, and . . . *Jesus*, she must be lying on her stomach right out in the open, with only a cleat the size of a peanut to conceal her from Xing Guan's whole damn assassination squad!

When she looked back at him, her brilliant smile was gone. Her eyes darted from him to the mooring lines and back again, looking anxious and worried. Like maybe she was wondering how he'd get back aboard *Île de Cœur* at all, let alone in one piece.

He ground his teeth. *She* was worried about *him*?

He wanted to shake her silly!

And hug the daylights out of her. And then—

Before he realized what was happening, she disappeared.

Wait! Where—

No. On second thought, it was good she'd come to her senses and backed away. He willed her to stay safe. He needed to focus on what was happening with the tangos, so he could seize the first opportunity to get himself off this tub. His hiding spot was far from ideal. When he'd sneaked on deck he'd wanted to go straight to the side and jump off, but he'd barely made it this far. The gang of five had appeared at the rail, and he'd had to freeze where he was, melding into the shadows. Seven seconds of distraction, that's all he needed to be home free.

But *not* by her. Even though she'd probably want to help.

But she'd just end up distracting *him* and he'd probably—

Aw, hell.

A dozen yards beyond the trawler's stern, just above eye level, the small door next to the garage bay on *Île de Cœur*'s ro-ro deck cracked open. Two green eyes peeked out at him.

He didn't have to ask whose.

She opened the door a bit wider. Her face appeared, touched by a pale ray of early morning sun, framed with flyaway strands of golden hair that were blowing free. Where was her ugly cap? God, she was beautiful.

He couldn't quite decipher her expression . . . a telling

blend of fear and joy and disbelief and . . . something else, something warm and powerful, and . . . yeah, almost reluctant. He knew that look. It was the same one she'd given him earlier when he'd left her behind in the room where they'd made love.

He swallowed. *Made love.* Good old-fashioned sex was all he'd had in mind when he'd followed her into that secret room nearly fifteen hours ago. But it had turned into so much more.

Hell, no wonder she looked reluctant. It scared the crap out of him, too, this thing arcing between them like one of those detonators in his dry-bag. Neither of them needed this happening right now.

But Jesus, the feelings were too overwhelming. He was already in way over his depth, and she was the air he needed to survive this dive into the unknown.

As he gazed up at her, he hoped to hell she felt the same about him.

With all five tangos staring down over the rail— thankfully they couldn't see her from where they stood—he couldn't move, couldn't speak, couldn't do what he devoutly wished to do. Which was to get up there any way he could, sweep her into his arms, and kiss her until neither of them could breathe. And then make love to her until they couldn't walk.

Her lips parted and the tip of her tongue wet them, as if she were thinking exactly the same thing.

Ho-boy. The damn wetsuit was shrinking by the second.

Suddenly, a rope ladder came hurtling down from above and to the side, jerking them back to the present. They ripped their startled gazes from each other. Unfurling as it flew, the ladder smacked against the big ship's hull a dozen yards aft and bounced. On the trawler, Tango One caught the bottom rung, and a chorus of orders erupted from the gang of five. Most of the men looked downright suspicious; Xing Guan looked royally pissed.

About what?

He really hoped this wasn't about the dead guy. *Damn.*

Had Tango One gone below again and found the bathroom empty? Realized the other man wasn't on board at all and already warned the others? He'd hoped for a bit more time before all hell broke loose.

Clint tensed, willing Tango One to start climbing up the ladder. "Go on, you little prick," he muttered under his breath.

The little prick didn't go up. The others started to climb down. Guan came first, agile as a monkey, the rest close on his heels.

Clint gave a silent, virulent curse. *Shit.*

The good news was the tangos had their backs to him. So he moved in the opposite direction, following the shadows, dodging equipment lockers, and rolled under the fish sorting table to land in a tight crouch at the edge of the gunwale.

Giving the dry-bag and dive knife quick tugs to make sure they were clipped fast, he grimaced at his ripped wetsuit and bloody arm. Yeah, this should be fun.

He grabbed the taffrail, braced himself for the icy bite of Arctic water, and dropped over the side into the sea.

For the second time today, Sam was forced to watch Clint die.

Almost die, she told herself firmly.

Which was just as bad, she thought in despair.

Almost.

He'd moved like a shadowy apparition flowing across the deck as he made his escape in plain sight of all six hijackers. Her heart throbbed painfully in her throat, terrified for him, both hands pressed against her mouth to keep herself from crying out as he leapt into the sea and instantly disappeared under the waves.

She just stood and stared, scarcely able to believe she'd gotten him back only to lose him again.

No, she *wouldn't* lose him. It had been a miracle the hijackers didn't see him cross the deck, but they hadn't.

And the ships were lashed together—he'd find a way back on board *Île de Cœur*. *Before* he froze to death in that water. He was a SEAL. This was what he did. He'd be *fine*.

She hadn't lost him.

A joy-filled wonder flooded through her. He was *alive*!

My God! Clint was alive!

He hadn't been shot! What had happened to the man with the gun? How had Clint escaped? Her mind buzzed with questions.

He surely must have nine lives.

Thank God.

She stepped back from the crack in the door, blinking against the inside darkness and a new onslaught of ragged emotions—fear, elation, hope, and profound relief.

But the relief was short-lived. Clint was alive, but not safe. Not yet. She wouldn't stop worrying until he was back on *Île de Cœur*, and safely in her arms.

Blindly, she eased the heavy door shut, giving the wheel a twist to lock. She realized she was shaking. For a long moment, she closed her eyes and clung to the solid steel, battling for control. But it was no use.

She wanted to see him. To touch him. She needed to put her arms around him and hold him. Just hold him. To have solid evidence she wasn't losing it, that the shadowy figure in black really had been Clint, not some PTSD-induced vision playing cruel tricks with her mind.

Don't be ridiculous, she told herself firmly. She wasn't that far gone. It was him.

And there was only one place she could think of to get back on board where the hijackers couldn't see him: the matching bay doors on the opposite side of the ship.

She turned and started to run.

When she got to the matching port bay, she threw open the smaller door and started to lean out so she could see better. Her foot caught on something. Still in her slippery stocking feet, she lost her balance and nearly catapulted over the side. With a yelp, she grabbed the rusty frame and dragged herself back inside by her fingertips.

Her heartbeat thundered. *Good lord. That* would have been just great. She really needed to retrieve her shoes.

She looked down for what had tripped her. A long, thin line had been made fast to a ring on the outside of the door. The end was almost touching the water. Instantly, she realized Clint must have left it there for his return trip.

Obviously, he'd done this before.

She eased out a breath to steady her nerves, hung on tight, and carefully leaned out again, scanning the waves for him. A cold breeze teased the straggling ends of her hair, and she pushed them back, shading her eyes.

The midnight sun had turned to dawn in a bright, fiery ball. It broke its kiss with the eastern horizon, sending shafts of brilliant orange and yellow streaking across the surface of the sea and breaking into glittering shards on the blue-gray waves. Between the shiny reflections and her tired eyes, it was hard to see anything at all.

She searched in a slow half circle for a sign of his black wetsuit. There was only water.

"Come on, come on," she murmured, growing more anxious with every passing second. He should be here by now.

There! A black dot appeared in the morning chop and then disappeared again. *Was that . . . ?* Heck, maybe she was so tired she was seeing spots. *No!* There it was again. She had definitely not imagined the flash of black that time.

Her heartbeat sped with anticipation as she caught more glimpses of him. Why didn't he come up to the surface? The tangos on the trawler couldn't see him over on this side.

Maybe it was easier to swim underwater. She frowned. Okay. But why was he so far out?

The black spot surfaced once more, this time clearly visible as it glided through the water, coming toward the ship.

Her eyes bugged.

Oh, God.

It wasn't a wetsuit hood, or a snorkel. . . .

But a distinctively curved fin.

21

///////\\\\\\\///////

A shark!

Horror filled Sam to the soles of her feet. Frantically, she scoured the sea for Clint as the curved fin cut through the water, coming closer and closer.

Suddenly, it veered off at a sharp angle, sped up, and vanished into the deep—in exactly the direction Clint would be coming from.

"No," she murmured desperately. Please, God, this could *not* be happening. "Please. Please, *please*," she whispered over and over, white-knuckling the metal doorframe until her fingers ached.

All at once, something big and black broke the surface just below her and shot up from the water in a spout of foam. She gasped and instinctively jumped backward. The line at her feet jerked taut. Then it started to whip back and forth like a manic metronome. She jumped out of the way with a curse, but after a tense moment, decided to risk a peek over the edge.

Her heart nearly leapt from her chest.

Clint!

At least . . . she hoped it was Clint. The hood and mask obscured most of his face.

He was coming up fast, hand over fist, body straight, and flippered feet pushing off the hull like Spider-Man. Or maybe Waterbugman.

In places, his wetsuit carried a sheen of red. And there was an ugly gash across his forearm. *Oh, no.*

But to her confusion, his lips were curved in a diabolical grin that grew wider and wider the closer he got. Within seconds, he was at her feet.

"Showed that fucker," he said in a gravelly rumble that sent a chill down her spine. "*Damn*, I needed that."

Her jaw dropped. Was he *crazy*? A *shark* had almost—

She didn't have time to complete the thought. He was up and through the door, flippers and snorkel were flying, and suddenly she was in his arms. "Damn, I needed this, too," he said. And then he was kissing her, and kissing her, and kissing her.

"Oh, Clint." She melted into his embrace, weak with relief. "I am so glad you're—"

"Show," he interrupted, pushing her up against the bulkhead. "Don't tell." His mouth covered hers, swallowing her gasp at the icy wall of metal at her back and the frigid, wet wall of man against her front.

His tall, hard body pressed into her and his strong arms lifted her off her feet. Suddenly she was warm all over.

With a sigh of intense pleasure, she raked her fingers through his short, thick hair and held his face to hers. He smelled of the sea and tasted like the salty spray on a windy day—two of the things she loved best in the world. The man himself was rapidly climbing her top ten list, too.

She kissed him back, deep and thorough, opening her mouth and her body to him. Showing him all the feelings she'd been holding inside all day. Everything she'd regretted not telling him . . . and never thought she'd get the chance to. He was so right, showing was better. Much better.

He groaned at her eager response, and something hard hit the deck at his feet. His hand went to his wetsuit jacket, and the zipper flew down as they kissed feverishly, their tongues blending and swirling.

Her fingers bumped up against the ragged rip in the thick fabric on his arm. How could she have forgotten? She pushed on his shoulders to put a sliver of space between them. "My God. You're bleeding!" she said, blanching at the sight of his arm. "Did the shark—"

"Hell, no. It's nothing." He set her on her feet and yanked impatiently at the jacket. "Help me take this thing off."

She peeled it over his shoulders, unzipped the wrists, and tugged it off his good arm. He did the other side himself and tossed the jacket away. Blood trickled down from the wound, but he didn't seem to care.

With a masculine grunt, he pressed her back onto the bulkhead. Harder this time. His free hand dipped under her sweatshirt, leaving no doubt what was on his mind. "Now where was I?"

With a laugh, she attempted to elude him, glancing up toward the quarterdeck.

"But the hijackers—"

"Are busy on the trawler. We've got time."

"But—"

"Don't worry. We'll hear them."

His nails raked lightly up her ribs, erupting in trills of arousal everywhere he touched. She forgot all about her reservations and arched against him, humming with need.

He cursed at the wet, rubbery fabric between them. "Damned wetsuit," he muttered, and shot the zipper of his Farmer John down, frowning when it got stuck just below his chest.

She took the opportunity to pull off her sweatshirt. He forgot all about the zipper.

Just as she'd intended. They might not get this chance again. She wanted to take full advantage.

He reached for her bra and found his totem bracelet hidden there, next to her heart. He touched it, and the look he gave her melted her to a warm puddle.

The wetsuit splayed open across his broad chest at the

parted zipper. "Now you," she said, returning the look. She found the jerry-rigged ropes at his shoulders and began untying them. Or tried to. But her anxious fingers were useless.

He dropped the leather thong with her bra and ran a calloused hand over her breasts. They zinged in pleasure, and she fumbled with the knots. And fumbled some more.

Oh, why had she tied those knots so well? Tight and wet, they were impossible to unravel.

Unlike herself.

Tight and wet, *God, yes*, but she was about to come apart at the seams.

His tongue licked at her pouting lips . . . and teased them into parting.

She gave up on the knots and moaned in frustration. "Fuck," she breathed into his questing mouth.

His response was instant, whispered in a gravelly, possessive rumble. "Oh, I intend to."

Goose bumps spilled over her whole body. She believed him. Her insides clenched with exquisite arousal. Being so desired by this incredible man was the most powerful aphrodisiac imaginable.

The hilt of his dive knife prodded her palm. "Hurry," he urged in that same seductive murmur.

She needed no urging. Quickly she sliced up through the cords on one shoulder, then the other. The straps snapped apart, leaving his broad, masculine shoulders bare. *Finally.*

He took the knife, tossed it to the deck, and reached for her again.

"No. My turn," she murmured, blocking his hand. She brushed her fingers reverently over the muscular ball of his shoulder, lingered on his rock-hard bicep. He felt so incredibly good. So buff . . . and male. His were muscles honestly earned. Such a turn-on. She had no use for a man afraid of hard work.

And yet, he was so damned beautiful. Despite the flaws—or maybe because of them. She trailed her fingers down to the jagged slice on his bronze forearm, stopping just short. *There'd be a scar.* And it wouldn't be alone. "This has to—"

"There must be more interesting places to touch me," he suggested darkly, reaching up to draw his thumb over her pebbled nipple.

She inhaled sharply, a piercing pleasure zinging through her breasts. God, he could lay her down right now and she'd be hot putty beneath him. "Yeah? Like where?" she managed to say past her desire-tightened throat.

"Shall I show you?" He drew his thumb back again.

She quivered all over. In a good way. "And spoil my fun?" She pushed his hand away, as much to get control of herself as him. She was so aroused she could already feel the slick moisture pooled between her legs.

But she wanted him as desperate for her as she was for him.

She caressed the beautiful wolf inked on his perfectly sculpted bicep. Then ran the backs of her knuckles over the eagle and anchor navy tattoo on his pec. She'd never been into tattoos before, but on Clint they were incredibly sexy.

And speaking of sexy . . . She dragged her nails down to the flat male nipple below. It sprang to attention. She couldn't resist; she leaned down and licked it, then gave it a little bite. Just one. Any more, and she'd be all over him.

He didn't make a sound, or move a millimeter, but something changed. A subtle shift charged the atmosphere around them. It sizzled, giving her another shower of goose bumps.

She straightened and met his dark, hooded gaze. His mahogany eyes bored into her. Hot, potent, hungry. The eyes of a dangerous predator. *Making an even more dangerous promise.*

She shivered—an electric, full-body shiver of anticipation. She knew what that gaze meant.

It was the look of a man who knew what he wanted, and meant to have it.

Her.

Helpless.

Naked under him.

And she was going to like it.

He stepped closer, crowding her. Her pulse sped, but she
didn't back away. In a single, unyielding motion, he hooked
her sweatpants and panties and sent them down to her ankles. He lifted her out of them, then kicked them aside.

Slowly he set her down. His predator's gaze traveled
over her naked body. Focused on it with single-minded intent.

A shuddering chill of desire burst through her. She was
ready for him. *So ready.*

"Cold?" His strong, steady fingers returned to her achingly tight nipple. He toyed with her lightly. Then pinched.

She nearly detonated.

"No," she gasped as he squeezed harder and rolled the
burning tip between his fingers. "Hot."

He thumbed the other one. "How hot?"

She hesitated, and he squeezed them both. She cried out
as a shock of pleasure-pain streaked through her breasts and
straight between her legs like a lit fuse.

"Wh—" She was suddenly so close to coming she could
barely speak. She shut her eyes tight. As if that would stop
the tidal wave. "Wh-white hot."

A zipper rasped. "The hottest flame of all," he murmured, as though expecting no less.

She felt his cock bump against her belly, thick and hard.
"Hotter," she whispered, opening her eyes to look.

He'd peeled the wetsuit down to his hips, spreading it
open to free his sex. It was big. And long. And fully erect.
She couldn't take her eyes off him—his perfect body or his
smoldering gaze.

She licked her lips and waited breathlessly for him to
move. She wanted him. No, needed him. *Now.*

He stood for a tense moment regarding her, then turned
his attention outward and did a careful scan of the vehicles
on the deck around them, then glanced up for several seconds at the companionway, crew deck, and quarterdeck
landing at the other end of the ship. Apparently satisfied, he
turned back to her.

He grasped her arms and pulled her against the solid
wall of his body. "I want to be inside you," he said, his
voice low with intent.

She swallowed. "Then take me."

His mouth descended on hers, demanding her surrender.
She gave in to him willingly. She no longer felt a need to be
the strong one, the one in charge. Not with Clint. It was a
strange sensation. One she didn't entirely understand. But
it felt good. Liberating. And intensely arousing.

He kissed her hard, and she opened for him, reveling in
the dark taste of his desire for her. His hands molded her
backside, then his fingers slid between her legs. A very
male growl vibrated up his throat. "God, you're wet."

"Your fault," she breathed.

He touched her clit, and she almost came.

With a whimper of acute need, she wriggled away from
his hand and groped for the wetsuit, shoving it farther down
his thighs. "I want you naked."

She went to her knees and made short work of pulling it
off him, raw need fueling the effort. She looked up when he
was as naked as she. His cock pulsed inches from her lips.
Her position before him felt erotic and insanely arousing.
She'd tasted him yesterday—more than once—and knew
that he liked it. She liked it, too.

Her pulse pounded. She moved her body forward and
put her lips to his cock. Then took him into her mouth.

After three seconds, he gave a harsh, guttural curse, and
his hands were gripping her, lifting her off. His arms banded
tight around her, and before she could think, he'd taken
several swift steps, and suddenly she was on her back on
the hard deck, lying between the treads of a giant orange
vehicle. Blinking up into his unsmiling face.

She could feel her pulse thundering in her throat.

He parted her legs with a knee and lowered himself between them. She swallowed heavily, more aroused than
she'd ever been in her life. My God, what the man did to
her!

He stared down at her as he gripped the backs of her

knees, lifted, and spread them wide apart. His cock prodded her slick flesh. She moaned softly. Her center blossomed. Her blood raced.

When he didn't move, she clung to his shoulders and tried to wriggle herself onto him.

"Please," she begged. She was on the very edge.

He rocked his hips back, regarded her for a breathless moment, then began to thrust. "Scream," he demanded, and scythed hard and deep, to the very hilt.

She cried out, a keen of pure carnal pleasure. Before it passed her lips, he sealed her mouth with his and captured the sound, swallowing her cry like succor.

He even tasted different now. Darker. Hot and musky, like liquid bliss.

Holding perfectly still within her, he deepened the kiss. Deliberately . . . provocatively . . . his tongue penetrated her mouth, full and bold, just as his cock was doing. Marking her with his essence, laying claim to her with the dominance of his body in hers.

The power of his seduction took her breath. She trembled, and wrapped her legs around his waist, helplessly trapped in his erotic spell. She felt taken as never before, and totally possessed.

She should be terrified.

Instead she felt profoundly wanted.

And with a flare of insight, she knew she'd never been truly wanted before. Not by any man. Not like this.

He took her jaw in his hand and held her fast for his kiss, demanding her complete attention, and the thought was gone.

Sheltered from reflection by the sheer force of his passion, her shaking body was coiled and throbbing with need for him, her mind blank of anything but Clint. Never had she felt so totally . . . visceral . . . with a man.

Or vulnerable.

Somehow, her unheeding heart had opened wide and let him in, ready to surrender to a deluge of feelings and emotions she'd been starving for all her life.

It was exhilarating. And not a little frightening.

Especially when a quiet voice inside her head whispered, *Careful! Love always leads to betrayal by those you love. . . .*

She stilled. Wait.

Love?

Who said anything about love? She tried to push the thought aside and back to Clint's heated kisses.

But the quiet warning in her mind grew to a dull roar. She felt dizzy with the overwhelming sensation of being poised on the brink of a treacherous precipice.

Because of another blinding insight.

She was about to fall for this man, and fall hard.

A soft noise of desperation escaped her at an even worse realization.

It may already be too late.

She was already hurtling off that cliff, falling at the speed of light. And there'd be no one at the bottom to catch her. Certainly not a man on a mission, a spy who lived halfway around the world.

Clint must have heard her soft mewl of panic and sensed some measure of her sudden inner chaos.

He broke their stalled kiss, his hand still wrapped around her jaw. "Samantha, look at me."

She shook her head.

She couldn't face him. Not yet.

What was she *doing*, so vulnerable in this man's arms? Offering her heart to him on a platter, like some lovesick fool? Had she not learned the painful lessons taught to her by an indifferent father and faithless husband?

She couldn't bear it if Clint turned out the same. And how could he not? He'd never pretended this was anything but temporary.

"Samantha."

She heard the steely command in his even tone and wanted to bristle against it, but couldn't summon the will.

His body stirred within her, urging her to forget the past. And, oh, how she wanted to!

She was a such a fool!

Because even now, after her fateful realization, she still wanted him. She craved him with such an overpowering need that her body didn't give a damn that his brand of macho was all wrong for her. Or that he would surely break her heart when he walked off the ship.

"Look at me."

She touched her lips with her tongue, and the taste of him flooded through her. It was like a drug that robbed her mind of all sense, and her body of its willpower.

She looked up at him.

His shadowed eyes were nearly black. They pinned her like a butterfly, watching her with lethal intensity.

He shifted his hips and slowly withdrew his cock from her. Inch by slow inch, he pulled out until only the rigid flare of the tip remained. Leaving her cold and empty, inside and out.

This was worse than a broken heart. Far worse. She couldn't stand the thought of being without him here and now, regardless of future consequences.

Besides, he might never walk off the ship.

Neither of them might survive long enough to do that. Or to have a future at all.

She'd be an even bigger fool to push him away. She'd deal with the heartache if and when it came.

"Don't," she whispered, and tightened her arms around him.

For a long moment he studied her. She could feel the barely leashed strength in his tall frame, his muscles taut and corded. And sense the weight of his decision.

"Give me a reason," he said at length, his voice low.

In the set of his mouth she saw his own need for her, and for this overwhelming connection between them to continue. For now, anyway. And yet . . . his need seemed equal to hers in strength and vulnerability . . . as well as in reluctance.

He needed her, too.

Could it be true? Not just for now?

It didn't seem possible. And yet . . . there was something in the tightness around his eyes. He seemed . . . hurt.

Or was it an illusion . . . just wishful thinking on her part? Could she really trust what she was seeing?

Could she trust *him*?

She touched his face, smoothed the lines between his brows.

Did it really even matter? Either way, her heart was his.

"A reason?" She swallowed. And admitted the frightening truth. "I don't want you to let me go."

Ever.

His eyes didn't soften, but his forehead lowered to hers. His nose flared as he jetted a sigh through it.

He needed her, too.

That's what she chose to believe.

For now.

She lifted her lips and kissed him. Slid her arms up around his neck and pulled his mouth to hers, enticing him back to her with long drugging strokes of her tongue. He smelled of the cold, crisp sea and tasted like heaven. She subtly rubbed her breasts back and forth against his chest, drowning in the starbursts of pleasure in the friction. Loving the groans she was finally able to coax from his throat, and the quivers she sent through his limbs when she touched him.

Until they were both back in the fever, breathing hard and fast as their tongues did battle.

To her sublime frustration, he would not thrust, but kept his cock poised just at her entrance. Waiting for . . . what?

She reached down to touch him. To urge him—

"No."

He clamped a hand over her wrist and brought it up over her head. He held it pinioned against the deck.

"But—"

"You'll do as I say."

Taken aback by the growled reprimand, she opened her mouth to retort, but the words became an "Oh!" of surprise when his hand slipped between their legs. His fingertips went to the place of their joining, sliding around the neck of his cock, touching, exploring, his own flesh as well as hers.

And turning her on even more.

Her cheeks flushed. The man liked an edge to his sex. Yesterday, he'd done things like this, too. Not exactly dirty. Not even kinky or weird. Just . . . slightly naughty. Enough so to make her blush. And usually come. Immediately.

His fingers brushed over her clit. He watched her face as she writhed at his silken touch. He knew exactly what he was doing to her. He'd touched her there enough times yesterday with hands and tongue to be a goddamn expert.

"What are you doing?" she managed, though she knew very well. Driving her mad.

A muscle along his jaw twitched. "Anything I want." He watched her eyes flare at his impudence, and he touched her again, deliberately letting his thumb ride her. "Problem?" he asked as she sucked in a gasp.

She wanted to punch him, the cocky bastard.

Right after he got her off.

"Fuck you," she told him.

Far from being angry, he looked gratified at her reaction. Even more so when, despite her pique, she moved her legs farther apart for him.

His thumb slicked over her, increasing its pressure. Fountains of pleasure shot through every nerve ending. It was impossible to stifle her moans. He kept at it, bringing her right to the sparkling edge of orgasm, then leaving her hanging in frustration.

"Fine. What do you want?" she ground out.

She dug her fingers into his shoulders, attempting to wriggle down onto his rigid length again. To push herself over.

So . . . close . . . So . . . close . . .

He didn't answer. He fisted his cock and held it in position, so close yet so maddeningly far away from where she wanted it, that she held her breath in suspense.

"You want me?" he asked.

God, yes. She felt the first electric tingle of orgasm at his question—that was how much she wanted him. "Yes."

He pulled his cock out of her and guided the head up over her clit. Hot and smooth as a steel piston, it glistened with his essence. She writhed against it and moaned, reaching for the climax that was still just out of her reach.

"Please," she rasped, and opened her legs wider for him.

"Say my name," he ordered, his voice like rough cut velvet.

Her throat ached for a taste of him. For the feel of him crushing into her. "Please, Clint."

He stared down. The angles of his face were harsh, uncompromising, his lips a tight dark slash in his flushed bronze skin. *Not good enough,* his expression said.

She shivered.

"Clint . . . Wolf Walker." This time it came out like a hushed vow.

His cock thickened, sucking at her clit. She felt another tingle, stronger this time. He pulled it away. She inhaled a stuttering breath of protest.

Then he guided it to her entry, and pushed in. Slick and hot, he slid home, stretching her, filling her, in an almost painful pleasure. She was drowning in desire, mindless with need. She arched up to meet him and felt the throb of orgasm take hold.

He flexed deep within her, then withdrew once more to the quivering verge. His thumb found the center of her pleasure and teased it. She cried out as the throb grew stronger.

"Say it again," he demanded, his voice low and rough in her ear, "while you come for me."

Climax seized control of her body just as his name left her tongue. "Clint"—she gasped—"Wolf Walker."

From far away came the hushed echo of a quiet question. "And who am I to you, Samantha?"

Clinging to him, she gave herself over to the rush of the inevitable, and whispered her answer. *"My man."*

22

\\\\\\\\\\\////////

Five minutes later, Clint cleared his throat. *Wow. Okay, then.*

"That was . . . interesting," he said, striving for neutrality. *And powerful.* And probably the best . . . and worst . . . sex he'd had in his entire life.

Under him, Samantha didn't move. "Um. Yeah."

Not to mention the most disturbing.

What did a guy say after doing something like that to a woman? *Talk about your average elephant in the room.* Hell, he couldn't even meet her eyes.

Clint rolled off Samantha and stared up at the orange snowplow chassis above them. What the *hell* had just happened to him?

She'd had—or *seemed* to have—a minute or two of hesitation about . . . well, God knew what—it wasn't like there was any big shortage around here of things to hesitate over. Naturally, he'd jumped to the conclusion it had to be *him* she didn't want. That she'd changed her mind about having sex with a raving lunatic on the cold, dirty deck, in the middle of a goddamn siege for godsake.

Because, yeah, *that* was a totally unreasonable hesitation.

So what did he do? Ask her nicely what was wrong? Whisper sweet nothings in her ear to change her mind back again? Admit he was being a prick for making her fuck him under those deplorable conditions and let her up? *Hell*, no. He'd gone all *Blue Velvet* on her.

Because, of course, that made *perfect* sense.

Jesus.

Sure, he'd engaged in power sex before. Handcuffs, role play, spankings and the like. But he'd never actually meant any of it. And he'd certainly never initiated it. But if some woman wanted him to tie her up and play cowboys and Indians, what the hell, he'd go along with the fantasy. Made the sex he got that much hotter.

But this . . . this was different. *He'd* been the one to start it. To force his will on her. He'd wanted to *own* her. Control her every thought. *Make* her want him. He'd meant every fucking word and action of his attempt at total domination over her.

At the time, anyway.

Now he was just plain embarrassed.

Hell, his usual demeanor might be a tad macho— according to certain parties—but he'd never been a controlling asshole. Not at work. *Definitely* not with women. He *liked* a woman with spunk, with a streak of defiance and independence. A woman who enjoyed being on equal footing with him. Who insisted on it, really.

That was one reason he'd never hooked up with anyone for more than a few months, or days. He'd never met a woman like that who wasn't also a ballbuster.

Until now.

And he'd just given this woman a damn good reason to bust his balls from here to the North Pole and back.

Yep. Way to go, asshole.

He raked his fingers through his hair. "You must be freezing," he said, and started to rise.

"No, I . . . Yeah. I am." She started to crawl out from under the giant snowplow.

"They'll be back soon, too." He took a second to grab the

SD card from its hiding place, then scooted out and helped her up. He deliberately avoided looking at her gorgeous naked body as he gave her an awkward peck on the lips. He was in enough trouble. A fresh hard-on wouldn't help.

She blinked, then wordlessly handed him his bear claw and went to gather her clothes. He looked down at it and realized that, naturally, he didn't have any clothes to gather.

And wasn't *that* special.

He watched her slide on her panties and sweats—he couldn't help himself—and as she was pulling on her hoodie she caught him looking. She froze uncertainly, the hem of the hoodie halting just above her breasts. Which was too much of an eyeful for his dick to take sitting down.

Outwardly, he remained determinedly impassive as it rose to attention. Inside, he was tearing it a new one.

Her eyes flitted down, widened, then darted back to his. She yanked down the sweatshirt. *Too late, baby.*

"You aren't getting dressed," she observed, her voice somewhat strangled.

"No clothes," he said, trying not to grit his teeth. "And I'm not putting that damn wetsuit back on."

Her lips formed an *O*. For a second she just stared at him. Was that *amusement* that darted through her eyes? "Okay," she said.

Okay?

What was that supposed to mean?

He began, "My clothes are down in our—in the room we—I mean, um . . ." He stopped in irritation.

"The hideaway?" she helpfully supplied.

"Yes," he said, and turned abruptly to gather his gear. Heat stung his neck as he tied the leather totem back around his wrist, then scooped everything up and flung the soggy wetsuit over his shoulder. "Ready?"

Again she nodded, and silently followed him across the ro-ro deck and down the ladder to the orlop. He didn't feel a *bit* self-conscious having her eyes on his bare backside the entire way.

"Warriors in ancient Sparta used to fight naked," she

ventured conversationally as they headed for the hidden room, treading cautiously through the empty passageways. "Went to war and everything in the buff. Except maybe, you know, a bracelet or something."

He turned to glare at her.

There wasn't a hint of smile on her face. "I'm just sayin'." It was her eyes that gave her away.

"Keep it up," he warned.

Her cheek twitched.

He realized what he'd just said, so he turned on a heel and started walking again before he could dig himself in even deeper. When they got to the hideaway, she busied herself with a black duffel bag he hadn't noticed before.

"What's that?" he asked.

"I managed to get to the staterooms. Our guns were gone, but I picked up some clothes and a few other things." She pulled out his black T-shirt and tossed it to him.

"Thanks. Is that a laptop?"

She nodded. "It has the ship's logs and such. Figured I should keep it with me."

He stared at it for a moment, then turned to look for a place to hang the wetsuit to dry. "Too bad we can't get the Internet on it."

"Yeah."

He settled on the empty hammock hook for the wetsuit. The hammock was still on the floor where it had fallen when she cut the ropes. It was a shame. It had been a nice one. And they'd had a good time in it. Real good.

He turned to find her watching him, a first aid kit in her hands.

"I should see to that wound," she said, studiously ignoring the hammock, acting as if she offered first aid to naked men every day. *Naked Spartan warriors.*

Hell, if she could take it, he could, too. "Sure," he said, and held out his arm.

She came over and opened the kit, picking through the contents and comparing bandage sizes to his cut. She swayed a little.

He grabbed her arm. "Hey, you okay?"

"Yeah." She gave him a smile that looked more worn than reassuring. "Just a little tired."

A little? He suddenly noticed she looked completely exhausted. Which made him feel even better about practically forcing himself on her. "What time is it anyway?"

She checked her watch. "Five thirty."

They'd been up for over twenty-four hours. Twenty-four highly stressful hours. On so many levels.

"Sit," he said. Taking the first aid kit from her, he urged her down to the deck. "Forget about my—"

"No." She reached up and took it back. "It might get infected. Who knows where that wetsuit's been."

He raised a brow but didn't argue. He saw it would be faster just to give in. He sat down next to her and held out his arm again. "You need sleep, honey."

"And you don't?"

He winced as she poured some foul, painful liquid on the cut. "I have things to do first." Number one being the sat phone in his dry-bag. He wanted to check on the Coast Guard's status. He hoped to God the battery was charged.

"So do I. I know where they've got my crew."

Wait. What? He gave her a narrowed look. "And?"

"I'm going to get them out," she said as she closed up his wound with a butterfly bandage. "This is deep. It needs stitches."

He hissed a breath at the sting. "Over my dead body."

Her fingers paused for a moment on a second bandage, then tore it open. "Wimpy baby."

"You know very well what I mean."

She stuck the bandage on him. "I don't suppose you made it to *Eliza Jane*'s radio?"

The change in subject didn't fool him for a nanosecond. "I did. But I'm telling you, Samantha. Do not even think about—"

Her expression went at once to astonished and hopeful. "You got through to the Coast Guard?"

He gave up. *For now.* "Yes. But—"

"You told them we're hijacked? And they're coming to help us?"

"Yes, but probably not in time to do any good," he reluctantly told her. "The GPS was smashed so I couldn't give our exact coordinates. It'll take them a while to find us."

He could see the gears turning in her head, calculating the odds. She looked less hopeful, but a lot more determined. "Okay. Then we just need to keep everyone alive until they get here. Right?"

He let out a long breath. He couldn't put it off any longer. He had to tell her everything.

"What?"

"You want the good news or the bad news?"

Her face fell a little more. "You choose."

No use sugarcoating. "The hijackers are probably planning to blow up your ship. Along with the hostages, is my guess."

To her credit, she barely flinched. "How?"

"I found a couple of military packing cases on the trawler. They were mostly empty, except for some spare ammo and a few other things." He jerked his chin at the dry-bag. "I brought back the ammo. And the box of detonators I found."

"Detonators?" As that sank in, she swallowed. "That's the good news, right? You took them away."

"Two were missing from the box."

"Oh." The last gleam of hope in her eyes flickered and nearly died, only reviving at the last moment. "Okay. We'll just have to find the bombs before they go off."

He had to hand it to her. The woman did not give up easily. Samantha Richardson was a damn good captain. And one hell of a woman.

"Know anything about bombs?" she asked.

He gave a tired smile. Not his main specialty, but . . . "I get by." His smile faded. He really needed to tell her. "There's more."

Her fingers gripped the first aid kit with a slight tremble. "You're killing me here, Walker."

"You deserve the whole truth."

She licked her lips and nodded reluctantly. "Thanks. I appreciate that. Most men—" She cut off abruptly and darted him a quick glance. Their eyes met and held. Her cheeks colored. And suddenly, it was back again, prancing around them. That giant elephant in the room.

Yeah. No fucking shit.

Most men wouldn't have forced himself on her and then acted like a paranoid pricktard when she objected. Most men wouldn't have led a frickin' foreign assassination squad right to her frickin' doorstep. Most men wouldn't be lying to her—*and himself*—about how much he was starting to like her. Hell, more than like. And wanted to keep her around . . . for a whole lot longer than they probably had left.

And most men couldn't kill another man and shove his body over the side of a ship.

The whole truth? Who was he trying to kid?

She tore her gaze away and swallowed. "So tell me everything."

For a split second he almost spilled his guts. About his guilt. About his feelings for her. He even opened his mouth to do it. But what came out was, "They've got two 120mm antitank missile launchers and a case full of rockets. I disabled one of the launchers, but . . ." He shook his head. "Not enough time."

He really was a wimpy baby.

She took in the information, and frowned. "Antitank rockets? Can they sink a ship?"

"They did a pretty good job on that Russian submarine I was on last week," he muttered distractedly, "with a little help."

She blinked owlishly. "Russian submarine?"

Ah, shit. He cringed at his slip. "Shouldn't have told you that. Now I really am gonna have to kill you."

She opened her mouth, then closed it again. He couldn't begin to read her expression. But this time it wasn't amusement.

"Sorry. Not funny."

"Someday," she murmured, "you'll have to tell me that story."

"Sure," he said, forcing himself to refocus. "The thing is, that help I mentioned?" He could literally see her heart sink. "It was a Chinese nuclear submarine. And it's probably still lurking around the Bering. Whether it's working with our boys"—he shrugged—"who knows."

She gaped.

Speechless.

Yeah, that about summed things up.

Her mouth snapped shut. "Clint. I could have sworn you mentioned *good* news."

He smiled weakly. "Well, I have a gun now. Bullets, too."

She stared at him in disbelief. Then shook herself. "Well great. Wow, we're totally saved." She turned back to the duffel bag and stuck the first aid kit into it with a vengeance. Then she spun back to him. "Clint, you really need to tell me what's going on. Why the hell are these guys after you? What did you steal from them that's so damn important?"

He stared back at her. "Who says I stole anything?"

She gave him a death-ray glare.

"I didn't steal it, technically, but, okay. I do have something they want back."

"Let me guess. A data card. What's on it?"

His jaw dropped. He shot a hand through his hair. "Ever think about becoming a spy?"

"No." She kept glaring at him.

"I can't tell you what's on it. But it's important to our country. Trust me on that. And if anything happens to me—"

She whipped up a finger at him. "Do not even go there, Clint. You are *not* leaving me alone in the middle of this mess. It was bad enough I had to watch you—"

Before she got really wound up, he cut her off. "I thought you wanted to hear the good news."

Her mouth snapped shut in midword. She huffed out a breath and hiked up her brows.

"I found a sat phone on the trawler." He smiled.

She gasped. "What?"

"Satellite phone."

"Are you serious?" She started to jump up. "And you didn't think to lead with that? My God, Clint. Call the navy! The air force. Hell, the president! What are you waiting for?"

He grasped her arm. "I plan to, but it won't work down here."

She shook him off. "Where's the phone?" She scooted out of reach and grabbed for the dry-bag. "We'll go topside."

"No," he said, hating this next part. "Wait, I—"

"You're kidding, right?" She ripped open the dry-bag seal and flipped out the folds. "We need to get up there ASAP."

"Yeah. But first—"

Something in his voice must have alerted her. She paused in midmotion. "What? You're telling me there's *more*?"

Damn. Until this very second he hadn't realized how much he didn't want her to know that other side of him. The side that was every bit as ruthless as the enemy they were fighting.

"I killed one of them. On the trawler."

She stared. "Killed? As in—?"

"As in dead. I gave him a burial at sea."

This time she didn't even try and stop her dismayed flinch. She sat down abruptly. "Oh."

Yeah. How to make a good woman run screaming in horror from you in one easy lesson.

"It was him or me," he said. "I chose me."

"I saw," she said, her voice hollow. "At least, I think I . . . So they know? That he's dead? Which means they also know about us . . . ?"

"You mean me." He shook his head. "Too early to tell. I covered it up as best I could. Tango One—the other guy—believes he was sick. Maybe they'll think he was puking over the side and fell in."

It could happen.

"Was he sick?" she asked, confusion banishing the worry for a moment.

"No." Clint waved a hand. "Long story. But if Xing Guan gets suspicious, I'm sure we'll know about it real quick."

"Xing Guan?"

"I'm pretty sure that's who the leader is."

"You've heard of him before?"

Clint nodded.

"Bad?"

"Yeah. Real bad."

"And if he gets suspicious, he'll start searching for us."

"For me." And then it would get really ugly, pronto.

Surprisingly, she didn't run screaming from him. In fact, she seemed to have completely forgotten the thing about killing a man.

"But he might not be," she said. "Suspicious."

He had to like her optimism. And he liked that she wasn't falling to pieces and going all hysterical. Face it—he liked pretty much everything about her.

He wasn't about to crush her hopes. "I'm taking it as a good sign that Xing Guan and his goons didn't come charging back from the trawler right away, hell-bent on hunting down the guy who made their compadre disappear."

Samantha's lips parted a fraction and her green eyes flared and met his. One second they were celery clear, the next dark and sultry like a Caribbean storm. "Yeah."

Suddenly, every cell in his body was remembering every single minute the hijackers hadn't come charging back after him.

She was remembering, too.

Her stormy eyes dipped to his body, and he realized with a start that he'd been sitting there the whole time naked.

"It's a darn good thing they didn't come charging back," she murmured.

Her meaning was impossible to miss.

He had to physically stop himself from reaching for her. *Not* a good idea. For so many reasons.

Besides, he was not about to go all caveman on her again. He was a civilized man who respected women, and by God, he would act like one.

Even if it killed him.

"I should get dressed," he said.

She nodded. And bit her lip.

The elephant nudged him. He ignored it. *Civilized.* "Maybe a quick shower first," he said. "If I'm going to die today, I'd just as soon—"

Her sultry expression morphed to taken aback.

Okay. Black humor not appropriate.

He forced his gaze away from her. "Actually, dried saltwater gets itchy." He brushed some nonexistent grains off his chest, and glanced a few inches farther south. "I'm also a little—" He grimaced. Hell. *TMI, bro.*

She shifted, trying not to look embarrassed. "Sticky?"

He gave her a wry smile. "How'd you guess?"

Her cheeks turned rosy. "Not exactly a guess." She shifted again. "We must really have—" Her words halted abruptly.

Her eyes went big and wide, and she stared at him askance. No. More like *horror-stricken.*

What?

A low buzz started in his head.

His mind swiftly hit rerun and fast-forwarded through what they'd just said. And came to a dead stop on one particular word. His stomach dropped like a twenty-pound weight.

Sticky.

From making love.

He looked down at his cock, and his heart literally froze in his chest for several beats. Then it took off into hyperspace.

There was only one reason they'd both be . . .

"Oh, hell," he breathed. The buzz in his head grew louder. "Oh, fucking hell."

She didn't make a sound. Just sat there staring at him, utterly aghast.

"Please tell me you're on . . ."

Her head shook side to side, in slow motion.

He'd known that. Yesterday they'd both been mindful of using protection. Neither of them was in the market for the kind of long-term commitment that could come of being careless.

How could this have happened? That they'd *both* been so . . .

"I—We—" He tried to think of something to say. Anything. But his tongue couldn't begin to form words. His brain was buzzing too loudly in his skull. Like propellers churning through the—

All at once he snapped to attention.

Holy hell.

He whipped toward the bulkhead and tried to listen. But the adrenaline surging through his ears made them next to useless.

Samantha also sprang to her feet, turning in the same direction. "Is that an engine?"

"Yes. And it's not ours."

She looked over at him, her face lit by a spangle of emotions.

They both spoke in the same instant.

"The Coast Guard!" she exclaimed.

Just as he gritted out, "The Chinese nuclear sub."

23

〉〉〉〉〉〉〉〉〉〉〈〈〈〈〈〈〈〈

Alarm shot through Sam. "God, the sub? You think?"

She'd been wishing so hard the Coast Guard would hurry up and find them, she hadn't even remembered the Chinese submarine he'd just told her about!

Clint's face was grim. "Let's hope not."

To be honest, she hadn't quite believed him when he'd mentioned it. She should have. The man might be guilty of a lot of things, but exaggeration was not one of them.

He closed his eyes and listened intently. "I should be able to tell them apart. But the sounds are different through this hull than what I'm used to. Too muffled."

She didn't even want to imagine what would happen to the ship, to them, if this was the enemy sub and not the Coast Guard. "We need to go up top and see," she said, starting to move.

"Yep." He hastily pulled on his clothes, carefully tucking his leather and ivory totem in the pants pocket, then glanced hesitantly around at their small sanctuary. Their few belongings were scattered around—her duffel and his dry-bag, the limping hammock, the dripping wetsuit.

She halted, realizing he hadn't budged. She followed his gaze. "What?"

He shook his head and bent to retrieve the sat phone. "Nothing." When he rose again, he looked at her. Really looked. His face went all serious and uncertain.

Crap.

It wasn't hard to guess what was on his mind.

She headed him off at the pass, raising a hand like a stop sign. "Clint, don't even go there. There's no need. Besides, we've got bigger problems to deal with right now."

He silently studied her, a frown slowly creasing his brow. "There is a need," he said at length. "But you're right, now is not the time."

Yeah. Hardly surprising he'd agree so quickly. No doubt, he'd conveniently forget to bring it up again.

Whatever.

Well, at least he'd lent lip service to giving a damn. She started for the door again.

There hadn't been time to process the fact that she may actually be pregnant with Clint's baby, let alone figure out the consequences if it were true . . . but she had to admit to a tiny sliver of disappointment that, in the end, Lieutenant Commander Walker was like all the other men in her life— ready to abandon her to her own fate and not want any part of it. Or that of his own child.

The age-old bitterness churned through her stomach and heart like a gristmill of acid.

He caught her arm. "Samantha."

She fought to keep her face neutral. And her eyes dry. "Yeah."

"Whatever you're thinking, you're wrong."

Her chin lifted a fraction. "I don't know what you mean."

His lips thinned. "Honey, I meant what I said. We need to talk about this, and we will."

Uh-huh. "Whatever you say."

His eyes narrowed. Beyond the hull, the sound of the other vessel throttled down to a low purr. He didn't look away from her. She tugged at her arm, wanting to get top-

side to see what was going on out there. Wanting even more
to escape his intense regard. He didn't let go. "Samantha, if
you're pregnant—"

"I'm not," she interrupted, tugging again. She couldn't be.

"And you know this how?"

"I just do."

A muscle in his jaw twitched. The knowledge in his
prickly gaze nearly flayed her. Damn it, she did not need his
sympathy. Did not want his pity. She was fine. *Fine.* "Let
me go."

"I don't know who hurt you this badly, Samantha, but
I'm not him. Remember that." With that, he dropped his
hold on her.

She spun away, terrified she was going to lose it. She bit
down hard on the inside of her cheek and strode to the door.
She didn't want to believe him. Hell, she *didn't* believe him.
She'd slid down that particular rainbow before, and the pot
at the end held only pain and heartache.

She didn't need Clint Walker. She didn't need her
damned father, either. She didn't need *any* man.

She was fine by herself.

She was fine, period.

Just fine.

She wrestled back the ancient demons, took in a deep,
calming breath, and opened the door a crack to check that
the coast was clear, then she took off at a trot for the ventilation shaft hatch.

Clint followed right behind her.

When they got to the chute, reaching into the darkness
for the ladder she suddenly became conscious of the shudder and roll of the ship. At some point during the past tur-
bulent hour, last night's rough waves had returned in full
force. No, they were even bigger now. How had she not
noticed?

She grabbed the bottom rung and started up the vertical
ladder. As always, pitch-blackness swallowed them after
ascending just a few feet. She clung to the cold steel bars,
swinging blindly back and forth as each wave hit and the

ship pitched forward and back. Still, it was almost a relief, because she was forced to concentrate on the climb more than she'd ever concentrated on anything since sitting for her captain's exam.

Clint kept pace just below her. His strong, muscular arms bracketed her as they climbed, so close their bodies constantly brushed. Even his scent surrounded her, masculine, ocean-salty, with a lingering hint of spicy soap from an earlier shower. He was sticking to her like a damn barnacle.

Her teeth clenched in resentment. Why did he even bother? She could take care of herself. *And* the baby, if there was one. His pretending to care just made her angry. She'd rather he'd just be *honest* with her. That she could respect. She had zero illusions about the scope of their relationship. He'd made it very clear from the get-go he'd be history the moment the boat docked in Seattle.

Which was okay with her.

Really.

A potential pregnancy was *her* problem, and she did not want any help from him. She wouldn't take it if he offered. She'd be too vulnerable, too open to the illusion of hope. Hope was such an insidious emotion, she knew all too well. One so easily betrayed . . . most often by one's own naïveté.

She couldn't begin to untangle the knotted skein of old hurts and unbidden hopes that had wrapped around her heart since meeting him. But whenever those feelings arose, a fall was sure to follow.

Hell, no. Been there, done that.

"Here, let me."

His deep whisper vaulted her out of her tangle of thoughts. She realized she'd stopped and was standing utterly still on the last rung before the rim at the top of the shaft. God, how long had she stood there immobile in the complete darkness, fuming over the past and terrified of the future?

"Sorry," she muttered. "Just catching my breath."

He grunted. "Duck." His fingers wrapped around her waist and lifted her to sit on the ledge.

"Would you *stop*?" she snapped, but quietly, mindful of their precarious position.

"No," he said evenly, and hoisted himself up next to her. "So deal with it."

He'd given her back her own damn line. Before she could retort, he carefully raised the hatch. Brilliant ribbons of sunlight streamed in through the two-inch gap as he peered out, illuminating the stubborn square jaw and the hard, determined cast to his dark eyes.

She counted to ten in her mind, praying the Coast Guard was even now boarding *Île de Cœur*.

So she could get away from him.

The man was maddening. No, insufferable. What part of *I do not need you* didn't he get?

"It's a Coast Guard cutter," he murmured.

She bolted to attention and looked. Immediately, her frustration evaporated. *Yes!* There it was, about a mile out, steaming toward them. The distinctive white and red hull stood out against the indigo sea, and a tall black radio array poked up reassuringly into the cloud-dotted sky. On the ship's side were painted the most beautiful words in the English language, *U.S. Coast Guard WMEC-39*.

"Thank God," she breathed. Tears of relief blurred her vision. The past twenty-four hours had been one long nightmare. She'd felt so responsible for her crew, so powerless to help them—or to do anything at all to stop what was happening—and so damn guilty that she wasn't with them, a hostage, suffering the same violence and enduring the same terror they must be feeling. If it hadn't been for Clint's knowledge and steadying influence, she would surely have dissolved and given up.

But now they were saved. Everyone would be safe now.

Without thinking, she threw her arms around him and hugged him tight. Profound relief poured through her body. "Oh, thank God."

The scuttle lowered as he returned her embrace. His strong fingers stroked over her back, and his cheek pressed warmly against her hair. It felt so good, and she felt so se-

cure wrapped in his arms that it took several long moments
for her to remember that hugging him was a bad idea.

Damn.

Rescue was imminent. He'd be leaving her soon.

Her heart squeezed, and she attempted to extract herself
from his embrace. But as she did, his lips found hers. He
kissed her so tenderly she totally lost the will to be strong.

He'd be leaving soon . . .

An unwilling tear trickled down her cheek—*from the
relief of being rescued.* Her crew would soon be safe. And
so would she and Clint. That was all that mattered. Not that
she would never see him again, because she didn't care
about that. She *didn't.*

She felt his thumb brush away the tear. More welled up
at the gentleness of the gesture. *Oh, God.*

Suddenly, she heard familiar voices from the deck. Clint
broke the kiss and quickly turned to lift the scuttle. They
both peeked out, raising their eyes to a commotion on the
gangway above them.

"The crew!" she whispered excitedly, dashing the moisture from her eyes.

Her joy at seeing her friends alive and unharmed froze
like ice in her chest. They were being hustled at gunpoint
from the mess hall out onto the narrow gangway. Their captors were barking orders, clearly agitated.

"What are they doing?" she whispered, watching with a
growing sense of unease. He didn't answer. "Clint?"

"I don't know," he returned, but it sounded to her like he
did know, and was not happy about it. "Is the crew all
there?" he asked.

She did a quick head count. Matty, Johnny and Frank,
Ginger, Jeeter, Carin, and Spiros were in a tight group as
they were herded forward. Bolun stayed one step behind
them, glancing all around. Keeping track of the bad guys?
Or their weapons? She saw exactly when he spotted the
Coast Guard cutter off in the distance. His step faltered for
a millisecond, but a gun barrel shoved into his back, prodding him forward.

A fierce pride in the second mate filled Sam. "Yes," she answered Clint's question. "They're all there."

She saw their wrists had been freed of the duct tape bindings, and their gags had been taken off, too. All except for Lars Bolun's. Still bound and gagged, he was looking a lot worse for wear, but definitely uncowed. As if sensing his defiance, the leader separated him from the rest of the group with a blow to his back with the butt of his machine gun.

"Oh, Lars," she whispered in misery, "I'm so sorry."

"This is not remotely your fault." Clint's voice was low but firm. It wasn't the first time he'd told her that, but the words didn't make her feel any better this time around than they had last time. "He's a good man. You're lucky to have him," Clint murmured.

Her gut knotted as she darted him a sharp look. Wow. Already trying to pass her off to the next guy?

"Yeah," she said, tamping down the inescapable hurt. "He is special."

For a split second she thought about Lars Bolun, actually trying to visualize him as a father for her child. But as good a man as Lars was, the image just knotted her gut even more. It wasn't Lars she wanted.

"I meant, lucky to have him as a second mate," Clint said.

The narrow band of light shining through the hatch opening was like a slash of golden war paint over his mahogany eyes. Beautiful. Impenetrable. It was a hopeless task to decipher Clint Wolf Walker, or his intentions.

Suddenly the sound of a terrified scream ripped her back to the present.

Carin! One of the hijackers had the petite redhead by the hair and was jamming a gun to her temple.

Sam gasped and started to rise. "What's going on?" she whispered, heart in her throat.

Clint put a hand on her shoulder and squeezed, keeping her in place. "I'm not sure. Wait and see."

It was the guard from earlier, from up on the crew deck. He dragged Carin away from the group, his ugly black gun pressed to the back of her head. The others called out and tried to rush to her aid but were quickly subdued and jerked back in the opposite direction. Lars Bolun looked like he was about to go berserk.

The leader strode over, grabbed Bolun's arm, and shoved him toward the stairs to the bridge.

The rest of the crew was herded in the opposite direction, over against the forward quarterdeck rail. They huddled together in a knot, staying as far away as possible from the edge, obviously fearful of what their captors would do next.

Sam was, too.

A stab went through her chest. *Oh, dear lord.* "They wouldn't dare throw them over—" She began in panic.

"No," Clint interrupted. "They need the hostages alive as bargaining chips."

Her alarm didn't subside, but she hoped to God he was right.

He swore softly as the leader forced Bolun up the steep steps of the forecastle ladder and into the bridge. "They're using Carin to make him radio the cutter."

"Why would they want to talk to the Coast Guard?" she asked.

"Good question."

"Do you think they want to negotiate?"

"For what? It's me they want."

She blinked at the reminder.

But all too soon their strategy became clear. Reluctantly, the crew raised their hands and started waving to the other vessel. The hijackers stood behind them, their weapons jabbing them, prodding the crew to show greater enthusiasm.

"Really?" Clint muttered under his breath in disgust. "*That's* your plan?"

Doubtfully, Sam glanced back up at the bridge. But sure enough, Bolun was standing at the helm, speaking into the radio's mike. "So, what, he's telling them everything's okay?" she guessed incredulously. "Will the Coast Guard actually believe him?"

"I hope to hell not."

Sam's heart pounded nervously as they waited. One minute. Two minutes. Three. And still the cutter maintained a steady course toward them. She was just starting to let out a small breath of relief when the red and white vessel began to slow down.

"Oh, no," she whispered, instantly horrified. "No, no, no. Do not do this to us! Please, not this."

About five hundred feet off the starboard quarter, the Coast Guard cutter churned to a stop.

On the poop deck above, her crew's hands halted in mid-wave, suspended in the air like a living tableau.

Clint cursed savagely.

Guns jabbed into flesh. Carin let out a terrified yelp.

On the bridge, Bolun's voice rose animatedly, his furious eyes never leaving the pretty young oiler. The crew resumed waving madly, as if their lives depended on it.

Sam held her breath, praying as she'd never prayed before.

A harrowing second later, the cutter's engines throttled up. The vessel began to move. It went into a wide, steady turn.

And started to steam away.

24

⫸⫷⫸⫷⫸⫷

What the *hell*?

"Oh, my God, they're leaving!" Samantha exclaimed, her voice strangled.

No fucking shit. Clint stared after the retreating ship. It didn't make sense. He knew how seriously the Coast Guard took their homeland security duties, and they were not that easily fooled. Especially after the mayday he'd sent them earlier. No *way* would the cutter be leaving. At least not without first boarding *Île de Cœur* for a look-see to make sure all was well.

Either Bolun had given an Academy Award performance on that radio, or . . .

Ah.

Clint smiled inwardly. He could almost hear Julie Severin, the CIA analyst he'd met on the Russian sub last week, quoting her favorite author, Sun Tzu. *In war, nothing is as it appears to be.*

Maybe the cutter's captain had also studied the *Art of War*.

In which case, the Coast Guard was not going on their

merry way, oblivious to the situation. They were probably falling back to regroup, strategize, and—

Above Clint's head, the scuttle suddenly whooshed up. Bright sunlight almost blinded him. Before he registered what was happening, Samantha jumped up and disappeared through the opening. Her dark silhouette scrambled across the open weather deck and crouch-ran toward the quartet of railroad containers lashed between the midstructure and the bow.

What the fuck? He caught the scuttle just before it slammed down on his head. Even so, he was seeing spots.

Adrenaline shot through his veins. God*damn* it! He should have known she'd go off half-cocked. That woman would be the death of him yet!

He started to vault out after her, but as if alerted, one of the guards up on the quarterdeck jerked his head around and scanned down at the weather deck. And looked right at him. Clint froze like a pillar of salt. Biting back a string of curses, he held absolutely still. For an endless minute the man studied the weather deck with a scowl. Had he seen the scuttle move? Worse, had he seen Samantha? Or heard her running?

From up on the bridge Xing Guan snapped out an order. Reluctantly, the suspicious guard returned his attention to the crew, as Guan prodded Lars Bolun down the ladder to join the others being herded back to their confinement inside the wardroom.

While the guards were occupied, Clint quickly slithered out through the scuttle and took off after Samantha.

He tried not to let his annoyance with her get the better of him. But seriously, what was *wrong* with the woman? She should at least have told him what she was doing, preferably *before* she did it. The problem was, she'd hardly even looked at him for the past half hour. She'd been acting weird ever since—

Yeah.

Okay. Maybe not so weird, all things considered. Truthfully, he'd barely kept his own head together.

A father. Him?

Jesus. The mere thought was overwhelming. Hard enough for him; he couldn't imagine what Samantha must be going through.

But he would not allow his mind—or his heart—to linger in that place of joy . . . and uncertainty. Not until every last one of the crew was safely aboard that Coast Guard cutter. Which *would* be returning for them. Any second now it would be coming about, the Coasties armed and prepared to board *Île de Cœur*, forcibly if necessary, and take down the bastards holding the ship and crew hostage.

No time for distractions. However mind-blowing. However terrifyingly tempting. Right now all he could think about was how best to help the rescue go smoothly. Unfortunately, he had the sinking feeling that whatever Samantha was planning would *not* help at all.

He had to find her. *Before it was too late.*

Clint spotted movement beneath the old trolley car by the railroad containers and veered off in that direction. Sure enough, Samantha was lying on her back under it, fiddling with something on the trolley's undercarriage that he couldn't see.

He did a homerun slide onto the deck and rolled in next to her. "Are you insane?" he asked between clenched teeth as he bumped to a stop against her. "What the *hell* did you think you were—"

"Crap!" she squeaked, nearly dropping whatever it was she held. She rolled around to him, eyes wide. "You! Get out of here! Now!"

That's when he noticed a smoking match in her hand. Clutched in her other hand was the end of a long, makeshift fuse that looked like it had been cobbled together from a bunch of smaller ones. The end was already lit.

Aw, hell.

Thankfully, the burn was slow. *Very* slow. It would take its sweet time igniting whatever it was attached to—two, maybe three minutes at least. He reached out to snatch the fuse away from her.

"Hey!" She batted at his hand, then shoved his shoulder hard enough that he rolled back out from under the trolley. She tucked the fuse carefully up into the undercarriage, then rolled out right behind him.

He sat up, patting his jacket pocket to make sure the sat phone he'd tucked there earlier hadn't fallen out. Its reassuring bulk still rested against his chest.

She shoved at him again, more urgently. "Go! Go! Go!"

He didn't think so. Not until he had answers. "Where does that lead?" he asked, pointing at the dangling fuse. "What the hell are you up to?"

"You're about to find out," she muttered, "and it won't be pretty." She leapt up, grabbed his hand, and forcibly pulled him to his feet. She dragged him behind one of the railroad containers. "Actually, it *will* be pretty spectacular," she amended almost gleefully, peeking around the corner and up to where the tangos were herding the last of the crew through the doors to the mess hall. Her voice flattened. "But not if those scumbags catch us here. We need to get below and hide."

Which told him exactly nothing.

He wanted to strangle her. "Not so fast. Answer my question," he demanded, though he was pretty damned sure he didn't want to know the answer.

She tugged at him impatiently. "Fireworks."

Excuse me?

She started past him toward the cargo chute, but he pulled her back like a yo-yo. "*Fireworks?*"

"Gotta work with what you have," she said, vainly attempting to peel off his grip. "Seriously, Clint, we need to make tracks."

He gritted his teeth. *So much for staying undetected.* When those suckers went off, the tangos would swarm this deck like flies on vomit. Unless, of course, they lit up whatever those detonators were rigged to and they all went up in a blaze of glory.

He darted a quick glance at the receding Coast Guard vessel. Before going below, he needed to make contact so they'd know what was up.

The disabled deck crane stood at the edge of his line of vision, the jawlike claw and steel net swaying in the brisk breeze. He shifted his focus onto the crane's cab. *Yep.* That worked. He tightened his grip on Samantha and took off at a jog.

"Hey! Where are you going? We have to—"

"You promised you'd follow my orders," he reminded her tersely. "Up," he ordered when they reached the king post. She put her fingers on the first handhold. "Quickly."

They scurried up to the crane's glass and steel cabin. As quietly as humanly possible, he eased open the door and boosted them both into the cab. Then he urged her down into the hidden well in front of the operator's seat, under the control panel, as far back as she would fit. If the hijackers found him, he wanted Samantha completely out of sight.

He silently pulled the door closed, latched it, and slid onto the floor next to her. His heart pounded like a bitch. He hoped to God he'd made the right choice. The ventilation chute would probably have been safer.

Squished into the cramped space under the console, she blinked out at him as if he were sprouting horns. "What the hell, Walker?" she asked, echoing his own earlier incredulity.

Instead of answering, he produced the sat phone.

Instant comprehension filled her face. He liked that about her. She might be a bit impetuous—okay, a lot—but she was also a damn quick study. Under normal circumstances that could be a very intriguing combination. He hoped he lived long enough to test the possibilities.

He punched the phone's "on" button just as the first volley of fireworks blasted out from under the trolley. He looked up to the cab's windows as he heard the rockets whistle out across the water. *Bang!* A spangle of red and blue lit up the air beyond the glass, then drifted downward in a glittering firefall of patriotic colors.

Muffled shouts started, then got abruptly louder as the quarterdeck mess doors smacked open.

"Damn. I wish I could see their reaction," Samantha murmured.

"No, you really don't," he returned, pressing the phone to his ear and listening for the connection. "Come on, come on." Out at sea, it could take endless minutes to find a signal. They did *not* need the delay.

Another high-pitched whistle sounded, and an explosion of gold burst through the sky. The accompanying metallic clang of gunstocks and boots against ladder rungs told him the tangos were rushing down to the weather deck.

The frustrating *click-click-click* of the sat phone searching for a signal continued in his ear. *Come on, come on.*

"Whatever happens, stay exactly where you are. Under cover," he said, turning to look at her. He wanted his expression to tell her how fucking serious he was about the order. "I mean it, Samantha. *Whatever* happens."

His severity must have penetrated. Her eyes met his and she went a little pale. She nodded. "Okay."

"Swear?"

"Swear," she whispered.

The clump of boots thundered across the deck straight toward them, gaining speed and volume as they got closer and closer. The crane was right behind the trolley.

She swallowed. He could tell she was terrified of what could happen next, but was determined not to show it. His heart melted completely. *Damn.*

He leaned over and tenderly kissed her, touching her jaw with the very tips of his fingers as he lifted. "You know I'm falling in love with you, don't you?" he murmured.

He didn't know who was more shocked by the unexpected admission, her, or himself. Her lips parted, and her green eyes filled with an emotion he couldn't begin to decipher.

Just above the crane, another volley of fireworks lit up the sky. Scarlet, like blood. On deck, the bootfalls skidded to a halt. Angry Chinese exclamations split the air as glittering gems of liquid red rained down the windows of the cab, painting streaks of crimson onto the shadows inside. It was poignantly beautiful.

As was the woman staring at him, speechless.

He softly cleared his throat. *Okay, then.* "Awkward," he sang under his breath, his voice too gritty to be heard above the bursts of fireworks and the shouts of the men who had splintered off in every direction, searching in earnest for whomever had set off the display.

Holy hell. Falling in love with her? What had possessed him to say such a thing? And *now*, of all the ridiculously inappropriate times!

A dial tone interrupted his mortification, giving him a much-needed task to drag his attention from his idiocy. "About fucking time." His fingers flew over the keys, punching in the number he'd memorized for the Coast Guard station in Kodiak.

"This is Coas—"

He interrupted the dispatcher's greeting before it was out of her mouth. Keeping his voice low and his words distinct, he said, "Kodiak Station, this is Lieutenant Commander Walker again, from commercial vessel *Île de Cœur*. Please advise your cutter *WMEC-39* they are not, repeat *not*, under attack. The explosions coming from *Île de Cœur* are harmless fireworks, repeat fireworks. Please contact them immediately with this information."

Another rocket went off as she replied crisply, "Roger that, Lieutenant Commander Walker. Stand by for a patch-in, sir. There's someone waiting to speak with you."

Clint's brows rose. "Who?" But he was speaking to static. It had to be Washington. On the radio earlier he'd requested they apprise his boss of the situation. Maybe the admiral was calling with good news—for instance that he'd finally managed to get a requisition for a helo past the bean counters.

Streaks of silver and blue glitter spilled over the cab.

From the phone, a cricket chirped in his ear, followed by a woman's voice, "Lieutenant Commander Clint Walker?" She sounded like she was calling from inside a tin can long, long ago in a galaxy far, far away. He didn't recognize the voice.

He frowned, tempted to raise the volume of his own in answer, but he didn't dare. "Yes, ma'am," he said.

Below, he could hear the tangos close in on the trolley, yelling dire threats at the person they thought was hidden beneath it setting off the firecrackers. The last thing he wanted was to tip them off they were wrong.

"I'm in-flight on a C-2 Greyhound," the woman on the phone continued in a raised voice. "I can't really hear you, Walker, but I'm aware of your present situation and the dispatcher assures me you're there, so I'll just talk and you listen." She muttered a girly curse that raised his brows. "Okay, click your signal button or tap the mouthpiece or something if you understand."

Who the hell *was* this woman? A C-2 Greyhound was a high-priority carrier onboard delivery plane used to fly to—or from—an aircraft carrier, but she was obviously not someone familiar with military protocol. He pulled the phone from his ear, examined the keypad, and pressed a button that had a bell shape on it, which produced a short mechanical tone. He put the phone back and listened to her with one ear and to the tangos with the other.

"Great," the woman shouted. "My name is DeAnne Lovejoy, and I work for the U.S. State Department. I've been sent to try and facilitate—"

Clint saw red. And it wasn't fireworks. *State Department?*

Were they *kidding*? Not a helo. Not a SEAL team. A goddamn *bureaucrat*?

Samantha's worried eyes glanced at him hopefully. He gave his head an angry shake. She looked away, but not before he saw the haunted shadows return.

"—understand the hijackers are Chinese? Tap the button once for yes, twice for no."

What he really wanted to do was smash the phone into a million pieces to show what he thought of this useless conversation. Instead he forced himself to calmly press the call button once. His grandfather would have been proud.

"Excellent. And you believe they are security service, or military?"

He pressed it again, swallowing his impatience. He'd already gone over all this with the Coast Guard! Typical that the bureaucrats didn't trust intel from a military source. That explained a lot about the state of intelligence gathering in this country.

Outside the cab, the air went abruptly and eerily silent. Clint whipped around. The tangos must have stormed the trolley and halted the explosion of fireworks. They wouldn't be happy they hadn't found the culprit setting them off. He itched to peek over the rim of the window.

Meanwhile the woman droned on. "—am aware of what has given rise to this incident, and I'll do everything in my power to resolve the situation favorably."

He returned his attention to her and gritted his teeth. Situation? *Incident?* That's what the State Department called one man dead, seven brutalized hostages, and two people evading capture like rats in a—

"Wait," the woman on the phone shouted. "I'm getting something for you from the Coast Guard vessel." There was a pause, then she said, "*WMEC-39* has received and understood your message. They've come about, and are closing in. The captain says he'll standby for my—"

Suddenly there was a loud pop coming from the forward deck, and a whistling whine whizzed out over the sea.

A surge of instant, icy horror flooded Clint's veins. He knew that sound. Swearing viciously, he flung the phone aside and lurched up to the window, searching for a telltale tracer. There! A glistening thread spun through the sky from *Île de Cœur*'s bow in a graceful arc toward the approaching Coast Guard cutter.

Oh.

Shit.

In dismay, Clint watched the end of the thread explode. Three seconds later, the cutter's bridge burst into a fireball of flame.

25

‖‖‖‖‖⁄⁄⁄⁄⁄⁄

Sam grabbed for the sat phone before it hit the deck and shattered. "What's happening?" she cried, pulling it against her chest like a recovered football.

"*Fuck!*" Clint growled, and ducked down, spinning away from the window. His face was etched with a volatile mix of fury, disbelief, and a powerful emotion she'd never seen before.

"Clint, you're scaring me."

His eyes clashed with hers. The look in them scared her even more. "They blew it up," he gritted out.

Her lips parted. She tried to sense the feel of an explosion somewhere on board . . . but nothing had changed. "Blew what up?" she asked in confusion.

"The cutter."

"*What?*"

"Well, the cutter's bridge. Obviously one antitank rocket isn't enough to blow up a ship of that size. But taking out the wheelhouse—"

"Sends a hell of a message," she completed, stunned that the hijackers would up the stakes this high. She stared at him. The question was, who was the message meant for? •

He swiped a hand across his mouth, then muttered, "Shit," and jumped up once again to look through the window.

"Get down!" she said anxiously, tugging furiously at his pant leg. "Are you nuts? They'll see you!"

He let out a grim laugh. "I doubt that. Things are about to get very—"

The last word was drowned out by a deafening explosion coming from the forward deck. The crane rattled and shook under them. She grabbed on to the console base with white knuckles until the worst of the shuddering stopped.

"My God!" She leapt up to join him, shaking like a leaf, and not from the shock waves. "What the hell was that?"

Below, the hijackers stood as motionless as the ashen citizens of Pompeii, apparently as stunned as she was.

"And then there were five," he said, sounding grimly self-satisfied.

She glanced at him but was momentarily distracted when the crane's metal claw and net swung past the window. The wind had really picked up. "What?"

"Remember I told you I sabotaged one of the rocket launchers I found on *Eliza Jane*?"

Right. She swallowed a sudden sense of dread as the Chinese commander snapped out of it and started barking orders, drawing her attention back to the deck below. At the shouts, the other hijackers sprang into action. One went forward to check on the men who'd been firing the rocket launcher, another surged up the ladder to *Île de Cœur*'s own bridge, presumably to monitor radio traffic, just as the man guarding the crew slammed out of the mess hall, teeth bared and machine gun clutched at the ready.

Well, better late than never.

Five, Clint had said. So where was the fifth guy?

"Hello? *Hello*?" a teeny-tiny feminine voice said from somewhere nearby, barely audible. "Are you there? Walker, what's happening?"

Sam started, realizing she was still holding the sat

phone, and apparently whomever Clint had been speaking with was still on the line. She pulled the phone away from her chest where she'd had a death grip on it, and grasped Clint's bicep. "Your friend sounds worried."

Hell, so was she. Clint seemed to think this development was a good thing, but she didn't. Those men down there were angry. *Really* angry.

Clint barely glanced at the phone she held out to him with a tremulous hand, but did a double take at her, ending with a death glare when he realized she was standing next to him. He put a hand to her shoulder and shoved her down below the window. "Goddamn it, Samantha!" He made a noise of frustration. "Do you *want* them to see you?" He ignored the phone.

She barely refrained from gritting her teeth. Had she not just said the same thing to him?

"Hi," she said into the mouthpiece, focusing her energy on trying to get them out of there instead. "We're fine," she told the woman on the other end. "For the moment. But Lieutenant Commander Walker is, um, busy."

There was a pause. "Doing what, exactly?" came the clipped response.

Sam blinked, her fear temporarily abated by the woman's tone. "This is Captain Samantha Richardson, commander of Île de Cœur. To whom am I speaking, exactly?"

Sam listened as the woman impatiently gave her name and went through her State Department credentials. Call her suspicious, but seriously, this woman could be anyone. How did the Coast Guard dispatcher know DeAnne Lovejoy actually was who she claimed to be?

She also noticed the background sounds on the phone had gone silent.

"What happened to all the noise?" Sam asked Ms. Lovejoy warily, and lowered herself to the floor, keeping her own voice at a whisper.

"Pardon?"

"The engine noise. You had to shout before when you were talking to Lieutenant Commander Walker."

There was shuffling on the other end of the line. "We landed. On the *George Washington*. Look—"

She was cut off by the blare of a loudspeaker announcing an all-clear-on-deck in standard navy lingo. Then a youthful male voice cut excitedly over hers that the captain was expecting Ms. Lovejoy in the wardroom, ma'am, ASAP, and something more Sam couldn't make out.

At that, all doubts evaporated from her mind in a cloud of relief. The USS *George Washington* was a Nimitz-class aircraft carrier stationed out of the navy base at Yokosaka, Japan. *Île de Cœur* had crossed paths with her several times on the leviathan's patrol circuit around the Pacific Rim.

Wow. Had someone actually sent the navy out to rescue her ship? Her father maybe? Had the Coast Guard notified Richardson Shipping and—

"Please, Captain Richardson, tell me what's going on out there," DeAnne Lovejoy interrupted her thoughts, clearly alarmed. "I'm getting reports that both you and the Coast Guard are under attack." The woman's concern was palpable, even over the phone.

"Yes, but probably not how you think," Sam said, still keeping her voice as low as possible. The sounds of the antitank rocket explosions had subsided, and she could no longer hear the hijackers' shouts. She shot Clint a questioning look, but he just returned another frown, so with an eye roll she tucked herself back under the console to please him, and quickly outlined for DeAnne Lovejoy what had transpired over the past few minutes, then answered the State Department officer's few precise questions concerning the takeover and the crew.

"I'm worried about retaliations," Sam told her. "Because of Clint's sabotaged antitank launcher. Damn, I was an idiot for setting off those fireworks. I thought— Oh, hell, I wasn't thinking," she lamented with an edge of despair. "I saw the cutter turning about and knew I had to get it to turn back any way I could. I never dreamed something like this would happen."

"Who could know?" Ms. Lovejoy returned, not unkindly. "You did what you thought was best. No one will blame you for that."

She gave a soft snort. "Yeah. Tell that to my father," she muttered. Not that it mattered what the old bastard thought. Sam harbored no delusions. Her job was already lost, and with it any interest she held in her father's eyes.

"Your father? Jason Richardson?"

The query surprised her. "Yes." Could she be wrong? *Had* it been her father who'd pulled strings to call in the navy? "Have you spoken to him?" She cringed inwardly, hating how she sounded. *Needy.* Like she actually gave a damn.

"Uh, no," DeAnne Lovejoy said, but with a circumspection that raised a red flag immediately in Sam's mind.

"But somebody else did." It wasn't a question.

Sam heard a puffed-out breath.

"Yes."

Her respect for the woman increased a little. "What did he say?" Sam asked, sitting up straighter. "He must be worried." She grimaced. *Fool.* "About the ship, I mean."

Ms. Lovejoy cleared her throat delicately. "Of course he's worried. But he has the utmost faith in your abilities."

Sam understood why Ms. Lovejoy worked in the diplomatic corps.

"That's a lie and we both know it," Sam said, deflecting the hurt before it could twist inside her even more. "Anyway, I'm worried, too. About the crew. That crazy Xing Guan has already killed one of them, and—"

Suddenly the cab door swung open with a loud smack. She whipped her gaze up.

Omigod.

A gun was pointing straight at her. Held by the missing hijacker—the fifth man.

Her heart seized. She dropped the phone.

The douche bag smiled.

She whispered, "Oh, crap."

26

ⱵⱵⱵⱵⱵⱵⱵⱵⱵⱵ

Before the man had a chance to shoot, or even blink, Clint was on him. He'd been half expecting the guy.

He lashed out with a crushing slash to the man's wrist, sending the pistol flying, then followed that with a combination of a chop to his throat and a powerful fist to his temple. The man went down like a rock, landing in a heap at Samantha's feet.

She jerked her shoes away from him with a croaked curse. "Holy cr—!" Then darted a look at Clint, her expression a volatile mix of stunned and wonder.

He dragged the tango's unconscious body fully inside the cab, and in a fluid motion snapped the guy's neck. "Now they're down to four," he told her. "Time to make our move."

"Wh-what?"

Her eyes were huge. With abject horror. At him, without doubt.

What the hell. Now she knew who he really was.

He picked up the dead man's weapon. It was an old-school SIG P226 Navy—formerly standard issue to U.S.

Navy SEALS—and he wondered grimly how the man had acquired it. Now he felt even less remorse about killing the bastard. He slid the weapon into his waistband next to his own. The serial number could be traced and the owner's unit notified.

Clint peered around the cab door. "Come on," he urged, beckoning Samantha with a hand, but he couldn't quite meet her eyes. "It's clear."

Her bottom lip was clamped between her teeth, and her face was pale as sea foam. She wordlessly scooted out from under the control panel, carefully avoiding touching the dead man.

"We need to go fast," Clint warned, preparing to climb down to the deck at top speed. But he paused for a split second and studied her. "You going to be okay?"

She nodded. He could see she was struggling. But to her credit she wasn't losing it. And the hell of it was, she still seemed to trust him. He didn't have time to analyze the emotions that set to roiling in the pit of his stomach—and clutching at his heart.

And she could be pregnant with his baby.

Jesus. He really couldn't think about this now.

After a final check to be sure the four remaining operators still had their attention elsewhere, he launched himself down the ladder, half sliding like one of Ma Bell's finest, and landing in a squat on the balls of his feet. He slid in next to the king post and blended, glancing up to signal Samantha. She was already halfway down.

Together they crouch-ran between the railroad containers and made their way back to the ventilation shaft. He lifted the scuttle, and she slipped into the yawning opening without hesitation.

He slid in after her and grasped her arm before she could start down the ladder. "Wait." He lowered the hatch and pulled her next to him on the narrow ledge. The complete darkness of the narrow space enveloped them like a coffin; the only sound was her shallow breathing. He desperately wanted to put his arms around her. He didn't.

"Samantha, what I did just now—"

"I know," she cut in, her voice sounding hollow. "You had no choice."

She was right. It had been them or the enemy. But that didn't make killing any more palatable. She must think he was a monster.

She'd be right about that, too.

Still. In the end, what difference did it make what she thought of him?

He'd told her he was falling in love with her, and damned if that wasn't true—much to his own astonishment. But they were from different worlds and different ends of the earth. It would never work, even if she would want it to. Which, it seemed pretty clear, she didn't.

And he wasn't so sure he did, either. They both had too many issues to overcome. And him snapping a guy's neck right in front of her? That wouldn't exactly bring out the warm fuzzies in her feelings for him.

"What are we going to do now?" she asked.

The roll of the ship brushed their bodies against each other, and when they touched he felt a jolt to the soles of his feet. He glanced her way, even though it was too dark to see her. But he felt her presence with every one of his other senses. In the air around her he could smell the womanly scent of her skin . . . and a musky hint of their lovemaking. He heard her soft intake of breaths, and the way her throat closed around her words when she spoke. He even felt her dismay at him—or was it disgust?—like a living thing crawling over his flesh.

He shook himself, pulled his wits together, and inwardly berated himself for getting so distracted. They weren't out of danger. Far from it. He needed to concentrate on survival first. There'd be time enough to think about this stuff if they made it off this tub alive.

"We've got two choices," he said. "The smart thing would be to stay in hiding until either the tangos track us down or someone comes to our rescue."

The thought hung uneasily in the air between them.

"Or?" she said at length.

"We go on the offensive. Try to free the crew and take back the ship ourselves."

He felt her stir. This had been her objective from the start. "You think we can do it?"

With just four enemy remaining, the odds were getting better, but they still weren't great. Two handguns against an assortment of assault rifles and submachine guns was hardly an even match. Particularly as the enemy still held the trump card—the crew.

But the thing that bothered him most was, he couldn't shake the memory of those missing detonators.

"What did the State Department woman say?" he asked instead of answering her. "Are they sending help?"

Samantha sighed softly. "No idea. Ms. Lovejoy didn't have a chance to say much. Her plane had just landed on the *George Washington*. That's an aircraft carrier."

He nodded, surprised, then realized she couldn't see him. "Yeah. I did an investigation on her once."

"Unfortunately," she said, "that's when all hell broke loose and we got cut off."

He thought about the implications—and sanity—of the State Department sending an officer to negotiate with Xing Guan's black-ops team. Christ, and the navy had balked over merely sending a helo to pick him up. Now they were diverting a whole goddamn aircraft carrier? He would definitely have an I-told-you-so for the bean counters.

Frankly, the move smacked of an official cover-your-ass. The media must have somehow gotten wind of the story. Like CNN media. A cargo ship being held for ransom might make the Alaska news, but a Coast Guard cutter hit by a Chinese PF98 antitank rocket launcher would capture international headlines.

Damn, he wished he knew what was going on out there.

The PF98's rocket hit hadn't been powerful enough to sink the cutter, but the explosion on the *WMEC 39*'s bridge had no doubt mucked up its controls enough to render the vessel dead in the water. Rescue would not be coming from that quarter anytime soon unless they came over in rubber rafts. Maybe the aircraft carrier was the closest military ship available to come. But that still didn't explain the State Department woman.

"You still have the sat phone?" he asked. He might risk another call to get a sitrep.

"Yes, but the housing cracked when I dropped it. I don't know if it still works. I'm sorry," she said, sounding ticked at herself.

Damn. "Well, at least they know we're still alive." *For now.* "Any idea of the carrier's position?"

There was another long moment of silence. "I'm trying to remember if it was listed on our charts." Her voice thinned wearily. "But it feels like a lifetime since the last time I looked at them."

Wasn't that the truth. Hell, maybe even literally. A growing sense of unease tingled Clint's nerve endings. The imminent arrival of the carrier would complicate things considerably, maybe even force the Chinese's hand.

"Never mind. They know where we are," he said.

"So they'll launch planes from the carrier to come help us right away," she ventured optimistically. "Won't they?"

"I'm sure they already have." How much those planes could do from the air was another matter entirely.

"And if that Chinese submarine really is out there," she continued, "it won't dare interfere with us now."

She sounded relieved.

He wasn't so sure.

Though by no means secret information, the general public was largely unaware that U.S. Navy SEAL operations were launched not just from helicopters and surface vessels, but more and more from submarines. There'd been evidence for a few years now that the Chinese were building up their own small but well-trained spec-ops force equivalent to the SEALs. The plans in Clint's possession proved they were aggressively pursuing undersea military strategies. He'd be shocked if they weren't employing their submarines to launch missions, too.

Clint was acutely aware that Xing Guan's mission had not changed. His orders were still to recover those same top secret plans or destroy the microcard and him along with it.

Hell, Guan's operators wouldn't even need to use those missing detonators. Chinese swimmers could be under the water right now, attaching explosive limpets to the hull of *Île de Cœur*. Problem solved.

"It would be an act of war to attack us," he agreed neutrally with Samantha.

However, if Chinese SEALs sank *Île de Cœur* with the black-ops squad still on it, who would know? To the world, it would just be another random act of terrorism, this time taking the terrorists down with it.

Not exactly a comforting state of affairs for him and Samantha. Or for the captured crew.

Something in his tone must have belied the direction of his thinking. "We'll be fine. Right?" she asked anxiously. "We just need to hold out until the carrier gets here."

"Let's hope so."

He felt her turn toward him in the dark. He wished to hell he could see her face.

"What are you keeping from me?" she asked, voice tense.

"Nothing," he said. No sense in both of them worrying.

"Goddamn it, Clint. Do *not* start lying to me now." The intensity of her low-spoken admonishment made him wince. He should have known he couldn't bullshit her.

"All right," he reluctantly said. "I'm thinking of those missing detonators." He didn't even want to consider the submarine scenario.

"The det—? Oh." Her last syllable was a strangled exhale. "Detonators. How could I have forgotten?"

"I expect you had other things on your mind."

"My God. You really do think they plan to blow us up."

He figured the statement was rhetorical.

Anyway, they'd lingered long enough in this precarious spot. "We need to move," he said, and started to scoot over to the ladder, to get her down from here to somewhere safer.

Her hand grasped his arm. "Clint. What are we going to do?"

"They're going to try like hell to find me so they can recover that data card. You can't be anywhere close to me when they do."

The sentence hung crackling in the air between them.

"You mean *if*."

"Right."

She was smart enough to know he intended to let them find him, if that was the only way to save her and the ship.

"Oh, no," she said, her grip tightening. "You said we're going to rescue the crew."

"Not we. I." How many times did he have to repeat this? "You need to find somewhere protected—"

"*No*. Have you not learned a damned thing about me yet? I am not going to sit idly by and let you—"

"Have *you* not learned a damn thing?" he shot back without thinking. "Because if you ask me, it didn't work out all that well last time you took matters into your own hands instead of listening to—"

She inhaled sharply. You could almost slice the hurt in the sound. "That's not fair."

Shit. He clamped his mouth shut. *No. Probably not*. But he was frustrated as hell. His game was totally off, and no matter what he did, things were only getting worse and worse. And yeah, sorry, it *was* her fault.

No, not because of the crazy things she did. But because of his own inability to think about anything but her. First about getting her under him, and now about—

Hell. His concentration was shot, his judgment seriously impaired, and his decisions thus far had landed them in nothing but a fucking huge goatfuck.

And if he didn't do something pronto, he may be about to get them blown up, too.

He needed to get away from her. So he could do his god-damn job. "This isn't reconnaissance anymore, Samantha," he said quietly. "To free the crew it'll be real bullets and

real blood. I can't— No, I *won't* risk you and the—" He
swallowed the word just in time.

She went absolutely still.

Three heartbeats went by. *Damn, damn, damn.*

Then he felt her warm breath on his cheek.

"You don't understand," she murmured in a barely audible whisper. "If anything happens to you, I won't care
what happens to me."

27

////////////

Clint's heart stalled on a breath of surprise.

Of all the things she might have said . . .

He gave up the fight and turned his face to nestle against hers, his nose and cheek brushing tenderly against her skin. "Baby," he whispered, the echo of longing he heard in his own endearment nearly breaking his heart. *This was so damn unfair.* "You don't mean that."

She reached for him in the utter darkness and put her arms around him, pulling him close. She didn't seem to care that they were perched precariously on a narrow ledge atop a three-story ventilation shaft.

"Yes," she whispered back. "I do mean it. I just . . . I needed you to know that."

"Honey—"

He felt her eyes close, her lashes tickling his cheek. "Don't worry," she said softly. "I won't take any chances. I want to live. But I want you to live, too, and I thought . . ."

"Believe me," he quietly assured her, "I have no intention of dying." She'd given him a vision of a future he'd never imagined for himself. He wanted to see if it was possible. If *they* were possible. Despite their differences and the not inconsiderable obstacles in their path.

She hugged him a little tighter. "We're going to make it through this, Clint. *All* of us. We have to."

He slid his fingers through her hair and cradled her head in his palm, holding her in place to brush his lips over hers. "I hope to hell we do," he murmured. "Because—"

Before he could say any more, her mouth covered his and she kissed him. He knew what she was doing, and he loved her even more for it, but she didn't need to give him an out. He knew what he wanted. More clearly than ever.

Her. He wanted her with him. He also wanted the baby she might be carrying. And if she wasn't, he wanted to make one.

They opened to each other, and their tongues met in an aching meld of need. The kiss was long and deep and bittersweet, and filled with emotions he'd never felt from a woman before. Emotions he'd never felt from himself before. Feelings he'd despaired of ever knowing, and which would take a lifetime to fully explore.

His heart swelled with joy at the discovery . . . and all the while it twisted painfully. If he was right about the Chinese sub out there, they might never get the chance to know that future.

Unfair? No. *Unacceptable.*

Anger swirled through him. *Hell*, no. He had *not* found the love of his life just to lose her. Not if he had anything to say about it. Which he did.

It was time to get back to his own mission. Get that microcard to D.C. any way he must. Then tell his boss he was done with fieldwork for good. No more lies. No more bullets. No more cloak and dagger, ever.

He wanted to move on with his life. Take the plunge into the unknown challenges of falling in love.

With Samantha.

He forced himself to pull away from her. "We have to get off this ship," he said resolutely, the weight of his unshared suspicions urgent in his mind. He unwrapped her arms from around him, holding her by the wrists so she couldn't fight him. "But not without the crew. There should only be one man guarding them while the others are distracted by the launcher explosion. I'm going up to free them."

"You mean we."

"*Alone*, Samantha."

She didn't resist his grip on her. He couldn't see her eyes, but her voice was firm and steady when she shook her head and said, "We've been through this. I'm coming with you."

He pushed out a sigh. God knew, the last thing he wanted was to place her in harm's way. But he also realized with dead certainty that he couldn't stop her.

"No," he said evenly. "You're not. You're going to hijack *Eliza Jane*."

28

‖‖‖‖∨⁄⁄⁄⁄⁄

Be careful what you wish for.

It was a hard-learned lesson Sam would do well to re-member in the future.

Just like in the movies, she and Clint had synchronized their watches, then set in motion their quickly devised plan to free the crew. She was now standing just inside the small portside door on the ro-ro deck—the same door Clint had come back in through this morning—anxiously awaiting the designated time to jump down onto the trawler. Clint had told her to give him a five-minute head start. But he'd refused to tell her what he planned to do with those five minutes. Which to her meant only one thing—she wouldn't approve, and he knew it.

When they'd parted earlier, their last kiss had been heartbreakingly sweet. But afterward, the savage look on his face as she'd watched him turn to go had sent chills down her spine.

Was he planning to do something else, something reck-less and life threatening, before heading up to free the crew?

She had a sick feeling he was. And the roiling knot of tension in the pit of her stomach told her it had something to do with those missing detonators.

God. Nervous wasn't even in the same universe as what she was feeling right now. For herself, but mostly for him.

Unbidden, her gaze sought the place on the deck floor where she and Clint had come together in a wild conflagration of relief and passion earlier. Heat seeped up her throat to suffuse her cheeks, and her mind flooded anew with uncertainty.

She eased out an unsteady breath and put a tentative hand to her abdomen. Could there really be a new life growing inside her? She knew it had been less than a day, weeks too early to tell, so conjecture was futile. But the question wouldn't let her alone. Ever since their realization, it had gnawed at the edges of her mind, like a dog with a bone.

What on earth would she do if there was a baby? How would she take care of it? Hell, how would she take care of *herself*, with no job now, and no family to help her?

Would Clint help? Dare she hope? Dare she trust?

Before, she'd been so certain he wasn't interested in anything long-term with her. That he didn't even want to continue their relationship, let alone anything as serious as having a child with her. But now? She was not so sure. Hadn't he said he was falling in love with her?

And when they parted, he'd seemed so . . . different.

It was almost ironic. Before this, he'd been relentlessly macho and overprotective of her, determined to relegate her to a strictly passive role, making her hide herself away while he took on the enemy single-handed and faced the danger solo. He'd soundly rebuked her each time she'd done anything to help him, successful or not. It wasn't so much that he didn't trust her judgment, but that he had an outdated sense of what a man had to be to live up to his own self-worth. Nonsense, of course. But there you go.

But now, just when it seemed he might have changed his mind about letting her into his personal life, possibly even wanting a true relationship with her, he'd also done a one-eighty and thrust her into the middle of a perilous plan that could easily get her killed, and indeed, he had assigned her a part in the rescue that all their lives depended upon—the crew's, hers, and Clint's, as well.

Did it mean he had finally started to let go of his macho sense of control and trust her to take care of him, too, at least in this?

Or was it just that he'd had no choice . . . ?

She squeezed her eyes shut, battling desperately to embrace the hope and ignore the fear that gripped her heart. Fear of being wrong about him. About his feelings for her.

Fear of being betrayed.

Again.

How could she allow herself to trust him? To entrust him with her fragile heart . . . ?

Did *she* have a choice?

For it was impossible to deny her growing feelings for him any longer. It had gone far beyond a crush, or sexual infatuation. This was the real thing, and it terrified her. She simply couldn't imagine spending a lifetime without him. Without the feel of his body next to hers. Without the tenderness in his eyes as he looked at her. Without the overwhelming security of knowing he'd be there for her, come what may. Every night. Every day.

But *would* he be there for her?

To trust, or not to trust. It all came down to that.

She dragged her gaze up from the deck and the aching reminder of their lovemaking. And of the momentous decision they would both soon have to make . . . assuming they survived.

Which brought her round to the present.

She checked her watch and straightened like a shot. Only sixty seconds left before she was to make her jump.

Turning back to the crew door, she twisted the wheel lock and pulled it open a slight crack. The red glint of the sun flooded over her as she peeked out, along with the cold rush of nervousness. She scanned *Eliza Jane*'s empty deck.

Long black shadows danced across the boards in time to the pitch and roll of the waves. The small fishing trawler swung away from the larger cargo ship, pulling the mooring lines taut, then swung back to bump against *Île de Cœur*'s hull with a squeal of rubber fenders. The trawler still looked deserted. Sam was ninety-nine percent sure it *was* deserted. But that one percent uncertainty had her sweating like a Coke can despite the frigid wind that whistled through the narrow crack lifting the ends of her hair.

The rescue's success—and possibly her own life— hinged on whether in the chaos that still reigned after her fireworks display, and the attack on the Coast Guard cutter, and especially the unexpected rocket launcher explosion, the hijackers who remained alive had forgotten they'd left *Eliza Jane* unguarded.

It was a huge risk to take. With enormous consequences for being wrong.

What would she do if confronted by the same choice Clint had faced in the crane cab? Her pulse went heavy at the thought.

Driving the fishing trawler she could definitely handle.

But killing another human being . . . She didn't know how Clint had snapped that man's neck with such calm deliberation. But if there was a guard hidden on the trawler, once again she'd have little choice.

It seemed like all the crossroads she was meeting in her life suddenly had roadblocks across all but one path. Like she'd lost control of her own destiny.

She swallowed, slid a hand into her jacket pocket, and touched the loaded semiautomatic pistol Clint had insisted she take with her, along with the cracked sat phone. He'd also had her fetch and bring her small laptop containing copies of the ship's logs and her captain's logbook.

The barrel of the gun was smooth and hard, the trigger an elegant curve against her fingers. This choice, if difficult, at least was clear. For Frank and Ginger and Smitty and Bolun and the rest of her crew, she would do whatever it took to set them free.

She looked at her watch again. Thirty-three seconds to go.

She glanced over at the long rope ladder the hijackers had used last night to reach the trawler. It was still hanging from the rail over the side of the ship, but rolled up, mocking her. Clint hadn't wanted her to use it, despite its convenience. Getting to it, taking the time to unroll it, the noise it would make, she'd be too exposed and vulnerable.

He was right, but it irritated her that she'd be forced to play Tarzan instead.

The line Clint had used earlier was still tied to the door's sturdy metal wheel lock. She tugged and tested the knot holding it there. Still tight and secure. Just as it had been two minutes ago.

Slipping on a pair of leather work gloves, she grasped the length of line, worried she might not have the strength to lower herself, hand over hand, the thirty feet or so down to *Eliza Jane*'s deck—without either tumbling into the Bering Sea, getting squished between the two vessels' hulls, or splatting like a bug on the trawler's scarred wooden weather deck. She didn't even want to think about the possibility of accidental impalement on all the fishing equipment scattered around.

Suppressing a groan, she glanced at her watch. Fourteen seconds.

In the few remaining moments, she went over the simple plan again in her mind: rappel onto the trawler, cast off the lines lashing it to *Île de Cœur*, do a search of the vessel to be sure she was alone on board, then station herself on the bridge and be ready to fire up the engines and take off as soon as Clint arrived with the crew.

Assuming he wasn't killed trying to free them.

No. Not thinking about that, either.

Her heart pounded hard in her chest as she watched the numbers tick down on her watch.

Three, two, one, *go*!

Pushing the door open all the way, she quickly sat, grasped the line tightly in her hands, and without letting herself think, shoved off the edge and swung in a tight arc out over the sea. Her shoulders protested taking her weight, and her hands stung with the effort of hanging on. As she swung back against the hull, she twisted her body around and lifted her legs to plant her feet firmly on the icy cold metal hull as she met it.

No going back now.

She hung suspended for several seconds, listening over the splash and suck of the ocean waves for shouts of alarm from above—or below. None came.

With a deep, shaky breath, she began to let herself down the rope. It wasn't pretty, but she made it down to about seven or eight feet above the level of the trawler's deck. If she went any lower, she wasn't sure she'd make it over the rail and the jumble of crab traps, gutting tables, and other assorted things between her and the small open area of deck. She halted, clinging awkwardly to the rope, waiting with aching muscles for the motion of the waves to cause the two ships to kiss hulls so she could make the final push-and-drop to the trawler's deck. If she jumped too soon, she'd miss the trawler and end up as a human sandwich pressed between the two vessels. Jump too late, and she'd miss the retreating deck and land in the icy sea.

She dangled like a fish on a line, praying, waiting an eternity for the trawler to swing out and away, then slowly pitch and bob back toward her. Her arm muscles screamed in protest. Her blood rushed in her ears. It drowned out the sounds of the crisp waves below and the wind whipping past, and the persistent voice in her head telling her she was insane for insisting on helping Clint instead of hiding away to wait for the aircraft carrier to come to their rescue.

But he'd been adamant. The crew must be freed at once, and they all had to abandon *Île de Cœur* without delay.

He was sure the ship was set to blow up.

But if that was true, shouldn't the Chinese special ops squad posing as hijackers be abandoning the cargo ship, too, so they could get away in time? There was something wrong, but she couldn't put her finger on it. And had no time to think about it.

Below her, the trawler's fenders squealed as the two ships bumped at last. *Thank God.*

With gummy bear legs she shoved off, swung out, and with a fervent prayer let go of the line. She wheeled her arms, dropped, and landed with a thud on the rain-wet trawler. She heard the crack of plastic. Swallowing a cry, she rolled as Clint had shown her, a sharp pain stabbing into her hip. Her body smacked into the deck lockers lining the bridge, and she started to roll back toward the rail as the small boat rammed the bigger ship's immovable hull, jerked back, and tipped sideways over a wave. *Shit.*

She grabbed a passing cleat and hung on. It was cold, wet, and slippery. Her body probably wouldn't fit between the rails but she wasn't taking any chances on ending up in the water. The trawler leveled off and started its outward drift. She shook off the dizziness and the searing pain in her hip from her ungraceful landing and scrambled to the nearest cover, under a gutting table, that also sheltered her from the fat raindrops that had begun to fall.

Her whole body was shaking, her blood surging through her veins. She took several deep calming breaths, then risked a look up at *Île de Cœur*. Immediately she saw two of the hijackers on the foredeck. One was on a knee examining the twisted remains of the antitank rocket launcher, the other was hurrying back and forth from the pile of debris to the rail, tossing pieces of something over into the sea. She blanched, shivering with revulsion when she realized it was body parts of the man killed by the launcher explosion.

Her stomach recoiled, but she forced herself to look for the third remaining tango—as Clint called them—Xing Guan, the team's leader. But it was impossible to see most of the weather deck because of the angle up from the trawler.

Suddenly she spotted Clint's dark form gliding up the ladder to the quarterdeck from below like a ghostly shadow, his black clothes gilded by the reds and oranges of the sun.

Her heart stalled. Did he know the leader was not with the others?

Of course he did. Conducting dangerous missions was his job. He probably knew the exact location of every person on board *Île de Cœur*.

Including her. He'd halted with his back against the outside bulkhead, next to the mess hall windows, and she realized with a start he was looking right at her. Obviously she was shit at hiding.

She licked her lips and smiled up at him, pretending bravery.

His mouth flicked in a tense curve, but his eyes seemed to soften as he gazed down at her. No doubt her imagination. Still, it sent a rush of warmth through her cold, trembling body.

He lifted a hand slightly and twirled his forefinger in a sign reminding her to check the trawler for company. Had he been keeping track of her movements? To be sure she was okay? Her heart swelled a little more. No one had ever taken care of her like he did.

At his signal, she figured he hadn't seen anything alarming on board the trawler from where he stood, so she nodded, crawled out from her hiding place, grimacing from the pain in her hip, and cautiously limped toward the bridge door.

29

|||||||✓||||||

Clint's breath hitched as he watched Samantha slip through *Eliza Jane*'s wheelhouse door, pause to glance back and give him a plucky smile through the rain-spattered window, then disappear down the companionway to the lower deck.

Wait. Had she been limping?

And where the hell was the gun? He'd *told* her to put the P226 in her hand the moment she got on the trawler and keep it there until he joined her.

Damn.

He inhaled through his nose and let it out slowly, steadying his splintered nerves. He hated this. Hate, hate, hated not being down there to help in case she ran into trouble.

She wouldn't, he told himself confidently. She'd be fine. Besides, *Eliza Jane* was the safest place to be right now. If *Île de Cœur* was wired to blow, Samantha's best chance of survival was being off the ship. At least he could take solace in that.

Besides, he'd sworn to himself he would *not* second-guess her any longer. He knew he could rely on her. On her intelligence, her instincts, and her abilities. When her emotions weren't involved, she made excellent decisions. It was only when she was too upset to think things through that she went off the deep end. And that was not going to happen here. She had just one assignment for this final operation—getaway driver. When it came to rescuing her crew, Captain Samantha Richardson could be relied on one hundred percent to fulfill that mission.

He tore his gaze away from her and checked his watch. She'd made good time. Just under three minutes had elapsed from her jump.

Now the rest was up to him.

Gathering himself inward as his grandfather taught him long ago, he closed his eyes and stilled his mind and body in preparation for the hunt. When he opened them a moment later he was centered and ready.

Swiftly, he eased over to the double doors that opened onto the mess hall, and bent to glance in past the edge of the glass door. The large room was empty, no one sitting at the long tables. Okay. The crew was probably confined in the wardroom. Good. It would be easier for him to take down the guard in the smaller space of the officers' lounge.

He crossed in front of the mess and moved stealthily along the rear bulkhead to reach the lounge, which had a door and a window overlooking the narrow poop deck. The window's curtains were pulled closed, as they'd been this morning, except for a narrow sliver at the center. A few steps farther down, the door's curtain had been left open, probably so the guard could keep tabs on what was going on outside. Clint made sure he kept well away from it.

After a quick glance around the ship to make sure he was not being observed, Clint leaned in to peek through the narrow crack in the window curtains.

Inside, the wardroom was unlit except for the last pink rays of sunset that painted a surreal glow over the littered interior and the seven humans huddled together on two couches, and the man standing guard over them.

It was the tango he'd identified as probably being the team's sniper. But for now the thin, long-haired man held a

T-85 submachine gun in his hands. His emotionless gaze rested on the door. His expression was neither bored nor attentive, but cold and impassive, as though totally unconcerned with the fates of either his captives or his own dead team members.

Fucking sociopath.

Clint shifted his focus to the bound and gagged crew, arrayed along the two couches in the same order they'd been in this morning.

Second Mate Lars Bolun had again placed himself closest to the guard—deliberately, no doubt—but his back was partially turned to the man. One of Bolun's eye sockets had turned a livid shade of violet. His bruised cheek was swollen to twice its size, and the nasty cut on his temple was crusted with layers of blood. But Bolun's good eye was hyperalert and had already fastened on Clint when he met the second mate's gaze. Bolun didn't move an eyelash, but Clint knew he'd been waiting for this moment ever since he'd gotten those short glimpses of him and Samantha this morning.

Bolun slowly flexed his fingers, bringing his taped wrists into view. His steel-hard expression said he was ready for anything, if Clint could manage to free his hands.

Clint nodded and tipped his chin at Carin, who sat catatonic at Bolun's side with her head resting on his shoulder. The second mate lowered and raised his eyelids once to show he understood he'd have to ease her away.

Clint didn't have a lot of options, or time for finesse. His only real weapon was the element of surprise, and he intended to use it. Although by the look of the Chinese sniper, Clint would be hard-pressed to surprise the bastard.

He planned to initiate his attack from the inside corridor, not from here on the deck where he might be seen. So he pointed to the rear door, the solid one behind the guard, then held up two fingers, letting Bolun know he'd be coming in that way in two minutes.

Bolun's cracked and swollen lip curled in a malevolent parody of a smile. Clint mirrored it back at him.

Oh, yeah.

That guard didn't stand an igloo's chance in hell.

Sam stood in the shadows of *Eliza Jane*'s pilothouse and anxiously trained a pair of binoculars on Clint's back. She hadn't let him out of her sight since coming up from the lower deck a minute ago, where, much to her relief, she'd confirmed she was alone on board the trawler. The fog was starting to thicken as the rain increased. She prayed it wouldn't obscure her view.

She shifted on her feet. Her hip throbbed like Rammstein's woofer. She'd found a first aid kit and thrown some disinfectant on the deep puncture wound a shard of her notebook lid had gouged into her lower hip, so now it stung like a wasp. But she'd live. She just hoped she could soon say the same of Clint and her crew.

The good news was, the fact that a guard had not been posted onboard *Eliza Jane*—the hijackers' only means of escape—was evidence their control over the situation was slipping big-time. She was more than gratified that despite being badly outnumbered and essentially powerless, she and Clint had managed to throw them so far off their game. Well. Clint had, anyway. She wasn't sure how much she had contributed to the effort.

And he was about to deal them their fatal blow. If everything went according to plan, moments from now her crew would no longer be captive, and they'd all be cruising away at full speed, alive, and with Clint's top secret data card still in his possession.

Clint ducked away from the window and crouch-ran the few paces back to the mess hall doors, then slid unobtrusively through them and disappeared. Her pulse kicked up.

She checked her watch. Five minutes and counting.

Right on time.

Even so, her mind filled with quiet terror that something would go wrong and he'd end up captured, too . . . or dead. She couldn't go through the agony of losing him again! It had been bad enough the first time she'd believed Clint had been killed—and that was before she'd realized how far she'd already fallen in love with him. The idea of losing him for real now turned her stomach to a boiling cauldron of eels.

She wished like crazy she could see what was happening inside *Île de Cœur*'s wardroom.

She sweated in fear, breath held painfully in her lungs, and waited.

All at once she saw the two tangos on the forward deck drop what they were doing and turn around. As one, they peered aft along the weather deck.

What now? The whole midstructure lay between them and Clint, so she was certain—okay, *nearly* certain—they hadn't seen him. But what the heck were they looking at?

Staying well back in the shadows of the trawler's pilothouse so as not to be seen, she carefully scanned what she could of *Île de Cœur*'s decks with her binoculars—which because of the angle and the thickening fog was barely anything. Fear and frustration kneaded together in her chest. Could the Chinese squad leader suspect something had happened with the hostages and be running aft to check it out?

If only she could see!

Her heart pounding in her throat, Sam watched and waited for Clint to reappear. And waited. And waited.

All the while fighting an awful feeling in her gut that something was about to go terribly, terribly wrong.

The radio crackled to life.

Sam jumped about ten feet in the air, her pulse going into hyperspace. *What the—*

A curse flew from her lips just as a static-y female voice scratched out from the two-way radio mounted above her head.

"*Eliza Jane, Eliza Jane*. This is the USS *George Washington* attempting to contact anyone aboard your vessel. Please acknowledge, over."

Sam blinked up at the unit, torn by indecision whether or not to pick up the mike and answer. She recognized the voice coming from the ancient speaker; it was DeAnne Lovejoy. Sam desperately wanted to talk to the woman from the State Department and find out when help would arrive. But what if one of the hijackers was also listening in? She'd give away her position, and thus Clint's plan, by answering.

The radio crackled again, and DeAnne Lovejoy's voice came through once more. But this time the words were unrecognizable. She was speaking Chinese.

Startled, Sam darted a gaze back up at *Île de Cœur*'s forward deck. But the attention of the two hijackers hadn't wavered. Their gazes remained glued to something out of Sam's line of sight. Obviously, they hadn't heard the radio call.

Oh, what the heck. She grabbed the microphone.

"*George Washington*, this is *Eliza Jane*." She dialed down the volume, in case the sound carried, and demanded, "Where the hell are you people, over?"

"Captain Richardson?" came the relieved response.

"Yeah, it's me, over."

"Are you and the Lieutenant Commander all right?"

"So far," she returned. "But things may get interesting any minute now." She searched the poop deck for any sign of Clint's progress. "At least I'm hoping it will," she murmured under her breath when nothing had changed. "When's the cavalry arriving, over?"

There was a brief pause. "Ninety minutes."

Sam swore. "Are you *kidding* me?" It would all be over by then. One way or another.

"I've been in contact with the Chinese government," Ms. Lovejoy hurried to say, "negotiating for them to intervene with the, uh, pirates, over."

Read: Trying to get them to call off their damn hit squad.

"Good luck with that," Sam muttered, then pressed the "talk" button again. "Let me guess. They're denying all knowledge, over."

She thought she heard a sigh. "I remain hopeful of their cooperation, over."

Right. And there was some swampland in Alaska Sam could sell her, too.

"Any news of the Coast Guard cutter?" she asked, and skimmed the darkening sky with her binoculars. She'd been worried about them, praying no one had been killed. "Was anyone hurt?" A pale spiral of smoke drifted in the foggy sky toward Île de Cœur, but the burning vessel remained frustratingly blocked from view. Was it getting closer? Or was it just the wind blowing the smoke . . .

"Communications are still down," Ms. Lovejoy said. She seemed to read her thoughts. "We'll be there as soon as humanly possible, Captain Richardson. The commander has the carrier on afterburners." She must have finally realized where Sam was, and abruptly said, "Wait . . . are you on the *Eliza Jane*? How did—"

But Sam had stopped listening. On Île de Cœur, the wardroom door had suddenly swung open. She froze. Even her heart stopped beating.

Then Lars Bolun stepped warily out onto the poop deck, a rifle raised in one hand and Carin supported in the crook of his other arm. He glanced from side to side, looking for danger.

Sam let out a cry of joy, nearly collapsing from the relief of seeing them both alive.

"Captain Richardson?" DeAnne Lovejoy was saying over the radio. "What's going on out there? Please. Do *not* do anything to provoke the hijackers."

Too late.

Sam's pulse sped with elation as Lars moved aside and stood a vigilant watch as the rest of the crew crept out the door and headed through the rain for the ladder down to the weather deck—and *Eliza Jane*.

Clint had done it!

Oh, God, they were really going to make it!

"Sorry," she blurted out to the State Department official. "I have to go now." She dropped the mike and flipped off the radio, cutting off Ms. Lovejoy in midprotest.

Screw the cavalry. She intended to be ready to crank this baby's motor and run for their lives.

She reached blindly for the engine controls while scouring the upper deck for Clint. *Where was he?* She wanted to see him! She had to know for certain he was alive and unhurt. She needed to meet his eyes and share a happy moment of triumph, knowing they'd soon be together. That nothing more would stand between them and the rest of their lives.

Above her, the radio squawked. She ignored it.

Clint finally appeared at the wardroom door, and her heart soared. Dressed in jeans and a black T-shirt, broad shouldered, lean hipped, a pistol gripped in each hand and a rifle slung across his back, he looked more like a pirate than a federal law enforcement officer.

But every inch a hero.

Her hero.

The radio squawked again. She clicked it over to "mute."

He strode across the deck to bring up the rear of the little group, protecting their flank as the crew hurriedly climbed and tumbled down the two flights as fast as they could to the rain-slick weather deck.

Her heart did a slow spin in her chest. She was so much in love with the man it hurt.

Their eyes met across the distance, and she smiled. His lips started to curve. Then stopped. His head swiveled sharply toward the front of the ship. His body froze.

Instantly, alarm swept over her. Her gaze whipped to follow his.

That's when she saw it. The deck crane's ladder. Someone was climbing it at breakneck speed.

The leader of the Chinese black-ops team, Xing Guan.

Her breath stalled.

Oh, no.

No, no, no.

But there was no mistaking it, he was headed straight for the cab at the top.

And for the dead body hidden inside.

30

〟〟〟〟〟〟〟〟〟〟

When it came, Xing Guan's reaction to the body in the cab was not the expected shout of anger nor a yell to rally his decimated team to exact revenge. It was a deep cry of anguish.

The howl poured over the ship in a thick wave of grief, backdropped by the mournful patter of the rain. At the sound, everyone stopped in their tracks.

Shock vibrated through Clint. Clearly, the man's pain was personal. A relative?

The similar features of the young upstart to the older head honcho suddenly made sense.

Sweet Jesus, this was about to turn really ugly.

Clint didn't stop to analyze. He simply went on instinct. "Get everyone moving," he ordered Bolun with quiet intensity. "Get them off this ship, now!"

Also spooked by the enemy's unexpected emotional display, the second mate immediately started issuing hushed instructions to the crew. Carin still clung to his side, refusing to leave him.

High up on the crane, Xing Guan had gathered the

young man's body in his arms and was attempting to carry
it to the deck below. But the crane's ladder was not a narrow
stairway like the ones that led up and down between decks;
it was more like climbing down a telephone pole. The Chinese leader struggled. The rain was coming down harder
now, sheeting over the cabin, slicking the ladder, the man,
and the body, making the descent even more difficult.

The good news was so far the crew hadn't been spotted.
Twilight was on their side, with its enveloping grays and
shadows, along with the obscuring fog and rain. But any
minute now the grief-stricken Chinese leader would look
around seeking help with his burden. He'd see them for
sure.

"Go!" Clint told Bolun urgently. "Don't wait for me.
Make Samantha take the trawler out of range!"

He hoped to hell he could make it to the trawler, too. But
if not . . . He'd cover their retreat as long as he could.

He risked a swift look down at Samantha, who was
standing openmouthed at the smaller boat's controls, staring up at him through the glittering raindrops, her face an
ashen mask of alarm. As though she could read his intentions. *Damn.*

"Don't let her do anything stupid!" he growled after Bolun, who'd lifted Carin like a rag doll and was about to
launch himself down the wet stairway with her. The last
thing he saw before they were gone was the second mate's
grim nod of understanding.

Clint retreated into the steel gray puddles of shadow cast
by the cloud-darkened midnight sun. Rain drizzled down
his face, and adrenaline sang through his veins as he turned
back to observe the old man.

Up on the crane, Guan continued to wrestle with the body.
He finally gave a frustrated shout and gestured angrily at the
two goons on the foredeck, who'd been watching him from
afar, aghast and immobilized with uncertainty. At his beck,
they jerked to attention and took off at a jog toward him on
the other end of the ship.

Putting them on a collision course with the crew.

Clint muttered a curse. This escape attempt was shaping up to be a serious clusterfuck.

By now Johnny and Frank had made it down to the weather deck; Frank had sped off to get the rope ladder over the side. Johnny stayed behind to help Ginger, Matty, Spiros, and Jeeter down the steep, rain-slippery stairs between the two decks. He then sent them sprinting across the deck to the rail where Frank was madly unreeling the rope ladder down to *Eliza Jane*.

Listening intently for the enemy's footfalls, Clint fervently prayed the crew would all make it off the ship before the distracted Chinese operators spotted them.

A split second too late, Clint saw his worst fear materialize.

The two jogging men reached the open expanse of the weather deck just as the last of the crew streaked across it toward the port rail. Seeing the fleeing prisoners, the tangos skidded to a halt, whipped up their T-85s, and began shouting and brandishing the submachine guns at the escapees.

Still on the deck above, Clint started for the ladder. But Bolun glanced up at him with a sign to stop and a grim shake of his head.

Clint froze as the second mate peeled Carin from his side and gently pushed her toward Johnny, then drew a .357 Magnum from his waistband. *Jesus.* The revolver was big, but hardly a match for the Type-85s. Bolun stepped fearlessly in front of the tangos and braced his legs apart like a gunslinger, making himself into a human shield.

The Chinese commander lost it then. Baring his teeth on a string of guttural expletives, Xing Guan dropped the unwieldy body back in the cab and started to storm down the ladder, spewing invective as he went.

Perfect. Clint wanted to growl in frustration. They'd been *that close* to a smooth getaway. Now they'd all be lucky even to survive this goddamn Mexican standoff.

Tell that to the crew, though. Partially hidden by the second mate, the group continued to move closer to the rail, inch by inch. He caught a glimpse of Carin's huddled form disappearing over the side.

With a cold stab of certainty, Clint knew Samantha would be waiting at the bottom of the ladder to help each one of her crew onto the trawler, whether there was a gun pointed at her or not. Which there would be any second, he was sure.

Christ. The woman's reckless defiance scared him witless. But at the same time, he was also so damn proud of his brave, sweet woman that his chest was about to burst.

With conflicting emotions, he glimpsed Matty slip over the side, then Jeeter. Every fiber of his being wanted to go with them. To drop onto *Eliza Jane*'s deck next to Samantha, swing her into his arms, and set the throttle at full speed to get them the hell away from this living nightmare.

But that was not going to happen. Not today.

Probably not ever.

The second he saw the cold, hate-filled fury on Xing Guan's face as the wiry leader jumped to the deck and marched toward the confrontation, Clint knew the man was beyond reason.

The long, distinctive shape of a Type-67 silenced pistol appeared in Guan's clenched fist, aimed at Bolun's chest.

Jerking up his SIG, Clint brought the crosshairs dead center on Xing Guan's heart. But again, he was a nanosecond too late. Guan had snapped a command, and his two assassins were instantly at the rail, their submachine guns aimed down at the crew.

Fear froze Clint's finger on the trigger.

Samantha!

A knife blade of hesitation sliced at him. He didn't dare shoot Guan or the two assassins would cut down the crew where they stood. Including Samantha.

Clint could drop one, maybe even both the goons in rapid succession if he took them by surprise. But he'd never get off a third shot for Xing Guan in time to save Bolun.

He closed his eyes briefly, eased out an infuriated breath, and lowered his weapon a fraction.

There was just no good option here.

Guan gave another command, and his men started shouting at the crew, gesturing insistently for them to climb back up.

It took all Clint's willpower to stay where he was as one by one the crew came up the rope ladder to *Île de Cœur*'s deck and huddled together in the cold rain. He went absolutely still, waiting for his heart to be ripped to a thousand pieces when Samantha appeared at the rail.

But she didn't appear.

The last of the crew ascended and the rope ladder was hauled up, and still no Samantha. In a silent pact of solidarity, the others didn't let on she was missing, counting on the fact that the Chinese were still not aware of her existence.

Clint stood rooted to the upper deck, hope for her surging through him. And gratitude to the crew. He felt utterly humbled by the fierce loyalty of the small group of strangers, which she had, through the fairness and compassion of her leadership, forged into a true family.

But his spate of optimism was short-lived.

When the crew was once again assembled under the cold, watchful eyes of the guards, feeling the merciless dominion of their submachine guns, Xing Guan pressed the long barrel of his pistol hard into Bolun's forehead.

"Where is other soldier?" he demanded in his clipped accent, and jerked his chin up at the wardroom to indicate he meant their guard.

Their former guard. Who was now dead.

Clint stilled. This was not good. Slowly he raised the SIG again, preparing for trouble.

Bolun stared unblinkingly back at Guan. "He decided to go for a midnight swim," he said evenly.

The blow from the gun cracked into Bolun's skull swift as lightning. Carin screamed, and the others exclaimed in protest. Guan's response was to strike him again. "You kill soldier!"

Bolun didn't reply. He was still visibly reeling from the blows. Guan shoved the gun barrel between his eyes.

"You kill son." The old man ground out the enraged accusation between his tightly clenched teeth. "You die."

Son?

Shit.

In a flash Clint moved to the rail, dropping the SIG and
kicking it into the shadows.

"No!" he shouted defiantly down at his nemesis. "*I*
killed your son."

31

'''''''''''''''''''''

Something bad was going on up there on *Île de Cœur*. Sam could feel it in the roiling of her stomach—and it wasn't from the storm kicking up outside, tossing the small trawler around like a football.

Had that been a scream she'd heard?

She rose up cautiously from where she'd been hiding, crouched on *Eliza Jane*'s wheelhouse floor, to crane her neck up at the weather deck of the big ship above her. Rain was coming down in buckets and it was tough to make out details, but she could definitely see the silhouettes of her crew standing in a ragged bunch near the rail, and those of their machine-gun-toting guards. They all seemed to be mesmerized by some drama unfolding in front of them, but it was past the point on the deck where Sam could see.

What she did see was Clint. A wave of shock hit her.

He'd been doing his invisibility trick, a midnight wraith blending into the storm-blurred lines of the shadowed poop deck. Now he deliberately stepped out from his cover and revealed his presence in no uncertain terms to those below.

Her eyes widened. What was he *doing*?

Instantly, the two men guarding the crew whipped their guns toward him.

Sam let out a dismayed gasp. "No!" Where was *his* gun?

The hijackers exchanged a look, and one of them took off toward the ladder to the poop deck. Clint made no move to flee. Fear and consternation swept through her. My God, he was giving himself up to the enemy!

But why?

These men had proven they were brutal and without conscience. What would they do to him when they took him prisoner? Or . . . would they kill him here and now, and be done with it?

Her heart quailed. *No! They couldn't kill him!*

They wouldn't dare! Not with the pride of the U.S. Navy minutes away, ready to retaliate in kind. They'd have to be insane to do that.

The thought tamed her wild heartbeat a fraction.

Still, she had to do something! Help him! Make them—

No. She grasped the edge of the console to stop herself from vaulting up the rope ladder and charging into the fray. He was doing this deliberately. He *must* have a plan. She needed to trust him, to trust he knew what he was doing. Not do anything impulsive to ruin it.

She needed to take a breath and let him do his job. But watching the armed hijacker shove his machine gun to Clint's back and force him to join the crew below was the hardest thing she'd ever had to do in her life.

Terrified, she strained to see what was happening. But the fog had started to swirl around both ships in thick claws, obscuring what little view she'd had.

Edging toward panic, she wondered about his plan. By giving himself over to the Chinese operators, was Clint counting on Xing Guan taking him and leaving the ship and the hostages while he still could?

Surely they'd only leave the ship if he also gave them the micro storage card in his possession. Their mission was to retrieve the stolen card at all costs, according to Clint. But he had been so adamant about getting it safely to

Washington, D.C. Could he really be planning to use it as a bargaining chip and give it up, along with the critical data it held, just to save the lives of the crew?

More important, would the Chinese include Clint himself in any deal of lives for the card?

Her eyes filled with tears of dismay. He'd admitted they were a black-ops assassination squad—whose mission was to kill the man who'd stolen the data card.

"Jesus, chill out," Clint muttered as he took another jab in the spine with a machine gun barrel. The asshole was really pushing his luck. He might be a great shot—though that was yet to be proven—but Clint had about nine inches and ninety pounds on the guy. The only reason Clint hadn't grabbed the fucker's gun and thrown him off the ladder was because Xing Guan still had *his* gun barrel pressed into Bolun's forehead.

As they descended, Clint had to fight the overpowering urge to glance down at *Eliza Jane*'s wheelhouse again to see how Samantha was reacting to all this. It worried the hell out of him.

She'd done exactly the right thing when the tangos had spotted the escape attempt, hiding herself away so she wouldn't be taken, too. He prayed she'd be as self-protective now and not do anything crazy. She couldn't have been expecting this kind of a move from him.

To be honest, neither had he. But when he'd seen the stalwart second mate with that gun to his head, about to pay for Clint's own sins, there was no way he could stand by and let it happen.

He swallowed a curse as he took another stab to the spine.

Hell, now all he had to do was come up with a plan.

32

"Ms. Lovejoy?"

"Captain Richardson? Oh, thank God. Please tell me you're all right."

Despite the dire situation, a smile toyed briefly with the corners of Sam's mouth. Familiar questions from a by now reassuringly familiar voice. Strange what passed for comfort now; but she'd take what she could get. She was just insanely grateful the badly cracked sat phone was miraculously still working. She didn't relish exposing herself by being in plain view behind the windshield in order to use the ancient radio.

"I'm good," Sam replied anxiously. "But I can't say the same for Lieutenant Commander Walker. Clint gave himself up to the hijackers. They've taken him prisoner."

"Oh! That's not good," Ms. Lovejoy exclaimed with genuine feeling. "But why on earth would he give himself up?"

"God knows. We were separated at the time." As she peeked up through the trawler's rain-sheeted windshield, she quickly explained what had happened. "He must have a plan . . . but the last time I saw him, he was at the wrong end of a gun."

"*So* not good," the other woman repeated, then said, "I'm trying hard to resolve the situation. But the Chinese government is being uncooperative—denying the hijackers are even Chinese, let alone part of a PLA military operation, secret or otherwise."

"I'm shocked. *Shocked*," Sam murmured beneath her breath, but the satellite reception must have been amplified by the fog rather than dampened by it, because she distinctly heard DeAnne Lovejoy swallow a troubled chuckle.

"Yes, well, I'm afraid their stance ties my hands quite effectively. I'll still pursue it, naturally. But I am not optimistic of making any headway in a useful time frame."

"I understand." Sam hadn't really expected it anyway. She asked about the Coast Guard cutter, if anyone had made radio contact yet. "I haven't been able to see the ship from where I've been hiding," she said. "Any idea what's going on over there?"

"Yes. Apparently a couple of the crew members own sat phones, so they were able to set up communication with Kodiak that way."

"Any injuries? How bad's the damage?" If it wasn't extensive, maybe there'd be some kind of help coming from that quarter, after all.

"I understand a couple of the officers were seriously injured in the blast, but nothing life-threatening."

"Thank God." Sam kept scouring the sky, hoping for a break in the fog. Praying nothing life-threatening was happening up on *Île de Cœur*'s deck while she was talking. She hadn't wanted to make a move herself until she knew the full situation.

"I have some good news," Ms. Lovejoy said, as though reading her thoughts. "The cutter's commander is planning an armed assault on your hijackers."

"Really?" Sam straightened like a shot, a deluge of relief coursing through her. "When? How?"

"They have a small boarding craft." There was a slight hesitation on the other end. "I shouldn't give any other details over an open sat line. I just thought you and your crew should be warned."

No details? Was she *serious*? "There are only three hijackers left alive," Sam said in frustration, "and I think they're a little busy at the moment."

"Just three?" Ms. Lovejoy asked immediately.

"The Lieutenant Commander has been busy," Sam said noncommittally.

"Wow, I—" She heard a throat being cleared. "Well. That's . . . good."

Sam could tell the woman was torn between admiration and horror. Kind of like Sam, herself.

As they spoke, Sam continued to stare through the upper reaches of the windshield, hoping for a glimpse of what was going on up on deck. All she saw were watery swirls of gray and white. Nevertheless, she was damned sure the remaining Chinese assassins were not monitoring cell phone traffic.

"Anyway, I doubt the hijackers are listening in," she assured the woman.

"I'm sure you're right," Ms. Lovejoy said, and cleared her throat again. "The problem is, there may be others."

Sam blinked, focusing back on the conversation rather than straining her eyes on the blanket of fog. "Other what?"

"Others listening in. SOSUS has picked up the signature of a submarine hovering in the vicinity." SOSUS—the navy's extensive network of underwater listening stations. A whale could swim past one of the sophisticated microphones a mile away and still be heard, let alone a submarine. "Sonar thinks it's probably Chinese."

An icy spike of fear speared up Sam's spine. In her experience, navy sonar operators seldom made wrong IDs.

Holy crap. Clint had been right! "A Shan class nuclear sub?" she asked in alarm.

"Shang. Yes, but how—" Ms. Lovejoy began, then broke off the question. "It appears to be hovering on the edges of the situation just observing for now. But that could change quickly enough. I've expressed my concern to the Chinese government, but that's another brick wall."

None of which made Sam feel any better. "The Chinese seem to be master wall builders."

"The Chinese are masters of a lot of things. You just never hear about them. That is what's so worrisome."

"Tell me about it," Sam said, her fear for Clint and the crew growing every second. Good lord, if the Chinese sub was really part of this . . . "Look, Ms. Lovejoy—"

"I think under the circumstances we can dispense with the formalities. Please, call me DeAnne."

Sam smiled briefly through her seeping panic. "Thanks. And I'm Sam." She glanced up. Was the fog thinning? Thankfully, the rain had stopped—suddenly, and completely, as it often did in the Arctic. "DeAnne, can you do me a huge favor and ask the Coast Guard to shake a leg with that armed assault? I could really use some help here."

God, she hated being alone in this. Hated being alone, period. She missed Clint's expert input. Hell, she missed *Clint*. Like crazy.

"I promise I'll do my best," DeAnne said. "I'm sure they'll be happy the number of hijackers has been so greatly reduced. In the meantime, try to give a heads-up to the others, if at all possible."

"I'll try," Sam said, though she couldn't imagine how she'd get close to anyone without being caught herself. But somehow she had to find a way. "I should go. Not sure how much battery is left on this thing."

DeAnne made an unhappy noise. "Dammit, Sam! I really hate leaving you on your own out there."

That was the worst swear word she'd ever heard the woman utter.

Sam was more touched than she could say by her sincerity. "I'll be okay," she managed to squeeze past a sudden lump in her throat from an unexpected realization. More people had shown her more care over these past hellish seventy-two hours than in her entire previous life. Adversity really must bring out the best in people.

Or ... had those around her always been this supportive ... and she'd just been blind to it, wallowing in past betrayals rather than present possibilities?

She swallowed down the lump. "Just tell them to hurry. Please."

"I will," DeAnne said. "But check in again in thirty minutes, if nothing's happened. Okay, Sam?"

"Roger that. And thanks, DeAnne." As she pressed the "disconnect" button, Sam sucked down a deep, steadying breath. It was getting to her—everything. The emotions hurtling through her were nearly overwhelming. Fear—no, make that terror, panic, confusion, loss of control ... love. As she stared upward, she laid her hand gently on her abdomen, fighting tears.

Oh, God.

An eddy of fog whirled and parted, exposing the big ship's upper hull. The weather deck rail appeared high above her, a shiny line of chrome reflecting the dim midnight sun.

She shivered, and a rash of goose bumps tingled over her arms. *Île de Cœur* looked like a ghost ship rising from a haunting mist. Eerie. Silent. Deserted.

A tear spilled over.

There was no sign of Clint, her crew, or the hijackers.

Like the fog, they, too, had vanished.

33

\\\\\\\\\/////////

"Where is it?"

Clint lay curled in a ball on the wet, freezing deck and steeled himself for Xing Guan's next vicious kick. When it ripped square into his kidneys, Clint grunted in searing pain.

"Fuck you, asshole," he gritted out between teeth clenched against the cold and the agony. Letting them chatter would be a sign of weakness.

The crew was huddled against the midstructure bulkhead, forced to watch his savage tune-up. Some of them, anyway. The two women had been permitted by the guards to turn away. The one he recognized as Carin had her face buried in Bolun's shoulder—opposite the machine gun muzzle to his neck. If looks could kill, they'd already be halfway to Seattle.

Another kick hammered into Clint's flesh, this time in the ribs. He heard two distinct snaps as a new bolt of pain stabbed through his side. Black spots danced through his vision.

"Give me computer card or I kill you!" Xing Guan barked. The man was incensed—and clearly in no mood for mercy.

Clint had no illusions about his chances for survival—with or without giving him the microcard—but he also had no fucking intention of making it easy on the bastard. "Go ahead," he wheezed, squeezing his eyes shut. "You're going to kill me anyway."

He heard one of the women gasp, while the other sobbed quietly.

"Just give him what he wants!" the young kid on the crew cried, his voice ragged. "Whatever it is ain't worth—*Oof.*"

"Shut up, Jeeter," Bolun hissed at the kid.

"But—" Jeeter's protest cut off amid the sounds of the other men's growls, which quickly also turned to protests.

A woman screamed. *"No!"*

Clint snapped opened his eyes. Xing Guan was jamming the long barrel of his pistol into the kid's forehead, his face ablaze with hatred. "I kill you instead! Your life for son's!"

Clint struggled to rise up a little. "Please. Don't," he rasped.

"You give card!" Guan demanded, taking neither his eyes nor the gun off the kid. Jeeter's own eyes were wide with terror and rimmed in red.

Clint swallowed. This was getting far too dangerous. Somehow he had to protect these people. Even if it meant . . .

Defeat curled like an electric eel in his belly. "Fine. You win," he ground out furiously, and let himself collapse back onto the deck in agony.

"Give now!" Guan ordered, obviously not believing Clint.

Clint shook off a nauseating wave of dizziness. "I'll tell you where it's hidden . . . after you let the others go."

For a second his torturer just stared at him, his gun arm held stiffly in place. Then he turned back and sliced his malevolent gaze along the line of hostages, following with the aim of the pistol. It halted at Bolun.

The second mate gently pushed Carin off his shoulder. She whimpered, tears soaking her face.

Guan sneered, twitched the gun's aim down, and shot her in the heart.

34

\\\\\\\\\\\v///////

Oh, Jesus God.

Clint froze as, for a split second, the whole world went perfectly still. After the sharp report of the gun, there wasn't a sound to be heard, not a movement to be seen. Not from the humans, nor the wind, nor the sea. Even the waves seemed to halt at their crests, causing the ship's motion to pause in midroll.

Carin inhaled a short breath of surprise, looked down to where her hand had instinctively gone to the pinprick of pain, and blinked. As an orchid of crimson blossomed across her chest, her uncomprehending eyes fluttered closed, her knees dissolved, and she began to sink. Frank and Johnny caught her in a tangle of arms, shocked horror etched on their faces.

Ginger started to scream.

And that's when all hell broke loose.

"You fucking *bastard*!" Lars Bolun boomed. He launched himself at Xing Guan, knocking aside his pistol just as it went off for a second time, going for the man's throat.

"*Sonofa*"—Clint forced his aching body from its fetal curl, grunting in agony, and dove for the sniper—"*bitch!*" He brought the unguarded tango down with a body slam to his legs.

The remaining assassin whipped his gun around to Bo-lun's back as the second mate struggled with Guan. But too late. Matty and Spiros were all over him like sharks on bait. Two shots went wild before the third man hit the deck amid a pile of flailing limbs.

Clint heard Bolun's fist smash into Xing Guan's face over and over as he grappled with the pistol, attempting to wrench it away. The Chinese commander was built like an ox and strong as a jackal, and should have been able to shake off the tall, lean second mate with little effort. But Carin's death seemed to have given Bolun supernatural strength. It was a dead even match.

But Clint was losing ground fast against the sniper. Ignoring the excruciating pain, he clung like a leech to the twisting man's legs. He kicked up with all his remaining strength to foil the aim of the man's T-85 as it swung around and targeted Bolun. Clint's bruised kidneys screamed in agony and the sharp bones of his broken ribs ground into his insides, sending razor blades of sickening sensation through his middle. The fucker kicked back at him, again and again, but he gritted his teeth against the blows and refused to let go.

A spray of submachine gun fire burst through the twi-light darkness, cut through abruptly by Bolun's shout of pain.

The second mate staggered. And lost his grip on Guan. Ribbons of blood flew from his shoulder.

Clint must have loosened his grip on the sniper for a millisecond. The man wrenched free and lurched to his feet.

Shit on a—

Clint steeled his muscles to fling himself into his adversary's knees in another pain-wracked body slam. But before he could execute, a single shot cracked through the air. The sniper went rigid, his mouth twisting in a slash of shock.

What the— Another shot whistled past. The tango's body jerked. His weapon clattered to the deck.

Clint didn't stop to wonder who was doing the shooting. He rolled, grabbed the T-85, and whipped around to save Bolun from Xing Guan's kill shot.

Bolun was on his knees, head down and grimacing, one bloodstained hand wrapped around a scarlet-drenched shoulder.

Clint spun to Matty and Spiros, but they were okay. Using the end of a cleat line, Spiros had his boot planted on the hijacker's spine, tying the glowering man's wrists and ankles together behind his bowed-up back like a hog on a spit. Matty held a gun in his shaking hands, pointed more or less at the top of the man's skull.

Six down, Clint thought with satisfaction. *Just one more to go.*

He quickly scanned the surrounding deck, squinting through the half light, his heartbeat thumping like distant depth charges in his chest.

Fucking hell.

Xing Guan was gone. How long had he—

A woman's scream shattered the night air. Clint darted his gaze to Ginger. But she stood wide-eyed, her hands plastered over her mouth, staring transfixed at the poop deck above.

Oh, hell.

Every cell in Clint's body lit up, electric with dread, as he realized who must have let out the terrified sound.

And why.

Oh, God!

Samantha!

35

////////×//////

Sam recoiled, attempting to avoid a second blow delivered with the butt of her own Glock, which the Chinese leader swung at her viciously. It glanced off her cheek, leaving a stinging slash of pain on her flesh and bringing tears to her eyes. She forced back another scream.

He'd surprised her, attacking from behind and disarming her in a swift, practiced move as she'd leaned trembling against the rail, shaken to the core after deliberately shooting the man with the dropped machine gun she'd found in the wardroom. She'd had no choice. *He would have killed Clint.* But now *she'd* killed a man. Oh, God, *oh, God*.

She'd killed a man.

And now she'd pay the price.

Instead of closing her eyes in revulsion at what she'd done, she should have been watching the scene below. Should have kept her attention locked on the bad guys. Made sure all three had been dealt with before letting the physical reaction take her over. But she hadn't.

The brutal leader reached for her. Terrified, she jumped back and tried to run, but he was too quick. His iron hand flashed out and grabbed her arm, then spun her and wrenched it up behind her back so hard, this time she couldn't stop the scream from breaking free.

He pushed savagely, marching her forward in the direction of the ladder.

"You won't get away with this!" she cried, struggling while trying to keep up with his pace.

He just pushed harder.

She stumbled, and he yanked her up by her back-bent arm. She gasped out a cry.

"Stop! You're hurting me!"

"Good. Who are you?" he demanded in a staccato accent, his mouth practically biting off her ear. "You are *spy*."

"No!" Her heart quailed, pounding with horror at the accusation. God help her if he thought she was involved in Clint's mission. She swallowed away the acrid taste of fear that flooded her mouth. Vivid images of Clint's battered face and Shandy's and Carin's blood-soaked, lifeless bodies flashed through her mind. "That's absurd," she croaked as he marched her forward along the narrow gangway. "This is a cargo ship."

She would *not* give in to the panic clawing at her chest.

The rest of her beleaguered crew was now safe, she reminded herself. And Clint was miraculously still alive—*thank God*.

Shandy and Carin had made the ultimate sacrifice with their lives. Could she do any less? If the worst happened and she had to die to keep the others safe, then she'd do it willingly.

But she'd damn well go down swinging, with her pride and honor intact.

She drew herself up, blocking out the stabbing pain in her upper arm, the rivulets of blood trickling down her cheek, and the trembling in her limbs. "I am *not* a spy," she said with as much dignity as she could muster. "I'm Captain Samantha Richardson, commander of this vessel. Who are you, and what do you want with my ship?"

He yanked her to a stop and gave an ugly, derisive snort. "Captain? You only a woman."

Her terror was momentarily eclipsed by fury at the chauvinist barb. Were *all* men like her father?

"And you are a murderer!" she retorted, but instantly regretted the lapse in judgment. *Crap.* Fear surged back in a tidal wave as she braced herself for a broken arm, or worse.

His voice hissed in her ear, "Remember that when you lie to me." He jerked her arm hard, to get her moving again.

She bit down on a yelp. "I'm not lying," she ground out, fighting tears of pain and rage. "I swear." She needed Clint. Needed his strong, steady presence to talk her down off this emotional ledge before she did something foolish. With blurry vision she sought out the deck below, where he and the crew were standing.

For a nanosecond, her heart stuttered to a stop, as did her feet.

Correction. Where he'd *been* standing.

There was no sign of him! Or of the crew, or the captured guard. Or even of the two dead bodies, other than a red stain spreading thinly across the rain-soaked deck.

She snapped her eyes straight ahead, praying her tormentor hadn't noticed.

"Walk! Fast!" he barked, pushing at her again.

Her heartbeat surged as she reluctantly obeyed. *Where were they all?*

Her mind whirled with possibilities. Probably they'd gone inside to stash their prisoner, tend to the wounded, and lay poor Carin somewhere more dignified than the open deck.

Or better yet, maybe they'd escaped onto the trawler and were getting the hell out of Dodge. She subtly cocked an ear, hoping to hear the sputter and fart of the fishing boat's engines.

But there was nothing. All around, it was still and silent as an iceberg. Only the suck and splash of waves breaking against the hull disturbed the midnight calm after the storm.

Her captor jerked her arm impatiently again, shoving her forward. "Not stop!"

Her gasp of pain echoed through the silence.

Hell, it was almost *too* quiet.

Had the crew heard her earlier screams, and were they even now rushing to her rescue?

Doubtful. Clint was in no shape to be rushing anywhere—she'd seen how much he was hurting after what must have been a brutal beating. And rushing around was also out of the question for Lars Bolun. He'd been shot, and it looked like he'd lost a lot of blood. As for the rest of them, well, they were the best crew of merchant marines on the planet, but none were exactly Delta Force material.

Honestly, she hoped they *weren't* planning an heroic rescue attempt. Not when—

All at once DeAnne's voice sounded in her mind. *I do have some good news.*

She'd almost forgotten. *The Coast Guard was coming!*

Surely, the Coastie assault team must be on its way by now. Not to mention the imminent arrival of the *George Washington* with DeAnne herself. Hadn't it been ninety minutes a long time ago?

Damned if an insidious trickle of hope didn't awaken within her, seeping through her veins like a shot of sloe gin.

In a muddle of conflicting emotions, Sam reached the top of the quarterdeck ladder. It descended steeply to the middle of the main deck where the trolley and the containers were lashed, and the big, square cargo hatches were located. The crippled crane listed crookedly above the locked hatches, its large, jawlike claw swinging precariously out over the side of the ship and back again with each roll of a wave.

"Down!" her captor ordered, startling her with a push toward the ladder.

As she climbed down, she slanted a surreptitious glance out over the Bering Sea, searching the waves for running lights, or the glint of weapons against black clothing, or the stately silhouette of an aircraft carrier steaming full speed ahead over the horizon.

Again, there was nothing. The only movement was wispy tendrils of fog drifting over slate gray water, the only reflections from the patches of storm clouds melting up into the midnight sun.

The feeling of hope fizzled. She should have known it would prove false, as always.

They reached the bottom of the ladder, and she stepped off feeling the kiss of the Glock's muzzle under her ear. "Walk!" the man holding it commanded, steering her across the deck with the cold steel.

"Where are you taking me?" she asked, panic beginning anew.

"There."

He indicated the crane. But he wasn't pointing at the glass and metal cabin. Rather, he waved the Glock toward the steel mesh net hooked to the end of the cable. It swung back and forth like a pendulum from the half-repaired extension arm. The arm Clint had warned her was in danger of breaking off . . . and plunging down into the black void of the sea.

She faltered. "What? No, we can't possibly go up there! It's not—"

The gun dug into the back of her neck. Her fine hairs rose to greet it.

"Not we," he sneered. *"You."*

36

////\\\\////\\\\

"Goddamn fucking sonofa*bitch*," Clint swore, clenching his teeth so hard he was amazed they didn't crack into bits. At least he wasn't cold anymore. He was sweating bullets.

"We're trying to be gentle, man," Frank said apologetically as he dragged the too-small Farmer John wetsuit up Clint's torso.

"Fuck that. Just do it," Clint ground out. "Quickly!" He felt like a goddamn invalid. He hadn't even been able to bend over to get the damn thing over his feet, let alone pull it on.

The fucking wetsuit was even tighter than he remembered. The pain was excruciating on his bruises, his throbbing internal organs, and in the purple mush that was his abdomen. But this was the only way he could think of to keep his body from literally falling apart at the seams—at least temporarily—so he could at least hobble about without risking an instant punctured lung.

So he was flat on his back and Jeeter was holding his shoulders steady while Johnny pulled and tugged at the Farmer John's legs to get them over his calves. Clint had his hands pressed onto a makeshift bandage tied around his ribs, attempting to hold it in place as the others adjusted the rubbery material around him.

"Damn it! Can't you go any faster?"

He had to get to Samantha. God only knew what that sociopath Xing Guan was planning to do to her.

Matty poked his head in from outside and announced in low urgent tones, "They're down on the weather deck now."

Matty was playing carrier pigeon to Spiros's recon. As soon as they'd heard Samantha's screams, Clint had sent the pair to find and follow her and Xing Guan and report back the instant it looked like she might be in imminent danger.

"Where is he taking her?" Clint gritted out, grateful for the distraction as Frank pulled the zipper up over his ribs.

Matty frowned. "Looks to me like he's heading for dhe crane. But . . ." He gave a Bollywood waggle of his head. "Dhat would not be smart. He'd be as good as trapped up dhere."

Clint agreed. It made no sense. The smart thing would be for Guan to head for the trawler and make a run for it.

He eased out a painful breath.

But if he'd learned one thing about his nemesis over the past two weeks, it was that Guan was twice as tenacious as a junkyard dog. Clint knew full well the Chinese operator wasn't going anywhere yet.

Not without the SD card.

Which was not good. For the obvious reasons, of course. But also because it left little doubt in Clint's mind exactly what the bastard was up to.

And what role he intended . . . *for Samantha.*

"Come out, spy!"

Clint froze in his tracks at the static-y command that boomed through the overhead deck speakers. In a Chinese accent.

Shit.

Matty turned back to blink at him owlishly. "Spy? What is he dhalking about?"

They were threading their way through the cargo containers, making for the crane as fast as Clint could drag himself. Which wasn't nearly fast enough. Moments ago, Matty had burst back through the door, extremely agitated, saying Spiros wanted him to come at once. Something was happening with the captain.

Something bad.

"Later," Clint said, and started hobbling forward again. He'd pulled on his regular clothes over the wetsuit, so not only were his injuries slowing him down, but the friction between the neoprene and the uniform fabric made movement not only painful but difficult. It was like running underwater and having electroshock therapy at the same time. But the adrenaline screaming through his system gave him the anesthesia to power through it.

"Lieutenant Commander Clint Wolfwalker!" the speakers thundered.

Double shit.

The bastard knew his name. His *real* name. How the hell—

Matty opened his mouth in astonishment but didn't get a chance to ask the obvious question.

"I have your woman," the speakers squawked harshly. "Come out or I kill her."

Inwardly, Clint swore a blue streak.

"Don't listen to him!" Samantha's reedy voice called from somewhere, without the benefit of an amplifier. "You can't—" Her words cut off abruptly with a shriek over the tinny sound of metal links clinking.

What the—

Fury flashed through Clint like a firebomb. Spiros tried to snag him as he shot past, but Clint shook him off. He charged peg-legged onto the open deck across from the crane, anxiously scanning the area for Samantha. Where the hell was she? He shot his gaze up to the crane's cabin, knowing that was where Xing Guan must be.

What he saw turned his stomach. Spiros and Matty edged up behind him, muttering in disgust. The body of Guan's son was propped up in the crane operator's seat, his head lolling to one side, sightless eyes staring down at Clint. Xing Guan stood behind the body, holding a Glock in one hand and the crane's portable control box in the other. There was an indecipherable look on the bastard's face—somewhere between hatred and triumph, glee and desperation.

At first Clint didn't understand. Then he heard a swallowed squeal and whipped his gaze in its direction. His heart literally stopped for several beats.

Oh. Fuck.

The two men behind him swore.

The cargo net was swinging precariously back and forth from the end of the damaged extension arm, suspended well over the side of the ship. Set against the black water, the diamond pattern of the huge steel net sparkled like the scales of a serpent coiled in the pale golden light of the midnight sun, its jaws closed around a smaller solid object imprisoned in its belly.

Oh, Jesus.

Samantha.

Her beautiful green eyes peered down at him, round and shiny as Caribbean tide pools. A tangle of blond hair surrounded her face like a halo, backlit by the rising sun. She looked like an angel. Her elegant fingers were threaded through the mesh, clinging to the strands of steel. *An angel in a cage*.

Clint took an involuntary step forward, his brain paralyzed by pure horror. What was the monster doing with her?

Spiros grabbed his shoulder. "Don't, bro."

A second later it became all too clear. *Insurance.*

The cable jerked, abruptly plunging the net toward the sea several inches before jolting to a halt. Samantha's eyes slammed shut and her fingers convulsed around the mesh diamonds. A squeak came from her throat though her full lips were pressed bravely into a thin line. Even from here he could see her body shaking with fear.

"Stop!" Clint roared, shaking off Spiros's grip to round on Guan. "What the *hell* do you think you're doing?"

His nemesis stepped to the open door of the cab and looked down his nose at him. "I get your attention," the bastard said just loud enough for Clint to hear.

His anger sharpened. It took all his willpower to say semi-calmly, "All right. You've got it. Now let the woman go."

Guan fingered the controller impassively. "Must give back first what you stole."

Clint's pulse sped. He wasn't about to argue. Behind him, Spiros and Matty whispered to each other.

"Fine," Clint said, and swiftly dug into his jacket pocket.

"Clint, no!" Samantha's anguished plea speared down from her high prison. "Please don't do this."

"It's all right," he told her, and pulled out the tiny memory card. He held it up between two fingers, showing it to Xing Guan. "Here. Take it."

Guan considered, then shook his head. "You bring up."

Was he *kidding*? He shook his head firmly. "Let her down first." Clint had no fucking intention of going up there, but he wanted Samantha out of harm's way before breaking that bit of news. He darted a glance up at her, his heart squeezing. If anything happened to her . . .

Guan's expression shifted. Could that have been a smile? The bastard lifted the controller. Put a finger to one of the buttons. "Down?"

Alarm ripped through Clint. He leapt forward, wincing in pain. "No!" The guy was fucking certifiable! "Hurt her and you'll be dead before you can take another breath," he spat out. He whipped the SIG from his pocket and took aim.

"Oh, God." Samantha's strangled whisper floated down.

Behind him, he heard Spiros rack his weapon and quietly urge Matty back.

Guan shrugged, seemingly unconcerned. "I fail mission, I have accident. Dead anyway."

The man's nonchalance was unnerving. And unnatural. Clint jetted out a breath and ratcheted down his weapon. "I'll give you the damn card! Just don't fucking hurt her."

He tipped his chin at the other side of the deck. "Take the trawler and get out of here before the navy comes. After that stunt you pulled with the Coast Guard cutter, you've got to know they'll be here soon."

Guan's eyes narrowed, and he slashed his hand angrily. "Cutter not my orders. Stupid men." He did a slicing one-eighty of the horizon. Suddenly, almost imperceptibly, he stiffened. Then he returned his focus to Clint. "Okay. I come."

Clint blinked at the abrupt about-face, and swiftly searched the horizon, himself. His eye skittered over a flash of something solid . . . a fishing boat? The Chinese sub? Or maybe nothing. The rising sun had thrown a spangle of gold across the water, turning the rolling waves into a kaleido-scope of light and shadow, making it impossible to distin-guish mirage from reality.

Guan lifted the controller again, placing his thumb over one of the buttons, and snapped Clint's attention back to him.

Guan growled in warning, "Do not be stupid, Wolf-walker."

"I won't," Clint assured him, raising his hands in the universal gesture for don't-freak-out-I-won't-try-anything. He turned and gestured to Spiros to put away his gun. That's when he noticed the other crew members watching warily from the shadows between two railroad containers. Frank and Johnny stood holding up Lars Bolun, who looked woozy but furious. Clint shook his head once, signaling them to stay back.

Before he'd turned around again, Guan had scuttled down the king post and landed like a cat on the deck before him, still holding the portable controller. He withdrew a small electronic tablet from his jacket and held it out to Clint. "Put card in and turn on."

The man was definitely no fool. Good thing Clint hadn't tried pulling a switch.

He accepted the unfamiliar device, examined it, and loaded the SD card into the appropriate slot, then punched keys until the thing turned on. He handed it back.

Xing Guan stepped away and used his thumb to type in
a few commands. Apparently he knew what he was looking
at; it didn't take more than a few minutes for him to nod in
stony approval. He handed Clint the tablet. "Take out now."

He did as he was told.

"Throw in sea," Guan ordered.

Clint's brows knitted. Unexpected—and annoyingly
smart. No chance of the SD card ever falling into non-
Chinese hands again. Setting his jaw, he threw it. The small
storage card sailed far out over the water and winked into
the darkness.

"Oh, Clint," came Samantha's soft lament as they all
watched it disappear.

For a moment, no one moved. Then Frank muttered,
"Fuckin-A. *That's* what this was all about?"

"Okay. I've kept up my end," Clint said, stowing his frustration with both Frank and this whole damn mission, and
started to turn back to Guan. "Now hand over that con—"

But he was talking to thin air.

Xing Guan had vanished.

Clint spun around. "Sonofa—" His pulse went into over-
drive. "Where'd he go?"

Spiros's jaw had dropped, and the other three just looked
flummoxed. They'd all been so intent on the SD card no one
had noticed the assassin slip away.

Clint whipped a look up at Samantha, his stomach
clenching in growing panic. Through the mesh, her surprised gaze met his. Her lips parted uncertainly. Slowly, her
expression softened into heartrending acceptance. Her fingers stretched toward him through the strands of her prison.
"Clint," she whispered.

Then the cable jerked, the hook opened, and the net
dropped like a stone to the sea, with Samantha trapped inside.

"*No!*" Clint bellowed, anguish filling every molecule of
his being. And then his feet were running, running, his
mind in a fever, toward the rail. He didn't think, *couldn't*
think, he just knew he must save her.

If anything happens to you, I won't care what happens to me.

He brushed off the alarmed calls of the crew behind him, ignored the agonizing pain in his body, and sprinted on with single-minded purpose toward his destiny. *One way or another.*

He hit the side with ferocious velocity, fingers brushing the top rail as he flew over it in a graceful arc. He stilled his mind as his grandfather had taught him, and dove down, down, down, into the freezing water below.

37

\\\\\\\\\\///////

Sam was wet and cold . . . so cold her skin burned, white hot flames licking at her flesh.

And she was shivering—deep, continuous wracking shivers that rattled her bones and teeth and skull.

The ship was shaking, too, or bouncing, or . . . She gave up trying to figure it out. It hurt too much to think. But the ship hit a massive wave, and her body slammed against something solid and . . . *warm*.

She gave a little moan, wanting to . . . wanting . . .

"Shhh," a sonorous murmur rumbled into her hair. "You're safe now. I've got you. Here, snuggle closer."

Strong arms tightened around her.

Oh, yes. *That* was what she wanted. Who she wanted . . .

She nestled into his warm, safe body, and sighed. *Safe* . . .

She felt herself start to drift away, and she fought against the darkness. She had to tell him . . . something. Tell him something important. Before it was too late.

I love you.

Had she said it aloud?

Yes! Maybe? She tried to open her mouth and form the words. But she was shivering too badly. She gave up, and let herself drift. Down, down, down, into the comforting warmth of his embrace.

I love you, she whispered in her mind. *I love you. I love you.*

I love you.

When Sam awoke, she was alone.

But not for long. Waking up must have triggered one of the dozens of blinking, beeping monitors surrounding the bed, and a few minutes later a nurse bustled in.

"You're awake. Excellent. How do you feel?"

Sam considered the question, mentally probing her body for signs of anything wrong. "Good," she concluded. "What happened to me?"

"Severe hypothermia. You don't remember?"

She thought back and felt a brief stab of panic. "Something about a net . . . and . . ."

The nurse gave a short nod. "Not to worry. I wouldn't want to remember, either. If your guy hadn't jumped in to save you . . . well, let's just say it's a good thing he did."

She blinked at the woman. "My . . . Clint? He jumped in?" This time the panic was longer. "In his condition?" That much she *did* remember. And . . . the drop to the water from *Île de Cœur*'s weather deck was— Her eyes widened. "Oh, my God."

"He's lucky he didn't kill himself," the nurse agreed. She gave a naughty smile. "Would have been a darn shame. Such a handsome man. And so devoted." At Sam's blank look, she said, "Why, he put up such a fuss about staying with you when you came in that the doctor had to sedate him in order to treat *his* injuries." The woman's lips curved up higher. "He didn't like that, I can tell you."

Sam could imagine. She smiled. And all the crazy emotions she'd felt for him came flooding back, jumbling in the pit of her stomach. She wanted to see him! She wanted to

hold him. She wanted to— "So he's all right? Is he . . . ?"
Gone? She swallowed, terrified of the answer.

"Oh, he's a stubborn one. He'll be fine. Checked out
early this morning, broken ribs and all," she said, efficiently
fluffing Sam's pillow.

At those words, those achingly terrible, but expected
words, Sam's heart died inside. "Ah," she managed.

"These are from him," the nurse said, adjusting a huge
vase of red roses on the nightstand, plucking at a couple of
dead petals. "Oh! I nearly forgot. He said to tell you he took
your laptop."

Sam blinked. "Why on earth would he do that? I need it
for my ship's logs." If it still worked. After falling on it and
shattering the case, she wasn't so sure.

"Not to worry." The nurse pointed at an envelope next to
the roses. "He left you a thumb drive with all your data on
it. He said he needed to take the hard drive with him." The
nurse made a face. "Something about getting it to the navy
because of some software or something he'd transferred
onto it. Didn't make any sense at all to me."

Sam's jaw dropped as she stared at the nurse. The SD
card? He hadn't lost the data, after all? Thank God! No
wonder he'd insisted she take the laptop with her when she
went to the trawler.

"No wonder he checked out and left so quickly."

She felt dizzy from the hurt that squeezed the air from
her lungs.

"Oh?" The nurse briskly deposited the dead rose petals
in the wastebasket. "Well. He did say to be sure and tell you
he'd call you, dear."

Sure he would.

She shouldn't be so surprised. Sam had known all along
he'd leave as soon as they reached a town with an airport.
And this town obviously had one. Wherever she was. The
fact that he hadn't lost whatever intel was on the data card
only made it more urgent he leave. He had an important job
and a life, and he'd need to get back to . . . wherever he lived

She'd known that. Hell, she'd *wanted* that. That was their deal.

She swallowed heavily.

Right?

"Did they catch the hijacker . . . ?" she asked through a tightening throat. "The man who—" Her voice broke.

The nurse looked at her with pity in her eyes. "No. I believe he got away, dear. Something about the ship exploding, and a submarine, I think, or . . ." She shook her head. "I'm not sure. All very hush-hush I understand. The rumor is—"

Sam couldn't concentrate enough to listen any longer. She let the woman ramble on about spies and terrorists and the terrible state of security in this country until she finally bustled out of the room.

Leaving Sam alone again.

To cry herself to sleep.

A week later Sam was still crying herself to sleep, but she'd managed to get through the entire day before without breaking down in the grocery store, or tearing up at stupid commercials, or wanting to hurl the phone through the window each time it rang.

It wasn't that he didn't call. He *did* call. Every day. At least once. Sometimes two or three times.

But she didn't answer. She didn't want to talk to him. Didn't want to hear his excuses for leaving, or that he wanted to "keep in touch." Didn't want him to ask her if she was pregnant, because she wasn't. Either she never had been, or her icy swim in the Bering Sea had made her lose it.

He left messages, but she muted the machine and deleted them unheard. The man was persistent, she'd give him that much. But his persistence only made it that much harder on her.

Why wouldn't he just leave her alone? He obviously didn't want to be with her, so what was the point of all this?

Finally, she changed her phone number, and the calls stopped.

Thank. God.

Now maybe she could move on with her life.

And today would no doubt be the first day of the rest of *that* wonderful adventure. Her father had summoned her for a meeting at the Richardson Shipping headquarters. That's where she was now.

She heaved a big sigh and checked herself in the ladies' room mirror. Her favorite suit was a little loose because she hadn't been eating much for the past week, but the color was good. A power color—red. To match her eyes.

Maybe she should think about getting some colored contact lenses.

She straightened her skirt and headed for the conference room. This should be a barrel of laughs. She knew what was coming—there couldn't be much doubt about that. Her father had not been pleased to learn his ship had been blown up with all its cargo.

Thankfully the Coast Guard had shown up moments before and gotten the crew safely off the ship. Which had happened just moments after a helo from the *George Washington* had arrived in the nick of time to pluck her and Clint from the freezing water. The exciting rescue had been captured on video by one of the airmen with his cell phone and been shown ad nauseum on news programs all over the world. Which had interested Sam only because she herself had no memory whatsoever of the event. No memory of anything after being forced into that awful cargo net. Amnesia. One of the symptoms of severe hypothermia.

It was just as well she was about to be fired. She didn't think she could ever look another cargo net in the face as long as she lived. Awkward for a cargo ship's captain.

She walked into the conference room with a confident stride and her head held high. No sense giving her father the satisfaction. But she had to admit she was a little surprised the entire board of directors was sitting at the long mahogany table. All men, of course. Big shock. Other than the secretary poised to take notes. Did they not even see what dinosaurs they were? They actually thought calling the secretary an "executive assistant" made it all better. She allowed herself an eye roll.

She glanced out the floor-to-ceiling windows at the Seattle harbor below and already felt a touch of nostalgia at seeing the bobbing boats and stately ships sparkling in the sun like a picture postcard. She'd miss the sea. A lot. Perhaps a kayak . . .

She turned to face the music.

"Samantha." Her father greeted her with a smile that didn't quite make it up to his eyes. "You're looking well, I see."

"Yes, thank you."

He put out a hand. "Please, have a seat."

She glanced at the offered chair and suddenly decided this was one exercise she would just as soon skip. She'd thought she could do it. But no. She was in no frame of mind to endure another humiliation, in public, by the one man who by any standard should love and support her . . . but never had. Too dangerous.

Hell, she'd killed a man. And no one had said a word. Not one. She'd gotten away with murder. That might give her ideas.

She tried to smile but her cheek kept jumping.

She cleared her throat. "Let's just cut to the chase, shall we? I'm fired, right?"

Jason Richardson suddenly looked acutely uncomfortable. He forced a jovial laugh. "Fired? No, no. Nothing like that. Please, have a seat, and let's talk about it."

Right. "Don't think so, Dad. Let me take a wild guess. After careful consideration, you're not renewing my captain's papers with the company, but would be happy to offer me a job as, oh, say, a secretary." She glanced at the woman taking notes. "Oh, I'm sorry, I mean executive assistant." She looked back at her father. "Close?"

He actually squirmed. She didn't know you could do that standing up.

She pushed out a breath and picked up her purse. "Yeah. I'll pass."

"But— Samantha, sweetheart, surely you must see it's impossible for us to entrust you with another commission." He smiled benignly. "Look what happened to the first ship we entrusted to you! Your poor judgment and—"

She held up a hand. "Stop. I don't want to hear the reasons. Let's just save everyone the trouble. I q—"

A deep voice from the corner of the room interrupted her. "I'd like to hear his reasons."

She spun to the sound. Her jaw dropped as the man rose. He stood tall and proud and wore a full dress naval uniform with a chest full of colorful medals. His cover was tucked neatly under his arm.

"Clint?" She was stunned. And a little taken aback. Please, God, not *another* humiliation. By the *U.S. Navy*? "What are you . . ."

He cleared his throat. "I've been trying to get in touch with you by phone, but I, uh, seem to have the wrong number."

And here, she'd thought he was calling for personal reasons. She hadn't wanted to hear them, but it had given her some small comfort that he had tried so hard.

Wow. How freaking wrong could one woman be?

"Yeah," she said. "I had to change it. Phone stalker."

The only indication that he'd fielded the barb was a slight flare of his perfect bronze nostrils.

Damn, it was maddening how exquisitely handsome he looked in that uniform. How handsome he looked, period. To think she'd had him—

She cut off the thought before the suit matched more than the rims of her eyes.

"Anyway," he said, and turned back to her father. He and the rest of the board were staring at Clint as though he had horns and a pitchfork. Or maybe a trident. The medals probably tipped the scales. "I'd like to hear your reasons for dismissing Captain Richardson."

Her father bristled. "I am not dismissing her. Merely assigning her a more appropriate job for her"—his words faltered for a millisecond—"experience." He looked to the other board members for support. They nodded solemnly.

"I see." Clint eyed them neutrally. "So you feel her performance as captain of *Île de Cœur* was . . . unsatisfactory?"

"Absolutely," her father said jovially. "Her judgment is sadly lacking, and her on-time record is dismal. She has questionable people skills. Why she fired one of our best—"

"Okay, enough, already," Sam gritted out. "I really don't think you need to—"

"I'm here on official U.S. Navy business, Captain Richardson," Clint cut her off in turn. "So I just want to be sure all the facts are presented." He smiled down at the secretary, er, executive assistant. "For the record."

"Are you a lawyer?" Sam asked in annoyance. She didn't remember him saying anything to that effect, but he sure as hell sounded like—

"No, ma'am. I'm just a SEAL."

"Former SEAL," she muttered, thankful at least it wasn't some kind of lawsuit.

His eyes narrowed ever-so-slightly. "Whatever."

"And what business?" she demanded.

"Who, exactly, are you?" asked her father.

Clint darted a glance up at the inlaid marble wall clock, then said, "Forgive me. I'm Lieutenant Commander Clint Wolf Walker." He handed the secretary a gold embossed business card. "I'm here on behalf of the Office of Naval Intelligence." He bent to pick up a briefcase that had been sitting on the floor at his feet, walked with it to the seat right across from her, and laid it on the table.

Sam frowned.

Her father did, too. "What in tarnation would—"

"And of Admiral Zeluff of Pacific Command," Clint added, snapping open the hinges.

Her lips parted. *Wait. What?* She was starting to get nervous.

"Pacific Com—" her father began on a laugh.

"And of Assistant Director DeAnne Lovejoy of the U.S. State Department," he went on, ignoring the interruption.

DeAnne? DeAnne would not be doing anything bad to her! Would she?

Clint lifted the lid of the briefcase, paused, and looked directly at her father. "Oh. And did I mention the President of the United States?"

She was pretty sure she and her father had never looked quite so much alike as they did at that moment. Their expressions, anyway. Pure incredulity.

Clint lifted a stack of parcels in Bubble Wrap from the case. Everyone sat dumbfounded as he unwrapped them. They were framed certificates. Five of them. He lifted them one by one and showed them first to her, then to the others.

What on earth . . .

"This one is presented to Captain Samantha Richardson from PACCOM for Distinguished Service in Homeland Security."

She gazed at it in astonishment. *Distinguished . . .* Wow. That was . . .

He picked up the next. "This is for Captain Samantha Richardson from the ONI for Outstanding Service in Naval Security."

Her jaw dropped. Naval security? But—

She needed to sit down. She felt for her chair and dropped onto it with a thud.

He raised a finger with the third one. "For Captain Samantha Richardson from the U.S. State Department for Grace and Honor under Fire and Risking Her Life in the Rescue of Five Captive U.S. Citizens."

Grace and honor? Her bottom lip trembled. She couldn't believe this. She thought of her battered and bloodied crew, and her heart ached with love. No, she hadn't saved them. They'd all saved each other.

Clint carefully lifted the smallest frame. "And this is from the White House. It's a certificate of intent to grant Captain Samantha Richardson the Presidential Citizen's Medal in the next nomination period."

She stared across at it through a blur of tears. Then up at
Clint. My God. This was all his doing. It had to have been
him.

"But why?" she whispered. No one had ever . . .

"What's the last one?" the executive assistant asked.
They all turned to look at the prim, gray-haired woman with
the old-fashioned steno pad on her knee. She pointed with
her pen at the fifth frame, which sat a little apart from the
others, and like a tennis match, they all turned to look at it.

"Ah," Clint said, and for the first time he looked a shade
uncertain. He picked up the frame and held it awkwardly in
front of him. He looked up at the clock again, then down at
the frame. He flipped it back and forth a few times between
his fingers.

"Well?" one of the board members asked.

Sam wasn't sure she wanted to know.

Clint cleared his throat. "It's a, uh, marriage license."

She blinked. Several times. "A . . . what?" He couldn't
possibly mean . . . Could he?

He'd *left* her.

"Marriage license."

Alone. In the *hospital.*

He handed her the frame.

Without even a *word*! Just a message through the freaking *nurse*. He couldn't *possibly* want to . . .

But sure enough, it had *Marriage License* printed across
the top and looked all official and legal. It even had their
names filled in. No date though.

"Clint?" She gazed up at him, totally floored.

"You said you loved me," he said, his voice softening.
"In the helo, after they pulled us out of the water."

"I did?" So many emotions were spilling through her
that she didn't know what to do. Or say. Or . . .

"Yeah." He gave her a lopsided smile. "Three times."

Her mouth opened and closed, then opened again. "Really? I don't remember."

His forehead creased a little. "So then, you didn't
mean it?"

She licked her lips and glanced around the room at the avid faces. There were a few scowls, too. On her father's face, for instance. Except he was looking at the other frames. Not the one that meant by far the most.

"Clint, I'm not pregnant," she said, her voice suddenly small and terrified. Terrified that *that* was why he was doing this.

There were murmurs around the table.

His face fell. Just a little. But she saw it, and her heart fell, too.

"Well," he said. "I guess we'll just have to try again."

Some of the board members grinned.

Her cheeks turned the color of her suit. At least it felt like they did.

"So . . . ?" he said, drawing out the syllable.

Her heart was suddenly beating so fast she thought it would fly away. "I, um . . ."

"Shall I read back the question, Captain Richardson?" the executive assistant asked helpfully. "Oh, wait." She looked pointedly at Clint, not her steno pad. "There *was* no question."

Sam put her trembling hand to her mouth. She didn't know whether to laugh or cry. "Oh, Clint, I—"

"Damn it, Samantha! I love you so much it's making me insane. Literally. I quit my job and bought this huge boat, and I was hoping we could—"

"What?"

"A boat," he said, and for just a moment he looked like a little boy at Christmas.

God, she loved him.

"It's a— Well, here, you can see it down in the marina." He turned to the acres of window and pointed downward to the dozens of boats moored in the marina. "See? It's the green one." He looked back at her, his eyes softening. "Celery green. That's kinda what sold me on it."

She smiled, so full of love she thought she might burst with it. "No, I meant about your job. Did you really quit?"

"I really did." He glanced up at the wall clock again.

"In . . . four minutes I'll be a civilian, and I can take off this uniform."

The executive assistant made a humming approval noise.

Sam's smile spread wider. "Hopefully not here and now."

Clint's eyebrow flicked up. "The boat might be a bit more comfortable."

She rose from her chair and tilted her head. "Is there a hammock?"

"Oh, yeah," he said, his eyes warm and his smile wicked.

Someone cleared their throat. "I think this meeting's adjourned," he mumbled.

The executive assistant stood and started gathering the frames. "I'll just take care of these for you, shall I, Captain Richardson?"

Sam nodded. "Thanks. And thank you, Clint, for arranging for them. That was truly the nicest thing anyone has ever done for me."

"Oh, those weren't my doing," he said. "They are all the real deal. You earned every one of those awards."

She didn't know what to say, so naturally her eyes filled with tears. But they were tears of joy. Such joy.

Clint said, "So, Samantha Richardson, will you marry a man with no job and only a boat to his name, but so much love in his heart he doesn't know what to do with himself?"

She didn't think it was possible to be this happy. "Yes. Oh, yes. But will you marry a woman with no job and no boat, either, Clint Wolf Walker? But a woman who loves you more than she can say."

In answer he slid across the wide table in an athletic move and scooped her up in his arms. "More than three times?"

"Many, many, more times."

And then he kissed her.

Many, many, more times.

Turn the page for a sneak peek at the next novel in
Nina Bruhns's Men in Uniform series

BLUE FOREVER

Available Summer 2013 from Berkley Sensation

A REMOTE MOUNTAIN VILLAGE,
HAINAN ISLAND, CHINA
AUGUST

It *would* be a woman.

Hell. Could his day get any worse?

U.S. Marine Corps Intelligence Operative Major Kiptyn Llowell swallowed a growl of irritation as he regarded the trim figure descending from a white SUV that sported a familiar sky blue U.N. logo on its door. He'd much rather deal with a man in situations like this. You could talk to a man. Reason logically with a man. Women were just so damn . . . illogical. And unreasonable. Not to mention unpredictable.

He jetted out a breath. At least there was little doubt of the woman's nationality. She had the look of a typical U.S. State Department geek. Gray suit skirt with white blouse. Leather shoulder bag. Sensible flats.

Whatever. She was his ticket out of this goatfuck of a day. Assuming he could talk his way into that SUV when it left this flyspeck of a village in the back of beyond.

Not that he'd give Ms. Sensible Shoes any choice in the matter. Women might be unpredictable, but he sure as hell wasn't. He'd do whatever it took to meet his transpo at the appointed time tomorrow.

No problem. She didn't look that tough.

Kip leaned against the rough trunk of a tamarind tree near the SUV and watched the woman from under the obscuring shadow of his billed cap. She said something to the Chinese driver, then turned and walked toward the nearby open-air market, chatting amiably with her traveling companion, an aging hippie-type wearing loose, colorful clothing and gesturing expansively with her hands. Ms. Sensible was obviously there in some official capacity—a trade liaison, a translator, maybe a cultural advisor to the other woman, who was clearly the party interested in the marketplace offerings. This village specialized in the highly sought-after traditional textiles and weavings of Hainan's native Li people. No doubt the artsy-fartsy woman was a gallery buyer or some such thing. Which would explain why they'd made the arduous drive to this remote mountain village rather than park themselves on one of the many idyllic beaches on this tropical South Seas island paradise.

The one bright spot in his day. If the women hadn't shown up, he might have had to do something a lot more dangerous to get down to the coast. As it was, no sweat.

The two women disappeared amongst the tall, primitive stalls festooned with a rainbow of handwoven textiles. Despite the village being so out of the way, there was a decent crowd of people browsing the marketplace, all of them Asian.

Kip didn't dare approach a single one. His Chinese language skills sucked. Besides, the last thing he wanted was to risk being turned over to the security police by some overeager Chinese national who'd seen his photo on the morning news—with the warning splashed across it in big red characters, "Beware! American Spy!" At least that's what he figured it had said.

So, Ms. Sensible Shoes it was.

Hiking his rucksack over the shoulder of his dirty, oversized cotton peasant shirt, he started after her.

He decided to separate the two women and get Ms. Sensible on her own. Ms. Hippy-dippy might be one of those conscientious objector types who opposed espionage on principle. But if it was as he suspected, and Ms. Sensible was attached to the consulate in any kind of official capacity, she'd have an obligation to help a U.S. Marine in need of aid on foreign soil. Especially when he told her it was a matter of U.S. national security. Which it was. Aside from the whole threat of torture and being hanged as a spy thing. Which he'd just as soon skip today.

Doing his best to shrink his six foot three frame down to blend in with the shorter tourists around him—the newscast would surely have mentioned his height—he slowly picked his way toward the woman until he was standing a few yards away from her at the other end of a large stall. Her companion had quickly become absorbed in examining the textiles on offer, and the stall's owner was smiling and chattering nonstop as she spread out more and more weavings for them to look at. Ms. Sensible was translating.

He waited patiently, hanging back until the stall's owner hurried off to fetch the inevitable offering of tea, over which they would start price negotiations.

He stepped in close to Ms. Sensible. She glanced up at him, startled, and started to say something in Chinese.

He cut her off. "I'm American. I need your help," he said in a voice for her ears only.

She did a double take, her eyes darting up to meet his in surprise. Hers were large and blue. And really pretty. He did his own double take.

Suddenly, they widened as recognition dawned. "You! Oh, my— You're that—" She swallowed the offending word, and glanced around nervously before turning back to him. "Major Llowell, I presume?"

It was his turn to be mildly surprised. "How did you know?"

Her brows flickered. Those blue eyes tracked down his body, then up again. "You really think that hat is a disguise?"

He stared back at her. Of all the— "It's what I had. Got a better idea?" he asked defensively.

Her gaze glided across the breadth of his chest. "Nope." She turned aside and cleared her throat.

For a second his jaw slackened. Wait. Was she *cruising* him?

An unexpected rush of physical awareness flooded through his body. He took another look at her. A good look. And his earlier opinion resolved into something quite different.

Yeah, she was wearing the typical drab uniform of a government bureaucrat, but the skirt actually hugged her shapely hips nicely, and her white blouse was soft and clung to a really outstanding set of—

"What do you want?" she asked, jerking him out of his reassessment.

He blinked. "What?"

"You said you needed help."

Right. Damn, what was wrong with him? He forced his focus back where it belonged. "A ride," he said.

She shot him a look.

"Down to the coast," he clarified with an inner wince. Had his voice betrayed his inappropriate thoughts?

Christ.

"You do realize," she said evenly, "there are at least three military checkpoints between here and Sanya."

He shrugged. "Yeah." They could be dealt with.

She didn't look particularly happy. She indicated his rucksack. "Anything in there I should know about?"

"No."

Which was true. She shouldn't know about it. For her own good.

She nodded, and he had the distinct feeling he wasn't fooling her for a nanosecond. His respect went up another notch.

"What the hey," she said at length, her eyes meeting his. "I've always wanted to see the inside of a Chinese prison."

———

U.S. Department of State Foreign Service Officer DeAnne Lovejoy almost smiled at his expression. The major looked majorly taken aback. Poor man. Apparently he wasn't used to a foreign service officer with a sense of humor.

Well, what was she supposed to say? "No, forget it, you're not coming with us?" Hardly. As an FSO, it was her job to protect American citizens abroad. Besides, her boss would kill her if she let anything happen to him. The hotlines to State and the Pentagon had been burning up since dawn with speculation as to the alleged spy's health and whereabouts, and here he'd walked right into her hands, healthy as a lion and asking her for help.

"DeAnne! Look at these fabulous— Oh!" Chrissie Tanner faltered at the sight of the tall, broad man standing so close to her.

Oops. DeAnne took a step away from him. "Chrissie, this is Mr. Llow . . . enstein. He's here, um . . ."

"On business," the major supplied smoothly, extending his large hand. Which was attached to a muscular arm. Which in turn led to an impressive body. "My rental car conked out and Mrs. . . . uh . . ."

A *very* impressive body.

He looked at her expectantly. Was she supposed to say something?

She lurched out of her lustful thoughts. "Oh. Lovejoy. *Miss* Lovejoy." Okay, maybe not completely out. "DeAnne," she said determinedly businesslike.

He inclined his head politely. "DeAnne offered me a ride down the mountain."

"Oh?" Chrissie appeared flummoxed for a moment as she tipped her head back to look up at him, but then brightened. "So you're here for the weaving, Mr. Llowenstein?"

DeAnne interrupted before the major could say anything. Lord, that body was a problem. It was far too noticeable. And not in a good way. "Chrissie, will you be all right on your own for a few minutes? I'm pretty sure my cell phone won't work up here," she said, "but I thought I'd give it a try, to see if I can get hold of the rental company for him. It's in the car."

"Oh. Sure," Chrissie said, and good-naturedly indicated the stall's owner returning with a tray of refreshments. "I'll just drink tea, nod, and smile a lot."

"Sounds like a plan," DeAnne said with a chuckle. "Sir?" She gestured toward where the SUV was parked. "Shall we?"

"Please," he said when they were out of earshot. "Call me Kip."

"All right, Kip. We need to get you out of sight. You stick out like a sore thumb."

He made a noise of agreement. They passed a vendor selling rolls of fried rice, lamb, and vegetables wrapped in pak choi leaves. It smelled delicious, and she could see him eyeing the food. She stopped and ordered a half dozen from the vendor, then glanced at that large body again and changed the order to a dozen with a cup of coconut milk to wash them down.

"When was the last time you ate?" she asked as they hurried on toward the car. The television "wanted" broadcasts detailing his "treachery" had started cycling yesterday afternoon.

"This morning," he said, as he accepted the newspaper cone of fried rolls from her. "There are fruit trees everywhere. But these smell great." He put a hand on her arm to slow her down. "We'll share."

She shook her head. "We really need to get you—" But the words died in her throat as he plucked a roll from the paper, pursed his lips, and blew on it. *Oh, man.* Those lips were— The guy was—

Oh my God. *Feeding her.*

She felt herself flush hotly as he put the roll to her open mouth and waited for her to take a bite.

This was crazy. Kiptyn Llowell was a fugitive. A *spy*. And no doubt was being hunted by every cop, security agent, and PLA soldier on Hainan. His life was in danger. Heck, *her* life was probably in danger just being with him.

And he was *flirting* with her?

Ho-boy.

She took a bite.

He smiled a slow, sexy smile, and her heart did a high dive off the cliff of serious attraction. Man, oh, man, was she ever in deep, deep trouble.

"Major Llowell," she said sternly after she'd managed to chew and swallow. And avoid looking at his mouth. "You don't seem to be taking me—your situation—very seriously."

"Hey, you're the one who stopped for lunch."

She glared at him. "And this is the thanks I get."

He waggled his brows. "I'd be happy to thank you properly," he said, and popped another veggie roll in his mouth.

She didn't know whether to roll her eyes or smack him. She definitely didn't want to think about any other possibilities. "The only thanks I need," she said primly, "is you staying well out of sight until we can figure out—"

He let out a curse.

She frowned. "I'm really not a big fan of profan—Oof!"

She suddenly found herself jerked to a halt against a set of hard masculine ribs. "Shit," he muttered.

"Honestly, Kip," she began. But that's when she saw them—a trio of army Jeeps, overflowing with soldiers, barreling up the dirt track toward the village. "Shit," she echoed, her voice going up two octaves as her pulse took off.

Kip grabbed her by the arms and pushed her toward the SUV. "Get in. Quickly." He sprinted around to the driver's side and vaulted in.

"But wait!" She looked wildly around for their hired driver, who was nowhere to be seen.

"Now!" Kip ordered, reaching across the seat to pull her inside. "Buckle up!"

The SUV's engine roared to life.

By now the Jeeps had reached the outskirts of the village.

Kip ground the SUV into gear and it lurched forward.

Her door slammed shut with a bang like a rifle shot. She nearly jumped out of her skin.

"What about Chrissie?" she squeaked, grappling for the seat belt.

"Forget Chrissie," he gritted out, steering the vehicle into a rooster tail to head in the opposite direction. He jerked his chin at the advancing Jeeps. "You've got more important things to worry about."

Her belt snapped home.

Just as the soldiers started shooting.

"A perfect blend of romance and suspense."
—*Fresh Fiction*

FROM

NINA BRUHNS

RED HEAT

MEN IN UNIFORM SERIES

CIA analyst Julie Severin poses as a reporter aboard a
Russian submarine—only to be unexpectedly reunited
with Captain Nikolai Romanov, with whom she had a
sizzling encounter just the night before.

"High-action suspense at its very best!"
—g author

to finish!"
—stselling author

sexy."
—ning author

facebook.com/Nina.Bruhns.Author
penguin.com

M1071T0212

FROM

NINA BRUHNS

A KISS TO KILL

"Suspense just got a whole lot hotter!"
—Allison Brennan, *New York Times* bestselling author

Eight months ago, Dr. Gina Cappozi and CIA black-ops commando Captain Gregg van Halen were lovers . . . until he committed the ultimate betrayal. She knows that Gregg lives in a shadowy world of violence and darkness—and that he is watching her every move.

But Gregg is not the only one following her . . .

With the threat of enemies at every turn, the passionate pair will be forced to realize that the power of betrayal and revenge is nothing compared to the power of love.

HILLSBORO PUBLIC LIBRARIES
Hillsboro, OR
penguin.com
Member of Washington County
COOPERATIVE LIBRARY SERVICES

M532T0312